About the Author

Natalie Tambini has more than thirty years' experience as a national newspaper and magazine journalist. She created and wrote Cosmopolitan's 'Confessions' columns, supplements and books and interviewed countless celebrities during nine years at TV Choice and Total TV Guide – infamously missing a slot with Julia Roberts. Her work has been syndicated worldwide, and she has acted as ghostwriter for several celebrity columnists on women's magazines.

Her fascination with murderers and the need to understand them stems from a childhood passion for Agatha Christie novels while growing up in Norfolk and Hampshire. She has also interviewed many victims of crimes as a real-life journalist, and those who endured miscarriages of justice, including an innocent man who spent 20 years on death row.

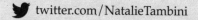 twitter.com/NatalieTambini

Also by Natalie Tambini

The Nail Salon

THE PUBLICIST

NATALIE TAMBINI

One More Chapter
a division of HarperCollins*Publishers* Ltd
1 London Bridge Street
London SE1 9GF
www.harpercollins.co.uk
HarperCollins*Publishers*
Macken House, 39/40 Mayor Street Upper,
Dublin 1, D01 C9W8, Ireland

This paperback edition 2023
2
First published in Great Britain in ebook format
by HarperCollins*Publishers* 2023
Copyright © Natalie Tambini 2023
Natalie Tambini asserts the moral right to
be identified as the author of this work

A catalogue record of this book is available from the British Library

ISBN: 978-0-00-858858-8

Printed and bound in the UK using 100% Renewable Electricity
by CPI Group (UK) Ltd

For mum and dad, and in memory of Ivy Read, who filled my world with love.

'I am the danger...I am the one who knocks.'

Walter White, *Breaking Bad*

Chapter One

LOLA

I t was dangling his balls in the prosecco that did it.

I've told him, a thousand times, that if you go to an awards ceremony, you're on show. It's all part of the job. You're there to be seen. Including the after-party. Did he listen? Did he fuck. Three bottles down and he'd whipped them out in front of the Head of Drama. His party trick. It was even her prosecco.

This is going to take some smoothing over. Damage limitation. That's my job. And why my clients pay me so handsomely. Personal publicist to the stars. I've got plenty of A-lister actors and footballers, but I'm not that fussy. Soap stars, snooker players and those actors who pop up in serial dramas – the ones where you know the face but can never quite remember the name – are just as rewarding. It's not all about the money, either. I get a kick out of keeping their sordid lives out of the press. Reputation management. When a celeb's in trouble, they'd better call Lola.

If the *Daily News* gets hold of this, it'll be all over the front page. But that's not always a bad thing. I've built careers back up after a fall like the fucking bionic man. Or woman. Depends if they've got that magical quality that means no matter what they do, the public is ultimately ready to forgive them. Because 'he's a nice boy really'. Or 'she didn't mean it'. For my clients, that magical quality is me.

It doesn't always work, of course. Like the prosecco. Some don't listen. Some – despite everything – are hell-bent on destroying the carefully manicured character you've created for them. Some just can't handle fame. And others are just shits.

Prosecco Guy falls into the first category. It's not the first time he's done it and it won't be the last. But I like him. He's a jobbing B-list actor who – unlike many – has accepted Hollywood isn't interested and just wants to enjoy his fame while it lasts.

My phone lights up. It's a message from my assistant, Olivia.

Only one person got that on camera. Kym Sylvian.

Ah, Kym. Also one of my clients. Word is bound to get out, but without video evidence, the papers won't run it. And even if they threaten to, I've got a few tricks up my sleeve. Offering them an exclusive on a footballer's wedding – I'm sure I can persuade one of them to tie the knot – in exchange for dropping it should work. I drain the rest of my sparkling water – I never drink on the job – and text Kym:

Meet me in the ladies by the entrance. Good news.
URGENT!

She'll be there, of course. Kym, like all my clients, is wedded to her phone. The London Sunset Plaza is a soulless place at the best of times, all glass, steel and fine dining dinners the size of a 10p, in a skyscraper with all the charm of a Travelodge. But I've done plenty of business here, especially in the entrance loos, which after the flurry of arrivals dashing in for their pre-party pick-me-up, is usually empty.

The attendant – whose main task this evening has been to clean the coke off the toilet seats – is quickly dispatched as usual with a twenty-pound note and a smile. 'Ten minutes, sweetie.' She nods. She knows me of old.

Kym sweeps in, her pale-blue Oscar de la Renta gown – loaned, of course, in exchange for a mention on the red carpet – showing unfortunate red wine drips. Inwardly, I wince. I can't bear red wine. Her eye make-up is smudged and she's slurring.

'Whassa news?'

'Kym, *darling*. I've been chatting to the Head of Drama. They think you're *wonderful*.'

'Really?' Underneath her up-do and borrowed jewels, she's a little girl from Liverpool, excited to be at the ball.

3

'Have a wee, now we're here, and I'll tell you all about it. Here, let me hold your stuff.'

Dutifully, she hands me her evening bag.

'Oh, darling, can I use your phone?' I add. 'I've left mine on the table. I know, I'm stupid. I'm always telling you never to do that. I need to call Olivia.'

'Sure,' she slurs. 'Passcode is… I can't 'member…' She puts her wobbly thumb on the phone and unlocks it before teetering into the cubicle.

The video is deleted in a flash. Gone, from her phone, the cloud, all her devices. Five minutes later, her ego pumped from top-secret tales of a non-existent drama series in the works, and which she'll have forgotten by morning, she's back on the cocktails. Job done.

It's four a.m. by the time my last client leaves, shoved into the back of a waiting taxi as the last few paparazzi by the exit grab a blurry shot. No one pays any attention to me as I leave ten minutes later, slipping out the front entrance and across Park Lane to the underground car park, where my black Tesla is fully charged, its blackout windows protecting anyone inside it. Three awards, two nominations, and apart from Prosecco Guy, no damage done. I'm tired, but elated. The Head of Drama had taken some smoothing over, but with a client list like mine, keeping me onside outweighed the 'pathetic schoolboy prank', which I promised would never happen again. I blamed it on the stress of his wife's fictitious *affair*. I'd dispatched him in a cab straight after Bollockgate, but I'll keep Prosecco Guy on the books because I like him. Because it was funny. And because – despite my 'no touching the talent' rule, I slept with him once. Just once. He'd got all emotional and said he loved me. I'd laughed, but I was touched. We'd never mentioned it again.

I'm just about to drive off when my phone lights up. It's Tim Thacker, the editor of the *Daily News*.

'Lola? What's the deal with Sam Stevens? We're hearing he's gone missing? Wasn't he at the awards tonight?'

I freeze, but my voice stays completely calm. 'Missing? I haven't heard anything. He told me a few days ago that he couldn't make it tonight. Just finished a shoot. Who says he's missing?'

'Police sources. Seems his latest boyfriend has turned up at Kingston Police Station just now in a right state. Says he's not at either of their homes and his phone is off.'

'Probably just gone off on a retreat. He's into that. Likes meditating and finding himself. Had they had a row?'

'That's all I know. If this has legs, we're gonna need a statement from you.'

'Sure. But keep this low-key for now.'

'He's A-list, Lola. If he's missing it's huge.'

'I know. But I'm sure he isn't. Just the boyfriend going off on one. Keep me posted, Tim. And thanks for the heads-up.'

Missing. Now I really do have a problem.

Because Sam Stevens *is* supposed to be at home. Dead.

Chapter Two

D etective Chief Inspector Sue Fisher rolled over in bed and looked at the crumpled pile of bedcovers beside her. Mike, her former deputy and now her boyfriend, was in the 1970s-style avocado bathroom, singing as he loudly brushed his teeth.

On the bedside table, her phone buzzed. Chief Constable Steve Biller. It was unusual for the boss to call.

'Sue? I need you in. Now. Missing person. Sam Stevens. The actor. This is obviously very high-profile and we need to show we've got the best team on it.'

'Sam Stevens? Doesn't he live in Hollywood?'

'Cobshott. Somewhere you're very familiar with, Sue. So the press will expect us to assign you to it. And he has a flat in Hampstead. One in LA too, though he hasn't been there for months, according to the housekeeper. Get in and I'll brief you. We'll need you on camera.'

Sam Stevens. Sue wasn't one for fangirling, but he was

7

up there with Tom Cruise in her book. Cobshott, though. Just a few miles away, but so many memories. Too many.

'That was the boss,' she told Mike as he emerged from the bathroom with a towel around his portly waist. 'Missing person. Sam Stevens. The actor.'

'God, even I've heard of him. Isn't he American?'

'No, just good with accents. British. Lives over here, apparently. Cobshott. Can you believe it? I thought I was done with that village and the super-rich. But they want me on it.'

Mike ruffled her hair. 'Only the best. The press will love you being on it. You did put Cobshott on the map solving the Medford case.'

Sue swung her legs out of bed and smiled. '*We* put it on the map,' she replied. Mike had never once appeared remotely jealous of the glory that had poured down on Sue after Medford, and she loved him for it. 'It'll feel weird going back there. I haven't set foot in Cobshott since.'

It had been four years since the Melinda Medford case had thrown both of them into the spotlight, and they'd started dating a year or so later. Sue shuddered as she recalled being left for dead in Cobshott, and what happened in the 'House of Horrors', as the papers had labelled the Medford crime scene.

'What happened to Medford's nail salon?' Sue called thickly from the bathroom, as she brushed her teeth. 'Surely it's not still there?'

'Funnily enough, I drove up Cobshott high street the

other day on that fraud job,' Mike replied. 'It's been turned into a Costa.'

Sue snorted. She loathed anywhere that sold overpriced coffee in toddler-like sippy cups.

'People still go there to take photos,' Mike went on. 'Even though that hideous house – Riverdell – was demolished, people still turn up in the village looking for it and wanting to see where it stood. Vultures.' He picked up his phone from the bedside table. 'That's history now, though. Do you want another cuppa, love?'

'Yeah. Strong one. Ta.'

She listened as Mike's slippered feet padded downstairs, followed by the predictable sound of the kettle. Cobshott might be history for Mike, but the scars still ran deep with Sue. She'd been lucky to survive the attack there.

Cobshott was bringing back too many memories, thoughts that she'd long driven deep inside, crunched so tightly that their darkness, their pain, rarely escaped. Memories of her late husband, Rob, exploded. How he secretly used to beat her, burn her with cigarettes. How he hated himself afterwards. And how, for years, she covered it up, pouring every scrap of energy into caring for their son, Tom, and catching men – and women – like Medford who inflicted such pain on others. Seven rapists and three killers were now off the streets thanks to her. Plus countless domestic abusers.

Sue turned the cold tap on full, splashing water on to her face. These days, her arms bore no bruises, and she no longer feared what might happen when she walked in the door at night. She was safe, free. But she still missed Rob. The part of him that, underneath the twisted, toxic mess he'd become, loved her.

Even though she cared for Mike dearly, and he'd been there for her and Tom during the most god-awful times, through the whole Medford case, she didn't love him like *that*.

Love, as she'd always known, was messy.

'Here you go,' Mike said cheerily, placing a steaming mug of builders' tea on the dressing table. He placed his arm gently round her shoulders. 'Don't worry, love. You've laid those Cobshott ghosts to rest.'

Sue wasn't so sure.

Dressed in a black suit, crisp white shirt and patent black shoes, with enough make-up to hopefully hide her late fortysomething wrinkles on camera, Sue drove to the police station car park, wishing she had Mike by her side. He'd been the perfect deputy, but police rules meant that once they were dating, they couldn't work as a team, and pleas to Chief Constable Biller to make an exception in their case had fallen on unsurprisingly deaf ears.

She missed having Mike by her side at work. These days they were more friends than lovers. Sex with him had always been more cosy than passionate, but even that had dwindled. With Tom now eighteen and preparing to head off to university, they'd settled into a routine. Mike made the six a.m. cuppa. He always sang in the bathroom – Abba, usually. Today was 'Fernando'. They tried to organise their shifts to spend time together. A curry on a Thursday – veggie korma for her, chicken madras for him. Cinema on a Saturday, if the job allowed. Occasional sex on a Sunday morning, always followed by Mike mowing the lawn. Sue hated him doing that, though she didn't really know why.

After the Medford case, she'd stayed in the same 1930s house in Surbiton, a commuter-belt town in Surrey. It was Tom's home, after all, and despite everything, it helped her feel close to Rob. His death was something that stayed with her every single day, something she felt responsible for. If only she'd got him the help he so clearly needed, to learn to cope with his anger rather than breaking her bones. If only she'd been *better*.

As the years had passed she'd go for minutes and then hours without thinking of Rob, but then it would come back, all of it, enveloping her in a thick, ugly fog, blotting out all that was good in the world.

Now she had to go back to Cobshott, where she'd almost died, and where the truth about her life, and Medford's, had come out.

A small group of paparazzi were gathered by the car park entrance. Clearly the story had started to leak. Recognising Sue from the Medford case, they thrust their cameras at the car windows and photographed her as she waited for the barrier to rise. Her knuckles whitened as she gripped the steering wheel, a sense of panic rising in her belly. Thoughts of the Medford case, of Cobshott, flooded back. But Sue kept her face inscrutable, her eyes staring straight ahead as she drove inside and parked. Mike's insight – and emotional support – on the ground would have been invaluable. But Sue was too professional to let her thoughts linger. There was a missing man to be found.

Inside the station there was a real buzz, an unspoken sense of urgency that always happened when a major case was brewing.

'Morning, ma'am.'

Sue's new deputy, DI Dev Basu, handed her a coffee.

'What's the latest, Dev?'

'Biller wants us to go straight to his office. I've never seen him so worked up.'

'It's a A-list Hollywood celeb missing on his patch, Dev. He's only eight months off retirement. I reckon he was hoping to sail quietly into the sunset.'

Dev was right. Chief Constable Biller was pacing around his office like a man possessed.

'Ah, Sue, Dev, come in. Here's the file. It goes without saying that this is seriously high-profile. We'll be under intense scrutiny. The whole world wants this man found.'

'Of course, sir,' Sue replied, calmly, fighting the urge to eye-roll. The *whole world*. Biller had clearly got his knickers in a twist. 'What do we know?'

'His boyfriend, Tyler Tipping, called it in. Turned up, actually, in the middle of the night. The duty sergeant did his best to cope as the man was *hysterical*. His statement's in there. The press office is setting up an on-camera appeal for later today. We'd like you to appear with Tyler. After the

Medford case, it's good for the public to see we've got you on it.'

'Of course, sir.'

'We've got officers at his two homes now. No obvious signs of a break-in, or anything untoward at all, but Forensics are on their way. The paps have already got wind of it. Christ knows how. Bloody leak at the station, if you ask me. More holes than a colander. Tyler's downstairs.'

'Any suggestion he's a suspect?'

'No. But we can't rule anything out. Including blackmail. There's been no ransom demand yet, but Stevens is *very* famous and super-rich, so it's a definite possibility.'

'What about activism?' Dev asked. 'Anyone or any groups he's annoyed lately?'

'Not that we know of,' Biller replied. 'His profile's been squeaky-clean up until now. No drugs, not even a driving offence. Doesn't even *drink* anymore.' Biller spat out the words as if being teetotal was utterly shameful.

'Almost too clean...' Sue pondered. 'Is Tyler up to being questioned?'

'He's pretty tearful, but yes. Keen to do anything he can to help.'

'What about Stevens' parents? Still alive?'

'Yes. Dafydd and Gwen Morgan. Stevens changed his name by deed poll. They live in the valleys in South Wales. Just outside a village called Tony-something. Tonyrefail, I think. Sounds like a dodgy cabaret singer. They've got a detached bungalow. Not at home, but neighbours say they're likely at their caravan, which is somewhere near

Porthcawl, so local force are checking the sites. Seem to keep themselves to themselves. Neighbours also said, as far as they know, the parents haven't spoken to Sam for years. What was the quote?' Biller launched into a thick Welsh accent. '"They don't approve of his *ways*." I'd hoped to notify the parents before we went public but as it seems they haven't spoken in years I won't lose any sleep over it.'

Sue picked up the file and stood up. 'We'll get straight on it, sir.'

Biller nodded. 'We need to find him, Sue. I don't want it to drag on. His agent is Lola Lovett, so if we put a foot wrong she'll be all over it. Bloody female Max Clifford. Without the paedophilia. I've asked Uniform to bring her in. She's bound to know more about Stevens' personal life than anyone.'

Back at her desk, Sue read through Tyler's statement. He claimed to have been with Sam for just under a year, ever since they met at an AA meeting. Tyler had addiction issues after growing up in care in Farnborough, Hampshire. Now clean, he worked for Climate Crisis charity as a campaigner, which, Sue noted, might explain Sam's recent Instagram posts promoting veganism to save the rainforests. Tyler's own social media was full of pictures of him at work, glued to petrol pumps and setting fire to a bin in Trafalgar Square, but for the last year, it was *only* work. No pictures in restaurants, bars, of him socialising at all. That made sense, Sue thought. Stevens – no doubt with the help of Lola Lovett – had always kept his private life private. Tyler was thirty-one, Sam was forty-two. Bit of an age gap, but nothing that remarkable.

'So they didn't live together?' Dev asked.

'No,' Sue replied. 'Looks like Tyler often stayed over at Stevens' house in Cobshott and the one in Hampstead. But he has his own rented flat in Soho.'

'How does he afford that as a charity worker?'

'Dunno. Probably paid for by Stevens. Get on to the lettings agent and find out whose name it's in. Tyler last saw him in Cobshott on Saturday. They went out for dinner, he stayed the night and went home Sunday afternoon. Started to worry when he didn't get his usual "goodnight" video call – I'm thinking phone sex – that night. No replies to anything on Monday including phone calls, and came in here panicking early hours of this morning.'

'What's your feeling, boss?'

'Multitude of options. A Grindr hook-up that went wrong. A crazed fan and he's tied to a bed like *Misery*. Stevens has fucked off somewhere for the hell of it. Gone all Stephen Fry on us and is driving to France or on a plane. Maybe the boyfriend did it. Get PC Evans to check all the passenger names on flights out of London to Los Angeles since Sunday afternoon, if he's got a home there. Like Biller said, we can't rule anything out. Let's go downstairs and talk to Tyler.'

Chapter Three

LOLA

S am Stevens was – sorry, *is*, if he's still alive – my biggest client. He was also one of the first actors I took on when I started my agency. After six years at the coalface with Soozie Lightwater's celebrity agency, I'd started my own. Lola Lovett PR. I still get a kick when I walk into our glitzy offices on London's Tottenham Court Road and off LA's Sunset Boulevard and see my name in lights above the doors.

Soozie took it badly when Sam first said he wanted to join me. Threatened all kinds of legal action, but nothing came of it. She didn't want the publicity. And Sam was adamant. He was an arrogant kid from a rough part of South Wales, with a pretty face – and a massive chip on his shoulder – who wanted to be a huge star. I set myself up as a 'personal publicist' to be at clients' every beck and call, to protect them from the press, from other PRs who wanted them to promote a film they hated that they'd done, but mostly to protect them from themselves. And as his star ascended, so did mine. We'd helped each other.

This could ruin me. Wreck my life and everything I'd worked so hard for. I'd be the one splashed all over the press, exposed as the desperate, deadly creature I've become. My hands shaking, I open the glove compartment and rummage around for a burner phone.

'What the fuck is going on?' I snap. 'Where is Sam? I've just had the fucking press on the phone tipping me off that he's been reported missing. By that money-grabbing weasel of a boyfriend. I thought you'd done the job.'

'I ran into a problem.'

'What sort of problem?'

'Someone else got there first.'

'Bullshit.'

'Straight up. A car was driving out of the gates of his Cobshott house just as I arrived. I let it go, slipped through before they shut – that saved climbing over the wall – went round the back and let myself in with that key. The utility room window was open, looked like it had been forced, and there were possible signs of a struggle – bedclothes on the floor, a lamp knocked over, but nothing much. And no Stevens.'

'For fuck's sake. Why didn't you follow the car?'

'No reason to think it was anything other than a friend leaving. Black Jaguar saloon. Expensive. I didn't get the plates. I've been trying to track him ever since. That's why I didn't tell you. I thought you'd go off on one, try to phone him, and that's too risky. My job is to protect you. I didn't think anyone else wanted him dead. Or alive. You said this is personal.'

'It is. So who took him?'

'None of the usual London gangs. Could be Albanians. My guess is whoever it is will deliver a ransom demand any day now. There's no other reason for anyone to kidnap him.'

A hundred awful, conflicted, confused emotions ran through my mind. I needed Sam dead. The deal was an overdose of heroin. Instant, no suffering. Just gone. Not this.

'What will they do to him?'

'Don't tell me you're getting a *conscience*.'

'I don't want him dead. I *need* him dead. Silenced. There's a difference. I don't think I can handle it if they start chopping off body parts and sending them in the post.'

His voice softens. 'Listen, whoever's got him will be after money. That's got to be the motive. I shut the kitchen window, so there's no sign of forced entry, tidied up a bit. The police will think he's done a runner and left in a hurry rather than been abducted. Should push a bit of suspicion on to the boyfriend. Buy us some time to find the kidnappers and deal direct with them. They'll just want cash – they won't be interested in your sordid past.'

That was probably true. But every second Sam Stevens was alive, I was at risk. I'd worked too hard to lose it all. The public shame, the humiliation. And I wouldn't survive a second in prison.

'Look, just find him. We've got to get to him before the police do, or before those kidnappers start torturing. He'll be in such a state that he'll spill *everything*. You should have told me straightaway. If he talks…'

'I've got contacts everywhere and no one's heard anything. Not a whisper. I thought I'd locate the kidnappers in a couple of hours, do business with them and get this sorted.'

'You mean pay them to do our dirty work?'

'Yep. Costly but effective. Once they've got their money, they'll probably kill him anyway. I just wasn't expecting the trail to be this cold. But whoever took him will surface at some point. Until then, sit tight. When the police come to talk to you – and they will, they're probably on their way now – stick to the story. You last spoke to him on Saturday afternoon. He was tired but fine. Happy to have finished the shoot. Didn't want to go to the awards with all that booze about. That call is logged on your phone. That's all you know.'

'OK.'

'And call me as soon as you've spoken to the police. Or if you get any ransom demands. They might come to you, as you're like family.'

I jab the off button and toss the phone on to the passenger seat. Family. I'm in far too deep, and I know it, but after everything that's happened, I can't see any other way out.

Chapter Four

TUESDAY

Tyler was sitting behind the desk, his face red, eyes puffy. Sue noticed how pretty he was, with a thin, chiselled face, floppy blond hair and huge, almond-shaped blue eyes filled with sadness. She had seen this sadness before, a pain that was clawing at his very soul, so if he had had something to do with Sam's disappearance, it was tearing him apart.

'Mr Tipping.' Sue held out her hand. 'I'm DCI Sue Fisher and this is my partner, DI Dev Basu. We're organising a TV appeal, but, in the meantime, I'd like to go over your statement. We're determined to find Sam, so this would really help.'

Tyler rubbed his face with his trembling hands. 'Of course. Anything.' He paused. 'I know you. Didn't you work on that other missing person case? The House of Horrors one?'

Sue nodded. 'That's right,' she said gently. 'So I'm very

familiar with Cobshott. Now, let's start with the last time you saw Sam. Saturday, wasn't it?'

'Yes. Sam had wrapped on his recent film – *finished* – on Thursday. I was working Friday, and he was shattered anyway, so I caught the train down on Saturday and he picked me up from Cobshott station.'

'What time was that?'

'I left home about eleven a.m. Got the Tube to Waterloo and then a train.'

'And your flat in Soho – is that Sam's too?'

Tyler reddened. 'It's in my name but he pays for it, yeah. I was in a flat share in Wandsworth before, so he couldn't come over. People would recognise him. Gossip, you know. Sell stories. He said this is more private.'

'So, you arrived at Cobshott station. Did Sam pick you up?'

'No. I walked. It's not far. He never learned to drive. Nor did I. Didn't need to in London, and now he just gets cabs or producers send cars for him. There was a paparazzi I've seen before hanging out at the end of his street. I'm sure he took a snap of me.'

'Do you know his name?'

'No. New one, though. Like a sodding fly, buzzing round Sam everywhere. The security guards on the estate usually move them on quickly.'

'So you went into the house. What happened then?'

'We, er, *chilled* for a while and then went out to dinner.'

'By chilled, you mean...'

'Had sex. I hadn't seen him for two weeks. He'd been on location in Ullswater filming a drama series.'

'Where did you go for dinner?'

'Our usual place. Riverside Vegetaria.'

'The one in Kingston?'

'Yeah. We're both vegan, and it's the best by far. They know Sam and always keep a secluded table for him. We got there about seven-thirty p.m. and left just after ten.'

'Did you take a cab?'

'Yes. When he's got a beard hardly anyone recognises him, so no one bothered us. Obviously neither of us drink. We're in recovery. Afterwards, we took a cab home.'

'Were any paparazzi still hanging about?'

'Not that I noticed.'

'How did Sam seem in himself?' Dev asked.

'Happy. He was relieved the shoot was over. I don't think he liked Ullswater.'

'What makes you say that?'

'Just a few things he said. We had a rule not to talk about work too much. But he said there was a toxic atmosphere on set. The director, Simon Omeria, had got everyone's backs up and Sam spent all his time trying to build bridges between people. Everyone went to Sam with their problems.'

'Did he mention anyone by name?' Dev asked.

'Only his co-star, Julia Peace. He said Omeria had really upset her all the way through the shoot, bossing her about, not listening to her ideas, pulling rank. And that he suspected the director had got too touchy-feely with one of the younger guys in the cast. Stephen Merryweather. Rumour was it had happened to other actors, too, in the past. Something had happened in Omeria's trailer, and Julia told Sam she'd seen the guy leaving in tears. I don't know the details.'

'Did Sam ask the actor about it?'

'He said he chatted to him but the guy didn't bring it up. And Sam didn't want to pry. But he took Omeria aside and told him to keep his hands off the cast. All of them. He said he didn't mention names. Omeria didn't say anything, apparently. Just walked off.'

'What did you do on Sunday?' Sue asked.

'Not much. It was a gorgeous day. We sunbathed in the garden, by the pool. Sam made some lunch. I went home about mid-afternoon as I'd promised to help a friend with their packing. They're moving house. Sam offered to get me an Uber but I said the train would be quicker.' Tyler scrolled through his phone. 'Look, Sam texted me to check I'd got home safely and said he'd video call me later.' Thick tears welled up in his eyes. 'That… that's the last message.'

Sue took the phone. The message said simply: *Home safe babes? Missing you already. Video call me when you finish the packing. I'm up for being big daddy again xxx*, followed by chatty messages from Tyler, which became increasingly desperate.

'Big daddy?' she said gently.

'It's a sex game we play. Sorry.'

'Nothing to apologise for,' Sue replied. 'So this text was sent at five p.m., and you replied about nine p.m....'

'That's right. I went straight to my friend's flat in Borough to help him finish packing, because he was moving the next day. Didn't see any paps at all when I left Sam's. I saw the message when I was walking to my friend's place but didn't get a chance to reply until later. I remember leaving around eight-forty-five p.m. because I texted Sam walking home.'

'We will need to speak to your friend, just to confirm your movements,' Dev said softly. 'Just routine. And it's best we hang on to this phone. We'll get any calls routed to us, in case someone's taken Sam against his will.'

Tyler buried his face in his hands. 'He's so gentle, Sam. Not like those tormented characters he plays. Something's really wrong. He wouldn't just disappear like this. He'll know I'm worried sick.'

Sue handed him a tissue and Tyler blew his nose loudly. 'What time did you get home?'

'I got the Tube so was home by about ten.'

'And that's when you tried video calling?'

'Yeah. But it wouldn't connect. I tried WhatsApping but my messages didn't show as delivered. Including that one I'd sent at nine p.m. I wasn't massively worried though. Often when he finished a shoot he'd be exhausted. I thought he'd fallen asleep, his phone had gone flat, and he'd call me full of apologies at six a.m. Monday morning. So I went to bed, and when my alarm went off for work at seven a.m. I checked my phone. Nothing. Messages still not delivered. I rang the retreat centre he sometimes uses, Hillmead Place in Kent, said I had an urgent message for him. He often goes there, and gets a cab to Camber Sands to walk on the beach. But he wasn't at Hillmead. Tried a couple of his friends too, casually. I didn't want to panic anyone. They hadn't seen him.'

'But you didn't contact us for help until the early hours of Tuesday?'

'No.' Tyler paused. 'He's *famous*. I didn't want this all over the press. So I rang in sick on Monday and got the train down to Cobshott. I have a key. There was so sign of him. Nothing. Same at the Hampstead flat. That's when I started to freak out. I thought maybe he'd met someone else.'

'You were feeling jealous?'

Tyler paused. 'Yes. Well, confused mainly. His bed wasn't made and Sam never left it like that. So yeah, I wanted to know where he was. He'd said he wasn't going to the awards ceremony on Monday night, and I couldn't see any paparazzi pictures of him on social media, but I wondered if he'd gone secretly to the after party by a back door, or hooked up with someone. I stayed at the Hampstead flat and when he didn't show up by three a.m. I got an Uber back down to Cobshott. I thought I'd turn up unannounced. He wasn't there. The house was just as I'd left it. That's when I knew something was seriously wrong and came here.'

Tears began to trickle down Tyler's face. 'He's going to be so angry with me if he's just gone off with someone. Or wanted to get away by himself for a few days and I've splashed this all over the papers. But I don't know what else to do.'

'Thank you, Mr Tipping,' Sue said gently. 'Like I say, these questions are just routine. Chief Biller said you're willing to help us by going on camera to put out an appeal for Sam. If he's having some kind of breakdown and has run away, hopefully he'll see it and make contact.'

'D-do you think that's what happened?'

'We don't know,' Dev said softly. 'But what we do know is an emotional appeal will have an impact on him if he sees it. Do you have some photographs of Sam with a beard? The public will be ready to help and that will make our chances of finding him much higher.'

'Sure. There's a few on the phone. They're all clean. Sam was really strict about photos and videos. Said they could get into the wrong hands.'

Sue nodded. 'Sensible. Let's get you another cup of tea. We'll finalise the arrangements for the appeal. I'll brief you properly before it starts. The key is not to reply to any questions, if the press start shouting them out. We'll run through everything. And thank you for your help. I know this can't be easy. Same goes for any paparazzi who approach you. Say nothing.'

Outside the room, Sue and Dev looked at each other. 'Jealousy,' Sue said. 'That's a motive if ever I heard one. And get hold of the paparazzi who took a shot of Tyler arriving at Stevens' house. They must have been hanging around the area. See if they noticed anything suspicious.'

'And what about this Simon Omeria guy?' Dev replied.

'If Sam confronted him about the casting couch, he's probably glad he's off the scene.'

'Yep. Do some digging, Dev. Speak to Omeria and the cast. Including Stephen Merryweather. But don't let on to Omeria that we know about him being handsy. Not yet. Are Forensics sweeping the house and flat?'

'They are,' Dev replied. 'Want to take a look at Cobshott?'

Sue nodded. 'Get Uniform to pick up Stevens' agent, Lola Lovett. Bring her in. They usually know all the skeletons in the cupboard. If he's got one, we'll find it.'

Twenty minutes later, as the morning sun glistened on the trees, Sue turned her unmarked Vauxhall Corsa into Cobshott's Crown Estate, a leafy network of private roads lined with sterile new-build mansions, home to Premier League footballers, city bankers and dotcom millionaires. A small group of paparazzi had gathered by the entrance, but the estate's private security guards were keeping them at bay. Each house was set behind imposing ornamental gates, and anyone who lived here was far too important to have a house *number*, so they'd been replaced by names even though that made them a nightmare to find. She shivered as she drove past the old entrance to Riverdell, which had been sold off, demolished and rebuilt after the Medford case, and renamed 'Chantry House'. But to her surprise, the thought of returning to Cobshott was worse than actually doing it. Maybe Mike was right. Maybe some of the ghosts had gone.

'Which one was it?' Dev asked.

'That one.' Sue pointed to a set of huge gates in front of a long driveway, which disappeared into the trees. Inwardly, she shuddered. 'You can't see the house from here. It's not the same building, anyway.'

'Do you think there's any link to Sam Stevens? It's quite close.'

'Doubt it. The only link is the location. But I'm not ruling anything out.'

'Who bought the house?'

'Developers. They erected a huge pile and some guy who owns an online betting firm snapped it up, according to the papers. I wouldn't live there if you paid me.'

'Really, boss? Don't fancy a swimming pool and walk-in wardrobe?'

'I do. Just not there.' She shivered. 'Bad vibes, you know.'

Dev nodded and pointed to a turning on the left. 'This is it.'

Sam's house, Appletree Lodge, was halfway down the street. The electric gates were open, with two uniformed officers standing in front of them, and the wide, tiled driveway filled with squad cars and forensics vans. 'Biller's really pushed the boat out on the one,' Sue said. 'Wants to get the job done *and* be seen doing it.'

'DCI Sue Fisher...' she began, pulling up by the young

officer, who waved her through before she'd even pulled out her ID.

'You're famous round here,' Dev grinned.

'Don't remind me.'

Sue parked the Corsa near the gate and walked up the sandy-coloured drive, scanning the house, while Dev chatted to the local officers. It was a wide, pale-red-brick house, built within the last ten years or so, with an imposing black front door framed with two Romanesque columns, and the ubiquitous triple garage to the right. Bit of a waste, Sue thought, given he doesn't drive. Something about it reminded Sue of the houses Tom used to draw as a child, with two windows either side of the door, three across the first floor, and a vaulted roof, though this one had a large circular window in it.

'Sue.' Dr Wei Zhao, the lead forensic investigator, came out of the front door, his clothes covered securely with a white hooded crime scene suit and his face behind a mask. 'Suit up if you're coming in. Biller's all over this case like a *rash.*'

'What's the latest, Wei?'

'We're taking samples, but, on the face of it, the place looks pretty clean to me. No blood splatters. There are fresh marks on the kitchen window – more of a utility room, really – which indicate it was jemmied open, but it was closed and secured from the inside. Could be Stevens locked himself out recently. Possible footprint outside the window, we're doing our best with that. No sign of burglary, or that anyone's been injured or killed here. So far.'

'I'm guessing you've checked the panic room,' Sue replied, with a half-smile.

'There isn't one. Unless it's got a secret entrance.'

'Very funny. I'll suit up and take a look round.'

Inside, the entire ground floor was covered in white marble tiles, with pale-grey walls and cool-grey velvet sofas. A copy of *Hello!* magazine lay open on one sofa, beside a TV remote control, which an officer was swabbing. Appletree Lodge was far more tasteful than some of the houses she'd seen on the estate. Unusual, brightly coloured abstract sculptures and paintings were dotted about, which she sensed were chosen out of love, not just to impress. Every room had a giant TV screen, including the kitchen, and vases of fresh flowers.

'Have we checked on the cleaner? He's clearly got one.'

'Uniform have talked to her,' Dev replied, joining Sue. 'Older lady, Mrs Deverish, lives on the council estate on the other side of Cobshott village. Looked after the house since he moved in six years ago, and did so for the previous tenants. She usually comes in every day, even when Stevens is away, to keep an eye on the place. But she'd had a text from Sam on Thursday morning to say he'd be back from his shoot later, to make sure there were fresh flowers in the main rooms, and that he wouldn't need her until Tuesday, as Tyler would be staying.'

'Was that unusual?'

'No. He sent a similar text to the pool guy, who also does

the gardening. Apparently he often gave them a few days off – on full pay – if he had people over. Both the cleaner and the pool guy have electronic keys to the gates and the house. Only other person with keys is his boyfriend, according to Mrs Deverish. The pool guy is newer and works for a local firm that seems to take care of most of Cobshott's hot tubs, swimming pools and gardens.'

'And Tyler says he left on Sunday.'

'Yeah. We're checking CCTV on the trains to confirm that. Maybe Stevens had someone else coming.'

DS Fiona Howe, one of the junior detectives on Sue's team, came in, speaking thickly through her mask. 'Burglar alarm was off, ma'am,' Fiona said. 'I've spoken to the neighbours and they insist Stevens was meticulous about leaving it on when he was out, as they had quite a few irritating false alarms over the past couple of years. Even had one last week.'

'Any CCTV?'

'Stevens didn't have it switched on if he was home,' Fiona continued. 'The neighbours say that wasn't unusual. He'd had them over for dinner when he first moved in and said he felt spied on enough by the paparazzi.'

'Thanks, Fiona. Keep me posted.'

'Ma'am.'

Sue walked up to the first floor, deep in thought. Abduction or a Grindr date gone wrong were top of her list. The giant spiralling staircase was perhaps Appletree Lodge's most impressive feature of all, a whirl of steel and grey glass. There were six guest bedrooms, each themed in a different pastel colour, all immaculate. Sam's bedroom was the largest, overlooking the manicured garden, an acre of brushed lawn and perfectly planted borders, with stunning dinner-plate-sized dahlias, giant swaying banana plants and palms.

'I'm definitely getting house envy,' Dev smiled. 'Knew I should have gone into movies.'

Unlike the rest of the house, which looked straight out of the pages of *Hello!* magazine, the bedroom had more of a cosy, lived-in feel. It was a huge room, but the mellow green carpet and yellow curtains gave it a homely air, and the bed was draped with soft throws and scatter cushions. The bed was one of the biggest Sue had ever seen, and only one side of it was disturbed, with the pastel-green duvet pulled back as if someone had just got out. The bedside lamp was on the floor, and a book titled *Viva La Vegans* lay on the table beside it. Sue picked it up. If Sam had been reading it, he hadn't bent the spine.

'Does this look a bit *staged* to you, Dev? The kimono neatly over the chair? The bedclothes pushed back just so?'

'Maybe. But the whole house is immaculate. Everything in its place.'

'Exactly. So if Stevens was going to do a runner, he'd either be in a right state – and so would the house – or meticulously plan it and leave it spotless. He'd make the bed. Something's not right, Dev. I can *feel* it. No matter what Forensics come up with, I don't think Sam Stevens left here of his own free will. So we're looking at abduction. Or murder.'

Chapter Five

LOLA

I wake up at 5:30 a.m., after half an hour's fitful sleep on the sofa filled with horrific nightmares about Sam. He's all I can think about. Images of Sam when we first met, laughing as we skipped though the wet, shiny Soho streets, promising each other we'd rule the world. Sam at a party, three lines of coke down, telling me I'm the only real family he's ever had. Drinking champagne in the Century Club's rooftop bar, surveying Soho below us, like a king and queen.

I should have seen his betrayal coming. Everyone stabs you in the back in the end, even if they don't mean to. Except for Rick, my fixer. He knows where the bodies are buried. And he's the one I tasked with silencing Sam. I trust him. Only him.

Rick and I were at school together. That's where I quickly learned to toughen up. It was a selective state grammar school, which meant most of the pupils were filthy rich, and their parents had had them tutored to the hilt to get them a place. I didn't fit in, and nor did Rick. While they went home to a warm dinner and – for the most part – parents who were interested in them, albeit for their success, I'd be wondering if Mum was out of bed yet.

Home was a council house on the outskirts of Farnborough in Surrey. Rick lived on the same run-down street, and even before we went to the Gram, as we called it, we'd see each other around, buying 10p pick-and-mix in the sweet shop or grazing our knees in the estate's playground. Dad was a hazy figure, who died when I was four, so my memories of him are blurry round the edges. I remember going to the hospital, only once, where Dad was lying in bed, asleep, tubes coming out of his stomach. He smelled of vinegar. I sat by the bed, wondering when we could go home. Days later, Mum told me he'd gone to Heaven. People came to the house, dressed in black. A long car with a coffin inside. A church service with people crying. Heaven sounded nice to me, much nicer than home, and I couldn't work out why they were sad.

Life wasn't too bad at first. Mum was working part time as a shop assistant, and my nan – a care worker and a big bear of a woman – sometimes picked me up from school. We'd have a Wimpy on the way home, and share Nan's favourite, a Brown Derby, which was a giant donut with ice cream in it. When I got into the grammar school, Nan was over the moon.

'You can make something of your life, my girl,' she said proudly. 'Don't end up wiping arses like me.'

That night she died of a cardiac arrest. And Mum started drinking heavily. She usually poured the first one around six p.m., always red wine, always out of those ghastly wine boxes so she didn't have to face how much she'd drunk. Even now, I can't touch red wine. Just the smell of it makes me want to vomit. By ten p.m. the tears or the shouting would start, railing at me or down the phone to anyone who would listen, until she passed out. The store sacked her, so we lived on benefits. I swore to myself that as soon as I could, I'd leave that hellish place and create my own life. Be someone. Make Nan proud. But she sure as hell wouldn't be proud of *this*, of what I've become.

Nan was in my dreams, too. I saw her looming over me, her eyes filled with anger, saying over and over. 'What have you *done*, Lola? What have you *done*?'

Pushing thoughts of Nan aside, I check my phone. The Sam Stevens story has clearly broken in the last hour, or been leaked, and my clients with the smallest hangovers have already woken up to it. *OMG Lola what's happened to Sam?* sums them up. I check the TV news. It's scrolling across the yellow ticker. 'Breaking: Sam Stevens missing' but the presenter is talking about politics.

I type a quick reply:

Don't worry, I'm sure he's fine. Probably just taken some time out. I'll talk to the police and find out all I can.

I have to keep them calm. The last thing I need is any clients falling apart while filming on set today because they're worried about Sam, while secretly enduring pangs of jealousy at all the press attention he's getting.

The showbiz reporter is on screen now. Sophia Scarlett. I detest her. Most of the magazine TV reporters play ball if you handle them right. Not Sophia. I took her on set for a drama once, to interview one of my potential A-listers, when she was on a TV magazine. To be fair, the client did get a bong out halfway through the interview and lit up. It happens. The other magazine journalists present didn't bat an eyelid, and listened to my heartfelt plea that exposing him as an addict would jeopardise both his recovery and his future roles. Sophia sold the story to the tabloids, earning herself both a new job and a truckload of cash. He's still a client, but never made it to the A-list, still struggles with addiction, and I still blame her for it.

'We're hearing reports that Sam Stevens has gone missing,' she trills, as the programme cuts to live shots of a police station. 'His latest boyfriend, charity worker Tyler Tipping, is believed to have reported it in the early hours, and is currently at Kingston police station in Surrey. We're expecting him to make a public appeal.'

My phone buzzes. It's Tim Thacker. 'A pap's got a snap of Tyler Tipping arriving at Sam Stevens' house on Saturday. We've got to run it, Lola. I can't sit on this one. Tipping's making a statement shortly, according to police sources. I need a quote from you.'

'OK.' I pause. 'I'm sure this is all a fuss over nothing, Tim. You can say I'm hoping to contact Sam and at this stage I'm not too worried as he's probably just taking some time out following a very successful shoot in the Lake District for the upcoming hit *Murder in the Lakes*.'

'Thanks. And will do. I'll keep in touch.'

Seconds later, the messages come pouring in. I send the standard reply to as many as I can, forward it to my assistant, Olivia, and tell her to mass-mail it to all our clients, asking them not to call me unless it's super-urgent. Exhausted, I haul myself off the sofa and pad softly across the deep white carpet through my bedroom to the ensuite bathroom.

My London flat is in a flashy blue-glass tower in Vauxhall, overlooking the Thames, not quite the penthouse suite – a politician lives up there – but high enough to give me an incredible view of the city and, I admit, a feeling of superiority. Across the early September sky, the sun is beginning to rise, streaking it with red and gold. The rays are slanting through the floor-to-ceiling window and landing on my black cat, Cleopatra, curled up in her basket.

'How was last night?'

Peter, my latest boyfriend, is stirring. I've been sleeping with him for a couple of months. I don't do long term. Too *messy*. The last thing I need is him sensing something's *up* and I really don't want to talk about Sam right now. 'I don't remember you coming in,' he yawns, rubbing his eyes. 'Did it go OK?'

'Really well, hon. I tried not to wake you. Only one incident involving balls and a glass of prosecco.'

'Oh God. Did he do his party trick again?'

'Certainly did.'

Peter yawns again and rolls over to go back to sleep. I close the bathroom door, place my phone carefully on the black marble top, and stare at myself in the mirror. Last night's blue eye make-up and one of my mink eyelashes are smeared down my cheeks. Despite the touch of fake tan, I look tired, haggard. I turn sideways and check my frame and belly. Still too fat.

I turn the power shower on full, pull a plastic cap over my hair – it still looks pretty much how the hairdresser styled it yesterday – and stand under the jets of water, running through what I'll say to the police. I feel soiled, dirty. Killing Sam was never part of my plan. Nor were the others. But I've waded in, I'm way out of my depth, and all I can do right now is try to stay afloat. To survive.

Peter's snoring lightly as I walk into my wardrobe. I've got clothes for every possible occasion, and this one needs to be formal. I choose a black trouser suit, a pink linen shirt – I don't want to look like I'm going to a funeral – and black Manolos. I keep my make-up light, and settle on sweeping my long blonde hair back into a smart ponytail.

The police will be here soon, I'm sure of it. They'll want to know all about Sam, and I need to be completely on my game.

Chapter Six

TUESDAY

Lola Lovett was exactly what Sue had expected. She'd seen photos of her in the press from time to time, and making statements on camera when any of her fiercely protected clients were caught partying with sex workers or snorting their salaries up their nose. Or both.

She looked in her early forties, and was wearing what Sue guessed was a very expensive suit, with ridiculously high heels for so early in the morning. Her thin, almost gaunt, frame, brown eyes that flitted rapidly around the room taking in everything, quick movements and slightly large, beak-shaped nose reminded Sue of a bird.

'Lola Lovett.' Her handshake was fast and business-like. 'I just can't believe this is happening. We must find Sam. Let me know how I can help.'

'Thank you, Ms Lovett.'

Sue led the way down the corridor to her office, with Lola's heels clicking loudly on the tiles behind her. To her relief, Lola wasn't one of those irritating PR people who felt they had to fill every silence with mindless chit-chat. She was business-like, to the point and, in that sense, rather like her. As they walked through the main incident room, Sue noticed officers glancing up from their desks to take a look at Lola.

'Please take a seat, Ms Lovett,' Sue said, closing her office door, and wishing she'd had a chance to tidy up a bit. Her desk was stacked with teetering piles of paperwork, scraps of paper and empty coffee cups. Lola's desk would be quite the opposite, Sue was sure of it.

She drained her mug and peered into it. 'Can I get you a coffee? In a much cleaner mug than this one?'

Lola smiled, revealing a set of perfectly white – but not too white, unlike many of her clients – and even teeth. It was a genuinely warm and friendly smile, Sue noticed, but she sensed steel behind it. Lola had clearly perfected it as part of the art of putting people at ease when she wanted to. 'Black, please. No sugar. Espresso if you have it. But anything will do.'

Sue gestured to Dev to come in. 'Can we get Ms Lovett a black coffee?'

'Of course.'

'Try and put a fresh pot on, Dev. The last one was thick as treacle. Tasted like it had been brewing for *days*.'

Dev smiled, and quietly closed the door. She'd already explained to him that she wanted to talk to Lovett alone. It was an instinct, a feeling that this powerful woman would respond better in a one-to-one situation, perhaps reveal things about Sam that she'd be more wary of if a younger and more junior male officer was present. Both women were in their forties, and although she was less well known than Lola, the Medford case had also made Sue a household name, for a while, at least. She felt sure that if it was just the two of them, Lola was more likely to open up.

'Thank you again for coming in, Ms Lovett. The more I can learn about Sam, the better chance we have of finding him. Is there anywhere else you think he could be that we're not aware of? A secret lover? Bolt-hole?'

'I wish I did. There are the three houses – Cobshott, Hampstead and LA – but no lover that I know of. Seems very taken with Tyler, his latest. He sometimes goes off to a retreat centre in the woods, but I'm guessing you've checked that. Hillmead Place? Markets itself as an "urban escape", but basically you pay them a fortune to switch off your phone, eat kale and shit in the forest.'

Sue couldn't help smiling. Lola was her kind of woman. No-nonsense. 'We have. He's not there. Anywhere else?'

Lola paused. 'What's Tyler saying? Had they had a row?'

'Not as far as we know. Any ex-partners?'

'There are a couple. Both actors, one currently shooting in Australia, the other in Northern Ireland on yet another *Star Wars* spin-off. Joseph Riller and Mark MacClune. I don't think either of them would have a hand in this. They're both younger, pretty boys in their late twenties, with hopefully terrific careers ahead of them. Sam was only ever a stepping stone if you ask me.'

'I'll need their details. We'd better check them out.'

'Of course. They're both on my books. What's your number? I'll email you their deets. Oh, and a girl he was dating before them. Not one of my clients, though. Emma-Jayne Lysette. She's with Robinson Sinclair Agency. I'll send you that too.'

Seconds later, the names, numbers and emails pinged on to Sue's phone, and she forwarded them to Dev. 'So they all split amicably?'

'Fairly.' Lola paused. 'Look, we've kept this out of the press and I'd appreciate it if you could support that, but Sam had problems with drugs, in the past. His partners got fed up with it. There were a couple of *incidents*. Sam had a habit when high of accusing people of betraying him. One was in a Brighton hotel when he was shooting down there, and he trashed it. Even chucked the TV across the bedroom. Very rock and roll. Though ironically the TV didn't smash to smithereens in the big, grand gesture Sam was hoping for. It just bounced. I've always bought a Samsung since then.'

'I'll make sure I do, too. They sound bulletproof. Though I don't remember hearing about that?'

'You wouldn't have done. The boyfriend called me straightaway in floods of tears, terrified his career was *over*, that he'd forever be known as Sam's toyboy shag. I made sure the hotel didn't report it and the press didn't get wind. I shut that down by assuring the hotel they'd be chosen to host a glittering awards ceremony. Which they were.

Brought them in hundreds of thousands of pounds' worth of business.'

'Must be an interesting job,' Sue mused. 'You must be pretty unshockable.'

'Fairly. Though I'm still constantly surprised by some of the scrapes clients get into. It's often sex. And drugs. Usually together. Or airing their bigoted views. But you didn't hear me say that.'

'So he's has the Cobshott place for six years? He would have been there during the Medford case. I'm sure you remember that. Did he ever mention the nail salon?'

'We discussed it at the time. He was horrified and even talked about selling up. Didn't want to live near a crime scene. Sam said he never met Medford or visited the nail bar. But the fuss died down and it was financially a bad time to sell, anyway.'

Sue was relieved that Lola didn't do what so many strangers did when they mentioned the Medford case: look at her in awe, with a quizzical look expecting all the gossip. To Lola, it was clearly yesterday's news.

'Cobshott is really just a show home,' Lola went on. 'For parties. To impress. As far as I know he has all his treatments done at a salon in LA. Botox and fillers, too, though you didn't hear me say that, either. He spends most of his time in LA or Hampstead.'

Sue smiled. 'When did you first meet Sam?'

'Years ago. I started out at the Soozie Lightwater Agency. He was on my books…'

Before she could stop herself, Sue interrupted her. 'Soozie Lightwater?'

'Yes. I'm guessing you came across her on the Medford case.'

'I did.' Sue recovered her composure. Soozie Lightwater. She knew her of old. Celebrity PR turned Stepford Wife and now the much-loved face of a children's charity. She'd known serial killer Medford well and had helped the police with the case.

Could it be coincidence? Probably. Cobshott was a small village that attracted the super-rich, and the world of celebrity PR seemed to have a handful of big names in it. So it wasn't that surprising that Sam had a place in Cobshott, or that the two women knew each other. Soozie had proved invaluable before. Perhaps she would again.

'I was at Oxford with her, before she started her agency. Sam was on her books,' Lola went on.

'I didn't know you went to Oxford.'

'I don't advertise it. Otherwise people think you've had an easy ride to success, made it on Daddy's money or contacts. I worked for Soozie and Sam was unknown then, a jobbing actor, like a lot of her early clients. For some reason, Soozie thought he'd never amount to much. She gave me him to manage, and I made it my mission to prove her wrong. Maybe that was her tactic all along.'

Sue smiled. 'I can imagine that.'

'He grew up in Tonyrefail, an absolute shit-hole in South Wales, only child, and didn't find it easy being bisexual there. Largely because of his parents. As far as I know, he'd had little or no contact with them for many years. They threw him out at sixteen and said he was dead to them. I thought they'd come crawling out of the woodwork when he found fame, but clearly their homophobia outweighed their love of money and their only son.'

'Did you become friends?'

'Not really. Clients are just clients, even if they think they're more. We went to parties, but that's just work. Networking. Being seen. I pushed him in front of the right casting directors and made sure that producers started to ask for him. His pretty face helped.'

'So you started your own agency?'

'Yes. By then he was clearly going to be a big star. Soozie was absolutely *apoplectic* when he told her he wanted to stay with me. His contract forced him to give her six months' notice and she held him to it. She refused to speak to me. Even when I bought out her agency a few years later. It was all done through lawyers.'

'So Sam's drinking and drug use came later?

'Once he was hugely famous, yes. Somehow he mostly managed to pull it together on set. Keeping it quiet for all those years was a problem. Finally stopped about three years ago. You probably saw a couple of stories in the *Daily News* about him breaking up with a partner and going to AA because he was worried about his drinking. The truth is, there was no partner. He just couldn't handle the fame, the money, the ability to have whatever you want, when you want it. I've seen it so many times. The *arrogance*. He started openly cruising on Hampstead Heath. I told him, the public have no problem with your sexuality. But they'll soon change their mind if images of you kebabbing up there are plastered all over the press.'

Sue smiled. In spite of herself, she liked Lola.

There was a knock on the door and Dev entered with two cups of coffee. Sensing he'd walked in at an inopportune moment, he placed them on the table and quickly exited.

'And surprise, surprise, someone videoed him,' Lola went on. 'We're talking five guys, and I don't mean the burgers. Sent it to the *Daily News*. I had to call in a few hefty favours to shut that down. Gave them the AA and the boyfriend break-up sob story and luckily they agreed to run with it instead. I know the editor, Tim Thacker, pretty well. He's got his hands on a pap shot of Tyler apparently arriving at Sam's house on Saturday, if that's any use.'

Something in her eyes told Sue that Lola knew Thacker *extremely* well.

'It will be,' Sue replied. 'We'll follow it up. Has Sam relapsed since?'

'Not to my knowledge. Been completely clean for coming up to eighteen months now. He's even gone militantly vegan since he met Tyler. I'm all for saving the animals and the planet, but it's a right bloody pain when I have to keep checking they've got special food and costumes for him on set. If they serve him up a lunch that's basically a roast minus the meat, or make him wear real leather, his toys are straight out of the pram. Even the make-up has to be vegan. He's gone all green with his transport, too. Sam never learned to drive and now he prefers electric cabs. Not easy to find in the middle of the fucking Lake District.'

'And does he have any other skeletons in the cupboard, apart from the Hampstead Heath escapades?'

'If he does, I don't know about them. He seemed very keen on Tyler, so I shouldn't think he's been up there cruising again, but you never know. It's worth checking out. I once spent six months restoring the reputation of a client who'd been caught by a tabloid hack posing as a rent boy, only to find he was back picking them up again. And this time they were underage. He said it was an *addiction*. I don't represent him anymore. And I tipped you guys off, too. He got ten years. Underage sex crossed the line and I wasn't having it.'

'So when did you last speak to Sam?'

'Saturday afternoon. Maybe around four p.m.? I called him. Let me check, it will be on my phone.'

Lola opened her crocodile-skin handbag and took out a large iPhone. 'Actually, 3:46 p.m. on Saturday,' she went on, scrolling through her call logs. 'I rang on the pretext of asking him how the shoot had gone. He wrapped on Thursday. But what I *really* wanted was for him to come to the awards on Monday night. He said the shoot was fine, he was tired and glad it was over, but he wasn't up for the awards. Said he wasn't nominated for anything this time and being around all that drink wasn't good for him. I said OK and hung up. That's all I know.'

'Why were you so keen for him to be at the awards?'

'It's good for business. My business. Reminds people just how many huge stars I've got on my books and keeps my profile high. Plus I hadn't seen him in a social setting for six weeks, so wanted to catch up with any gossip from on set. Out of earshot, of course.'

'Did he mention any problems on the shoot?'

'No. Why would he? Have there been? I'm sure he would have called me if so. We were in touch occasionally and he didn't even allude to anything.'

'Just covering all possibilities. Would you have copies of any texts between you?'

Lola shook her head. 'I chat with all my clients either on the phone, face to face or on WhatsApp. I delete everything.'

'That's no problem. We can sometimes retrieve deleted WhatsApp chats if we need to.'

'Really?' Lola raised a perfectly manicured eyebrow. 'I thought it was encrypted and secure. I'm always worried about the press hacking my phone and getting hold of anything.'

'We'd need a court order. But if you're sure there's nothing on there that will help, we won't need to.'

'I'm sure. If he'd said anything at all, I've have picked up on it. All part of the job. Keeping one step ahead of the clients. But you're welcome to look.'

Lola smiled, and for a split second Sue thought she detected a hint of unease. Probably just worried about dirt on her clients leaking if the IT team had access. There was bound to be stuff on there that the papers would pay through the nose for.

'We're just setting up the on-camera appeal,' Sue went on. 'Would you be willing to sit alongside Tyler? Maybe say a few words? The more famous faces we can call in on this, the better. If your clients could share the footage on social media, that'll help us reach so many people.'

'Of course.' Lola drained the last of her coffee. 'Anything that will help to find him.'

Sue stood up and extended her hand again. 'Thank you, Ms Lovett.' She paused. 'Do you mind if I ask you an unrelated question?'

'Please do.'

'I just wondered if you knew how Soozie Lightwater is doing? We were in touch for a while after the Medford case, but these things tend to drift. Everyone's so busy, you know…'

'Soozie? Last I heard was she's on good form. A friend was at one of her charity balls recently. It must have been hard on her. She called me once, years after I bought out her firm, asking if she could come and work for me. That must have taken some bottle. Her girls were growing up and she seemed, I don't know, *lost*.'

Soozie would have plenty to say about Sam and Lola, Sue was sure of it.

Sue opened the door and both women walked into the incident room. 'Thanks for the coffee,' Lola said to Dev, with a warm smile, as they passed his desk. He gazed back at her, with a puppy dog look in his eyes.

Sue had to hand it to her. Lola was a PR pro. A real pro.

The glare from the cameras made Tyler's red, puffy face look even worse than it already did. Still wearing the same, dishevelled, faded jeans and T-shirt he'd turned up in the night before, he followed Sue to the row of chairs neatly set out behind a stark metal table, wincing uncomfortably as the cameras flashed into life.

Journalists, camera crews and photographers were packed into the room, all straining to get a good look at, and picture of, Tyler. Sam was openly bisexual, and a proud supporter of LGBTQI charities, but snapshots of his private life or any boyfriends rarely made the papers. Word amongst the reporters was that his agent, the intimidating Lola Lovett, had an absolute stranglehold on the tabloid editors. Paparazzi pictures of Sam – unless they were carefully staged by Lola – were rarely bought or used even if they managed to snap them, so generally they left him alone. But Tim Thacker's *Daily News* had already posted the exclusive shot of Tyler from Saturday online. No photographer was credited, just 'SPA' – Soundbite Picture Agency.

Sue pulled out a chair and Tyler sat down beside her. Serena, the family liaison officer – FLO – whose job was to keep Tyler up to speed while quietly spying on him – was on his other side, with Lola on the end. 'Thank you for coming,' Sue began, addressing the press. She knew how important it was to get them on side. 'As you know, this is a missing persons appeal.'

She tapped her laptop and several large photos of Sam, with and without beard, appeared on the screen behind her. 'Sam Stephens was last seen on Sunday afternoon at his house in Cobshott by his partner, Tyler Tipping, who is joining us today. Cell site analysis shows Sam's phone was at the house until 8:50 p.m., at which point it was either turned off or went flat. Most of you know what Sam looks like, but we have additional pictures here, showing him with a beard, and others with a moustache. His disappearance is totally out of character, so we are very concerned for his safety. We won't be making any further statements at present, or taking questions, but Tyler and his agent, Lola Lovett, would like to say a few words. Tyler, you go first.'

Tyler blew his nose loudly. Sue gestured to the cameras, which were broadcasting live on all the news channels, to remind him to look directly at them. 'I-I just want to say that whatever's happened, Sam, please just come home,' Tyler stammered, thick tears pressing on his eyelids. 'I miss you so much. I'm so worried about you. I can't sleep. And if anyone has seen Sam or knows where he is, please contact the police. We can sort this out. No matter what's happened. All that matters is getting Sam home safe.'

'How long have you been together?' shouted one journalist.

'No questions,' Sue snapped, tapping Tyler's arm reassuringly. 'Ms Lovett?'

Lola stood up, and Sue marvelled at her naturally regal air, which instantly pervaded the whole room. 'Sam is a loyal client and a trusted friend,' Lola said, her gaze fixed firmly at the cameras. 'He's a wonderful actor who has brought a deeper understanding of what it is to be human into so many people's lives through his work. And he's done it against the odds, growing up in an environment where being gay or bisexual was seen as a *disease*.' She practically spat the word out and even the hard-nosed journalists seemed slightly intoxicated by her.

'We simply don't know what's happened to Sam,' Lola went on. 'I want to praise the police for acting so swiftly, but we also need everyone's help. Sam, if you're listening to this, please get in touch. Let us know you are safe. We are all here for you. If someone is holding him against his will, please make contact. Whoever you are and whatever you've done, it's not too late to put this right. The only way this situation can be resolved is by talking.' She gestured to a large banner behind the desk, with an 0800 number printed on it. 'This is the hotline. The call is free. Talk to us. You can ask to speak to DCI Sue Fisher, to me, to anyone on the team if you wish. We are here waiting, and here we will remain, until Sam, our prince, is home.'

It was a gloriously impromptu, rousing and passionate speech and Sue couldn't help but marvel at the echoes from Tony Blair's Princess Diana masterpiece. Camera flashes and a cacophony of questions exploded into the air, as the journalists all shouted over each other. Sue struggled to make out any individual ones but words like 'kidnapped', 'ransom', 'suicide', 'murder' and even 'alien abduction' were bouncing around.

Sue stood up, and gestured to Tyler to do the same. 'Well, thank you, everybody, for your time,' she shouted over the throng, ushering him out of the room, as Lola and Serena the FLO followed. 'We will keep you fully updated with any news.'

They walked deeper into the building, leaving the journalists and the chatter behind. 'Thank you again, Ms Lovett,' Sue said warmly, handing her a card. 'My mobile is on here. Call me, day or night. If you hear anything, remember something, whatever. Just call. We've solved cases on the tiniest of leads, things that people thought were insignificant.'

'I will. Can you point me towards the station? It'll be quicker than an Uber back to town.'

'Of course. I'll have one of the officers drop you at Surbiton. It's the least we can do. You won't be hassled by the paparazzi there.'

As Sue walked back through the incident room, Dev gave her a wide smile. 'Ms Lovett's quite something.' He grinned. 'I can see why the celebs love her.'

'So can I. If I wanted a personal PR, she'd be top of my list. We need to keep an open mind about any links to the Medford case.'

'Really, boss? Just because it's Cobshott? I thought that was done and dusted.'

'So did I. But Lola Lovett worked for Soozie Lightwater, whose husband owned Riverdell, the crime scene. They were both innocent as far as the Medford crimes went, but I'm not ruling anything out. Any luck with the paparazzi guy yet?'

'I'll talk to Soundbite Picture Agency. They're credited for it.'

'Good. I'll speak to Soozie Lightwater. And those journalists are relentless. Alien abduction, my arse. That's a new one on me.'

Chapter Seven

LOLA

I haven't been on a train for years. Even though I live in central London, I either drive everywhere or take a cab. It's a personal space thing. I'm not so well known that the public would constantly hassle me. To be honest, most of the times I've been on the Tube everyone looks so dead inside that Tom Hanks could get on and elicit little more than a couple of glances and a surreptitious snapshot. It's like everyone's souls have been sucked out. I like my space, Radio 4, a black coffee and tinted windows to keep prying eyes away from any clients I've got in the back.

It's lunchtime, and the carriage is almost empty. I'm sitting in a six-seat bay by myself, and beyond that, in the next bay, a teenage lad wearing giant purple headphones is nodding his head to a beat. The only other person in the carriage is an overweight guy about my age, dressed head to toe in unforgiving Lycra like he's about to ride the fucking Tour de France. He's standing by the doors, guarding his clearly very expensive bike as his pot belly strains at the taut fabric, and glancing suspiciously at the teenager, who is oblivious to it all.

I'm reasonably happy with how the meeting went. Throwing in the couple of ex-boyfriends and the true tales about the cruising should keep the police busy, while Rick tracks him down. That's our priority. Find him before the police do. Before he talks. Before he spills any of my secrets. And I had to mention the drugs. If they start interviewing any of Sam's co-stars, it will come out, and they'll never believe I didn't know. I need Sue Fisher to trust me.

The morning sun has turned to thick, grey rain, which streaks diagonally down the windows as the fast train speeds towards the city. I gaze at the rows of red-brick Victorian terraces as we slow down to pass through Clapham Junction, and spot my glitzy tower block as the train approaches Vauxhall. Every time I see it, it's a thrill. My nan would bring me to London sometimes, for the day, to 'give your mum a break'. We'd go to the Natural History Museum to see the big dinosaur and afterwards we'd walk up to Harrods so we could look in the windows. It was magical. Especially at Christmas, with the sparkles and the lights. Nan was always too nervous to go in, because there was a man in uniform on the door. 'I don't belong in a place like this,' she told me. 'But one day, my girl, you will. You'll have the best of *everything*. You deserve it. Always remember that.'

I promised myself that, one day, I'd earn enough money to buy *everything* there, and live in one of the glamorous steel skyscrapers rising up all across the city. And Nan could shop in Harrods every day and the uniformed man would open the door for her like a queen. She was the only family I'd had, the only person who really cared. Mum didn't count.

If Nan had lived, I would have made her dreams come true, like I've made mine. Instead, I spend my life doing that for other people. And if Nan knew the truth, she wouldn't be proud at all.

Thinking of Nan triggers a wave of sadness. My belly tenses, just like it always does when a wave of emotion threatens to get the better of me. So I count. One small apple and several black coffees so far. Forty calories. It's way past lunchtime and hunger gnaws at my belly but I shut it out, just like I have every single day since Nan died. Think of the numbers, Lola, focus on staying thin and you'll stop *feeling*. Being hungry all the time sharpens my mind, though I have to watch my blood sugar doesn't drop too far and make me pass out. I can pick up a Diet Coke and a low-cal sandwich in Boots at Waterloo. At 360 calories that will take me to a total of 400 and keep me going until the evening. Good. I'm well within my daily allowance.

The train's not stopping at Vauxhall, but that's fine, as I'm not going home. My laptop is open and I'm glancing constantly at the stream of emails, only to see if there's any contact from whoever has taken Sam. Everything – and everyone else – can wait.

DCI Sue Fisher wasn't quite what I'd expected. More thoughtful, more attractive in real life, with deep-brown eyes that held your gaze and a quiet, almost gentle confidence. Great sense of dry humour, too, and refreshingly different to the self-obsessed, vapid and anxiety-ridden souls I spend most of my life dealing with. The papers had portrayed her as a dogged, determined, tough-as-nails copper who rooted out serial killers for breakfast. I knew better than to believe anything they printed, though. Her messy, chaotic desk was a surprise, her nails and make-up were a disaster and she definitely needed a stylist – that cheap suit didn't work well on or off camera – but overall, she'd gained my respect. And fear.

Sending her partner out of the room was a good play. Made for a more intimate chat. She was clearly smart, much smarter than she let on, so I'll have to be on my guard. Keep in touch and keep her on side.

I feel a vibration in my left pocket. My burner phone. It's a text from Rick.

TV appeal looked good. What did you tell police?

I reply straightaway.

Nothing they didn't already know. Or will find out from Tyler & co-stars. Including drugs and rent boy thing. Said I called him Saturday afternoon. She asked about problems on set. Check that out. She asked about texts. I said we talked occasionally on WhatsApp.

Rick replies instantly.

WTF? Don't want her digging into your phone. Even if it's clean Sam-wise. There's other stuff on there. Bound to be.

I'm irritated.

Would've looked suspicious if I'd said we HADN'T been messaging. I'm his agent FFS. Agents message clients on there all the time. I do it with everyone else. Told her I'd deleted them & nothing to see.

A pause.

No new messages, right? You did everything with Stevens in person or by burner, like I said? Since he went off on one?

Of course I did. Not stupid. No messages between me and Sam for the last few weeks. Since he started threatening to spill.

Rick fires straight back.

No messages at all is suspicious in itself. Least of our worries tho. We just need to find Stevens before they do.

I stride across Waterloo station concourse and into Boots, choosing a calorie-controlled prawn sandwich, and eat it quickly before joining the queue at the taxi rank. Food isn't something to be savoured, like it was when I was a six-stone teenager in the full grip of not-eating, spending most of the day slowly drinking a single, watery diet hot chocolate. These days it's something I have to force down, to be rushed and forgotten about, once the number of calories is logged in my daily tally. Having an eating disorder isn't like being an alcoholic. They're lucky. They can just avoid booze, keep away from it. I *have* to eat.

My heels tap across the wide, tiled concourse, where the fine melting pot that is London is on full display. There's the suited and booted, the homeless, the tourists, the kids skiving off school, the blind dates meeting under the clock, the over-sixties squeezing every last drop out of their Freedom pass. I notice a couple of women in their fifties pointing at me, and realise the giant news screen is showing the appeal. There's Tyler, and Fisher, and that FLO woman, with me beside them, and a giant picture of Sam. I meet their gaze, smile and hurry past. Head down isn't my style. Like I tell my clients, confidence is key. If you're dripping with it, they're less likely to bother you.

It's after lunch and the taxi queue is short, so I'm soon in a black cab from Waterloo en route to my office, my brain in emergency planning mode as it always is in a crisis. I turn over DCI Sue Fisher's card in my fingers. Keep your friends close and your enemies closer.

Waterloo Bridge is at a standstill, and even though I'm

not on a deadline, I snap at the driver, a fat, cheery man about my age.

'What's going on?'

'Sorry, love, it's them protestors. The climate ones. They're at it in Trafalgar Square today and the whole ruddy place is seized up.'

'Christ. What are they doing now?'

'Glued themselves to the ruddy road. I mean, it's all right for them, with sod all to do all day and living off Daddy's money, but some of us have got to make a living. I've got a wife and four kids at home. She wants to go skiing at Christmas. Ruddy *skiing*. Costs a fortune.'

'I've only been once,' I reply. 'Hated it. Fell over and broke my wrist on the first day.'

The cabbie chuckles. 'That'll be the wife.' He pauses. 'I recognise you, love. Weren't you on that telly appeal earlier? I saw it in the caff over my cuppa. The one about Sam Stevens.'

'Yes. I'm his agent.' I really wish I hadn't started chatting.

'Had him in the back of the cab once. Pissed as a fart. Few years ago now. Flagged me down on Shaftesbury Avenue, outside the Century Club. I dropped him off in Hampstead. He had another guy with him. No hanky-panky though. Not that I mind,' he adds quickly. 'I ain't one of them *homophones*. Each to their own, that's what I say. But I don't like any hanky-panky in the cab from no one.'

This journey is taking forever. I'm hot, and slightly nauseous from the prawn sandwich. Food tends to do that to me. I haven't hit the full menopause yet but every now and then it's like someone's turned a hairdryer on me, full blast. My adrenaline is pumping too, so I'm keyed up and ready to deal with the backlog of emails and no doubt endless questions from my assistant, Olivia.

'Can you turn the air con on?'

'Of course, love.' A welcome rush of cool air wafts over my face and I catch his gaze in the rear-view mirror. He looks concerned.

'I'm sorry he's missing. Your Sam. I like his films. Always plays a baddie just right. Must be tough on you, love.'

I nod, unsettled. 'Thank you.'

Your Sam. That's what Sam used to say. I'm *your* Sam. *Yours* for ever. He said it to me the night we shared a bedroom in Paris, just as friends, when he was filming *The Last Star*. We were close, so close, and when it finally happened, just once, as sex was always going to do, it was magical. That was twenty years ago. We loved each other. Underneath the drugs, the addictions, the rent boys, we were soul mates. How the hell did it end up like *this*?

'I really hope you find him. They've got that copper on it, the one who did the Medford case. If anyone can find him, she can.'

That's *exactly* what I was worried about.

Chapter Eight

TUESDAY

The blindfold over his eyes felt like a thick piece of rag, pressing on his eyeballs painfully like a vice. His hands and ankles were bound together with something sharp and stiff, which felt like plastic zip ties, and one of his arms was broken, a searing pain slicing through it every time he tried to move. His collarbone, too. But it was the sack over his head and thick, wide tape over his mouth that were the worst. He had been claustrophobic since childhood. The sack scratched his face and smothered his nose, and even though it didn't stop him breathing, he constantly felt like he was about to suffocate. He tried to scream but only a muffled sound came out.

Sam had no idea how long he had been here, or where 'here' was. The last thing he remembered was sitting in front of the TV at home. The blackness, the disorientation, the dead silence, the fear of what might happen next, was so terrifying that for the first few hours – he guessed it was hours, but he had no way of knowing – he'd stayed huddled in one spot, rocking back and forth like a baby on the concrete floor, vomiting twice inside the sack at the stench of his relentless diarrhoea. He even cried out for his mum.

The fear didn't pass, but as the cold, black, filthy silence continued, it settled enough for Sam to be able to think. His first thoughts were for Tyler, gentle Tyler, who would be worried sick about him. Tyler would go to the police. They'd be looking for him right now.

Who would do this to him? Was it Lola, trying to scare him into silence? Never. Lola's cut of his earnings ran into millions. She wouldn't risk traumatising her cash cow. And underneath it all, she loved him. A crazed fan seemed unlikely, too. They wouldn't leave him in this state. And they'd have come to talk to him, fangirling or fanboying all over the shop. He hadn't heard or sensed anyone near him. It had to be a gang, kidnapping him for money. The thought triggered another wave of stomach cramps, flooding his body and mind with fear. Surely they'd call Lola and she would pay up? But what if she didn't? What if the police wouldn't let her do a deal? What if this stinking black hell was where he would die?

He had to get out. There had to be a way. Struggling to his feet, nauseous and shivering with fear and cold, the wet tracksuit trousers clinging thickly to his legs, he began to feel his way around. Sam's hands were tied behind his back, but his fingers could feel a cold, damp brick wall. It was some kind of room, possibly underground. The bricks were rough, unpainted.

With his ankles so tightly bound, Sam had to jump to move. Dehydrated and exhausted, it took every ounce of strength, but it helped focus his mind on something other than fear, and he made his way a couple of metres along the wall, the bricks scratching his arm, before reaching a corner. The next wall was shorter.

His body was screaming at him to lie down and rest, but Sam worked his way methodically around his prison, feeling every inch he could. And every inch felt the same. Cold, damp, rough bricks.

He couldn't find a door. But on the last, short wall, a patch of bricks felt different. The mortar between them felt softer, spongier.

Slowly, the sickening reality dawned. Whoever had done this had thrown him in here and bricked up the door.

Mike was out when Sue called home briefly at lunchtime, and her only child, Tom, was in his room, playing AC/DC at full volume. These days, she worried about Tom endlessly. One of the windows in his front bedroom was open but the blackout curtains were still closed, and Sue could hear the thumping bass as she parked on the tiny, weed-strewn run-off in front of the garage. It was a 1930s semi-detached house in the heart of Surbiton's anonymous Berrylands estate, where row upon row of practically identical-looking houses with deep, round bay windows and pebbledashed walls fanned out across the flat, soulless ground. Having grown up in a house on the estate, and gone to the local girls' school, there was something about Berrylands that she loved, though the twitching curtains did get on her wick.

Mrs Martin, her neighbour, was in the front garden tending to her tall dahlias, a riot of plate-sized colourful blooms and leggy green stems neatly planted in a row of huge pots. She was obsessed with them. Mrs Martin had lived there for years, even before Sue and her late husband Rob had moved in, which inflated her already grand sense of self-importance and gave her an irritating air of superiority on the street.

Dressed in her gardening trousers and a cotton shirt peppered with tiny flowers – an outfit, Sue noticed, that was smarter than many of her own suits – the grey-haired retired postmistress gave Sue a sympathetic look. Before the Medford case, she'd have berated Sue immediately for any perceived breach of acceptable behaviour, such as leaving the wheelie bins out after they'd been emptied or forgetting to cut back the front hedge. Loud music would *definitely* have been right up there on the list. Tom didn't play much music back then, and if he did, it was with headphones. He'd changed so much since his dad died, for the worse, and it broke Sue's heart every time she thought about it.

'How are you, Sue?' Mrs Martin began, putting down her plastic bottle of slug killer and taking off her pink paisley gardening gloves. She was clearly settling in for one of her nosey Big Chats, which was the last thing Sue needed. 'Popped home for lunch? I saw you on the telly earlier. Sam Stevens, eh? I know you can't discuss the case, but do you reckon he's dead?'

Sue smiled through gritted teeth, as she took her laptop bag out of the car and locked it. 'I'm not allowed to talk about it, Mrs Martin. I would if I could. We're all keeping an open mind.'

The music stopped momentarily as the track ended, and Mrs Martin nodded sympathetically, as the opening to 'Back in Black' blasted out.

'How's your Tom? Off to uni soon?'

'Yes. A couple of weeks. Sorry about the music. I'll get him to turn it down. Has he had it on like this all day?'

'Since Mike left for work. Can't be easy, being a teenager and what with his dad…'

Keen to change the subject, Sue gestured to the flowers. 'Your dahlias are looking lovely.'

Mrs Martin beamed. 'Thank you. They do take a lot of work, but it's worth it. Eggshells and MiracleGro. I swear by it.'

Sue slid her key into the front door. 'How's Mr Martin?'

'The same.' She picked up her slug pellets and busied herself with the flowers, avoiding Sue's gaze. 'I go most days. He doesn't recognise me at all now. Well, must get on.'

'Of course. Lovely to see you.'

Closing the front door behind her, Sue leaned against it, exhausted, the music screaming in her ears. The dahlias were Mrs Martin's distraction, just like work was for her. And for Lola. She wasn't fooled by Lola's expensive suits and sharp confidence. If the Medford case had taught her anything, it's that people just want to be happy. They do whatever they think it takes. Sometimes that's obsessing over hobbies or work. Sometimes it's murder. And when killing one person doesn't quite do it, they kill more. Whoever had taken Sam, their deluded quest for happiness was at the root of it. She'd never try and explain that to the public. But they either wanted money – likely a faceless gang who would soon surface with a ransom demand – or Sam wiped off the face of the planet. There was a reasonable chance it was the latter, Sue figured, which gave her a good shot at finding out why.

She walked down the narrow hall to the kitchen. It was a mess. Tom had clearly made a cheese omelette, and the eggshells were strewn across the surface, while the remains of a block of cheese was sweating on a plate as the congealed frying pan, along with a half-empty, lukewarm bottle of milk, glistened in the sun. The dishwasher Mike had carefully loaded before work hadn't been emptied, and the cat's water bowl was empty. She refilled it.

Walking through into the living room, Sue absent-mindedly opened her post and looked through the French doors to the shed. Rob's old shed. Mike had made a big thing of 'moving on' and had cleaned it out, putting all Rob's things into storage. He'd painted it white, put bean bags on the floor, bought a big TV, wired up an Xbox, and created a den for Tom to use with his mates. Tom had barely set foot in it.

She couldn't pinpoint when the shift happened. Tom had always been so loving towards her, protecting her from Rob, just as she'd protected him when he was a baby. But after Rob died, things changed. Not straightaway. It was gradual, so gradual that at first she barely noticed it. Despite going to bereavement therapy once a week, which she'd arranged for him, he withdrew from her. Then, nine months ago, he gave up his beloved chess. Said he didn't like people staring at him when he went to matches. Mike offered to take him away on a couple of camping trips, hiking round the Lake District and along the South West coastal path, but Tom refused to go. It was like the Tom she loved, the caring, kind, sweet boy, was locked away inside himself. He'd got a place to read Maths at the University of Southampton, so in two weeks' time he'd be moving into halls, and had made it clear he didn't want any help doing so. 'I'm *fine*, Mum,' he'd insisted, when she offered to take him to Wilco and stock up on bedding and essentials. She longed to be part of his journey, to help him navigate the big, wide and, as she knew too well, often dangerous world, but now Sue felt utterly rejected, redundant, and at a loss to know what to do. Their connection felt totally broken. It was like being bereaved when no one had actually died.

Tom's music seemed to be even louder now. Sue made her way upstairs and knocked on the door. 'Tom, love,' she shouted. 'I'm just grabbing some lunch. Can you turn it down a bit?'

The volume dropped, though it was no doubt still louder than Mrs Martin would like. 'Thanks, love,' she said. No reply. In the old days he'd have come bounding out, keen to hear about her morning, tell her about his, and chat about the case as she made them both something to eat. Losing his dad the way he did must have been hard, Sue accepted that. But this was something more. She missed the old Tom so much, and in spite of everything, she missed Rob. People had such a black-and-white view of domestic violence, as she'd discovered, and she'd put away a fair few perpetrators of it. But for those caught in its cruel grip, it wasn't just about love, or jealousy, or hate, or loathing, or passion, or desire, or rage, or intensity, or joy. It was all of those feelings and a thousand more, a potent, sick, addictive cocktail that they had both bought into, or become trapped in. She didn't blame herself for the violence, but she did blame herself for not walking away from it.

In a couple of weeks Tom would be gone, and who knew when he would be back. She needed to reconnect with him, break down the ugly, sprawling, tangled mess of emotions and resentment that had forced its way between them.

Sue knocked loudly on the door.

'Tom, love. Can I come in? I'm working on a new case.'

He'd always loved to hear about her investigations, and he'd definitely know Sam Stevens. Still no reply.

She turned the knob but before she could try to open it, the door opened a crack.

Tom was still in his pyjamas, and the room reeked of sweat and stale food.

'I told you the other day, Mum, I just want some *space*,' he spat. 'If my door's shut, I'm busy.'

'I know, love. But it's always shut and I worry about you. I miss talking. It's not like you to leave the kitchen in such a mess.'

'There you go again, *moaning*. I told you, I'm *fine*. I'll clear it up later.'

'I just popped back for a cuppa. We've got a big case on. Sam Stevens. The actor.'

Tom shrugged. 'What's he done? Murdered someone in real life? He's always killing people in his movies.'

Sue smiled. It was the longest conversation they'd had for weeks. 'Gone missing. Come down and have a cuppa with me and I can tell you all about it.'

'Can't. Got stuff to do. For, er, uni, you know.' His voice was higher-pitched than usual. Sue knew he was deeply stressed.

'Listen, love, if you're worried about going to uni…'

'I'm not,' he shouted. 'I can't wait to get away. From here. From *everyone*.'

The door slammed shut and a thick tear rolled down Sue's cheek. She brushed it away roughly with the back of her hand and went down to the kitchen, hoping she'd hear the click of the door and he'd come downstairs, full of apologies. He didn't.

Was he frightened of going to uni? Perhaps rejecting her was his way of preparing to go out into the world. She wanted him to go off to uni, to have fun, to make new friends, to take those important steps, and if being distant from her was part of that, then Sue knew she had to accept it. But giving up chess, his rudeness, refusing to go camping with Mike, losing touch with old friends – it was all so out of character. Gentle, loving Tom had been replaced by a young man she didn't recognise.

Half an hour later, the music back at full volume, Sue climbed helplessly back into the car. She just couldn't reach Tom, and the more she tried, the further away he ran. The pain tore at her soul, triggering waves of anxiety and nausea. All her life she'd protected him, and now he didn't want that any more. He didn't want *her*. Kids move on, she got that. But this was something else, a loathing that seemed to seep from his very soul. For a moment she thought of Rob. Surely, after everything, he wasn't going to turn into his dad?

Mike's car pulled up just as she was about to drive off. She lowered her window.

'You OK, love? Thought I'd pop home and see how the lad's doing. Sounds like he's having a disco.'

'He won't talk to me, Mike. I don't know what I've done.'

'It's just his age, love.'

'Will you *stop* saying that,' she snapped, roughly wiping away a tear.

'He's a teenager. It's what they do.'

'It's not his age. I'm his mum, and I'm telling you

something's wrong. You're not his dad, so how the fuck would you know?'

It was a wickedly low blow, and Sue knew it. Mike had been more of a dad to Tom over the years than Rob ever was.

'That's not fair, love,' he said gently.

'Life isn't fucking fair.'

Mike stood in silence by the car for a moment, as Mrs Martin's curtains twitched.

'I'm going in to make a cuppa,' he said stiffly. 'Do you want to come in and talk?'

'No, I don't,' she replied, closing the car window. 'I've got to get back to work.'

Sue blew her nose loudly, pulled out her phone and distracted herself by checking her emails, desperate to fill the gaping void that threatened to engulf her. She hated herself for lashing out at Mike. Stable, dependable Mike, whose love she couldn't return, and who would never be Rob. It made no sense, but some days she hated him for that.

Work was her refuge, her place of safety. She'd met mothers and fathers who beat their children, starved them, abused them, reduced them to emotional wrecks who grew up and vented their spleen on others. Had moving Mike into the house as a lover rather than a friend made life for Tom too blurred, too complicated? Was he *embarrassed*? Or had she, by staying with Rob for all those years, caused emotional scars in Tom that would never heal?

Sue couldn't go there, couldn't let herself think those

thoughts for a second. She looked up at his curtained window, silently blew him a kiss and drove off.

Sam Stevens had to be her focus. He could well be still alive, and she might be the only person standing between him and death.

Chapter Nine

LOLA

I step out of the air-conditioned cab into the light warmth of a sunny September afternoon. My London agency is here, on Tottenham Court Road, just a short walk from the space-age new tube station for those clients who can't yet afford to arrive by cab, and the handful who occasionally hop on public transport hoping to be seen as green. One of the newer paparazzi, an attractive, smiley, dark-haired Aussie in his twenties, is stationed by the agency's discreet entrance, a smart jet-black door between Caffè Nero and Habitat. Seeing me, he throws his cigarette on the floor and starts shooting. I put on my best worried-sick-but-not-despondent face. He might find a paper willing to take it. Keeping the paps on side was part of the job. They had their uses.

'Any news on Sam, Lola?'

I shake my head. 'Nothing new. Will let you know. Have you heard anything?'

'Nah. Jeez, I hope he's all right. Grew up watching his movies.'

'We haven't met properly. You're new, aren't you?'

He holds out his hand and I shake it. 'Jim. From Melbourne. Freelance. Been here a month or so. Worked for a couple of picture agencies back home. The other lads call me Jim L.'

'Makes sense. Not that anyone's going to confuse you with Jim B.' One of the oldest paps on the scene.

'Yeah. He's a legend.'

'Well, *Jim L*, we like to help when we can. Here's a tip for you. April Zebretti is having dinner at The Ivy tonight. Around seven p.m., I believe. The *Mirror* will be keen.'

'Cheers, mate.'

'You're welcome. But please don't ever call me "mate".'

I jab the intercom and the door opens instantly. Olivia must have seen me arrive from the window. The Zebretti tip-off should pay Jim's rent for another week. She was a household name, having worked her way through *EastEnders* and *Holby City* and had a bash at *Strictly* a few years ago, but work-wise things had been quiet for a few months. Finding decent roles for fifty-something women that didn't involve them staring moodily out of windows in the background, or being someone's demented mother, wasn't easy. April was up for a decent role in a Channel 5 drama, which actually featured a main character going through the menopause, so a few nice pics of her in the press wouldn't go amiss. I text her.

Be at The Ivy tonight. 7pm. Dinner. Take a friend.
Photo op.

I slip the iPhone back into my handbag, knowing she'll cancel any other plans to be there, and sprint up the gleaming glass staircase to the first floor, where, for security, we have a second intercom-controlled entrance. 'Lola Lovett PR' glows in soft blue above the clear glass door, and behind it, my receptionist sits at a long oak desk, uplit in warm gold. The floor is polished wood, and there's a scattering of soft armchairs and coffee tables for people to mix, mingle or wait. Framed photographs of my clients on set, on the football pitch or receiving awards adorn the walls, along with muted abstract paintings. Behind reception, screened off by a soft oak panel, is a huge open-plan office with black desks, a kitchen and several soundproofed, private meeting rooms. My desk is at the far end, separate from the others but still within earshot. Being cut off from the goings-on – and being gossiped about – is the last thing I want. They do enough of that when I'm out of the office. And I can't be doing with that hotdesking nonsense either. Everyone knows where they sit, and I don't care what state their desk is in provided the work gets done. Unless a major client – or potential one – is incoming. Then everyone is ordered to tidy up.

Olivia is already in reception with a black coffee for me. Lily, the receptionist, buzzes me in. 'Lots more calls, mostly clients asking about Sam,' Olivia says. 'Some in tears. Genuine *tears*. Twitter is full of rumours that he's being tortured by the mafia. Or dead. And Prosecco Guy's been on. Full of apologies. Nothing in the papers about *that*, thank God.'

'Deal with them,' I reply. 'The clients, I mean. And leave Prosecco Guy to stew for a bit. If he's worried he'll never work again he might think twice before whipping them out next time. He hadn't even *waxed*, for God's sake.'

'Will do. Oh, and Georgie Heaven is getting a lot of flak on Insta from animal rights groups after wearing that red leather suit to the awards.'

I sigh. 'How many times to I have to tell them? Leather is up there with fur these days. Get Zara to bike her over their latest vegan leather-look jacket, book her a table at Mildred's vegan restaurant and tip off the *Daily Mail* that she's embracing a plant-based lifestyle. Tell her I don't want to see her wearing or eating a single animal product till this bloody fuss has died down.'

'What about Twitter? #HaveTheMafiaGotSamStevens is trending.'

'The rumours we can leave. It's all good publicity for the fact he's missing. Might tap into the abductor's ego and flush them out. Oh, and book a table for two at The Ivy for April Zebretti. Seven p.m. Use my name to get a table if it's full.'

Her brown eyes widen. 'So you think he's been abducted?' She's sharp, Olivia. Determined, too. Doesn't miss a trick. That's why I hired her. She's been with me for two years after turning up with her CV and practically camping out on the agency doorstep until I gave her an interview.

'I bloody hope not. The police haven't got a clue. But if he has been, and it's about money, they're going to make contact at some point. Possibly with me.'

Olivia nods, and tosses her long brown hair over her shoulder. She's very tall and willowy, mid-to-late twenties. Very pretty despite a rather annoying nose piercing, with a penchant for wide-leg trousers, crop tops and colourful trainers. Not a look I'd ever try and pull off, but Olivia has body confidence in spades. That's posh parents and an expensive boarding school for you. She genuinely doesn't seem to care what anyone thinks. 'No one's phoned in so far,' she says. 'I was off Friday on that spa day, but I double-checked with Lily and no calls or messages then. A couple of crank callers this morning saying they know where Sam is. They sounded so *lame*. I passed their details on to the police.'

'How was the spa?'

'Fabulous. You should try it. I had this—'

I don't want to hear about Olivia's chocolate body wrap. Even a long shot was worth a go. 'Where did these cranks say he was?'

'One reckoned he'd spotted Sam in a baseball cap buying a chicken sandwich in Pret near Baker Street.'

'Obviously nonsense. Unless he's had a complete breakdown and pushed the self-destruct button, I can't see him stuffing his face with – what does he call it? – *rotting animal flesh*. And the other?'

'Pretty bizarre, to be honest. It was a woman. About five minutes ago. Possibly an Eastern European accent. Called the agency main line asking to speak to you about Sam Stevens and Lily put her through to me. Her number just said "unknown". It was over in seconds. She said "You need to go here", gave an address, and hung up. I just rang DCI Fisher and told her straightaway.'

'Good work. What was the address?'

'Here.' She handed me a post-it note. 'Seashore Cottage, Third Avenue, Camber, East Sussex. Right by the huge beach at Camber Sands. I looked on Google Maps. It's a real place. Tired-looking, rundown bungalow. Seems to have a Pontins right near it. What's a Pontins?'

'Somewhere you really don't want to go.'

I hand her my coffee and jacket. 'Take these to my desk,' I say, and head for the loo, the burner phone in my pocket.

Seashore Cottage, Third Avenue, Camber, East Sussex. Check it out fast. Police aware. Possibly a dead end. But it's all I've got.

Rick replies instantly.

On it.

~

I can't concentrate on anything and nor, it seems, can anyone else in the office. I've got six agents working for me, each with their own client list, while the select few – like Sam – get my personal attention. All my agents are in their late twenties or thirties, back-stabbingly ambitious, utterly determined and very, very good at their jobs. I can't be doing with employing someone straight out of uni and moulding them, as some of my rivals do. Better to let them gain experience and make their – sometimes costly – mistakes elsewhere, before I sweep in and headhunt the best.

I've given them all a rousing pep talk, about how it's our job to carry on business as usual because that's what Sam would want – he fucking wouldn't, the drama queen would want everyone sobbing their eyes out and combing every inch of the United Kingdom – and how I'm sure he's just gone off for a break at the end of his shoot. There was a burst of applause when I'd finished, which seemed genuinely heartfelt, though I know that each one of my staff will be secretly thrilled to be at the agency during the Sam Stevens Affair. No matter what happens to him, that's one for the CV.

Anastazia, a senior agent, is on the phone to one of the TV magazines, negotiating – or, rather, politely arguing – over a contract. Among my many tactics in making myself indispensable are Pieces Of Paper. Clients *love* contracts. If there's one thing that makes them feel important, it's knowing that interviewers have to sign a piece of paper before talking to them.

The paper's pretty worthless. It waffles on about how the magazine will only use their interview once, not taking quotes out of context, blah blah. I'm never going to hold them to it. But clients need to see me doing something.

Richard Riccardo, one of Anastazia's B-list-but-potentially-A-list-clients, is starring in an upcoming drama series on Netflix, starting next week. The channel's publicists have set up the interviews, Richard is happy to do them, and they'll be there on the day, standing guard, briefing him to the hilt on what – and what not – to say. Intervening if any journalists veer off track. He doesn't need Anastazia. But he doesn't know that. So we inject the Piece of Paper.

Some of the journalists – like the one on the phone to Anastazia right now – have seen right through our bullshit. They're refusing to sign on principle. It's a game of chicken. They want the interview, we want Richard in the mag. Someone's got to cave first.

Anastazia whips out her trump card. 'I hear what you're saying, but Richard is *insistent* on the contract. It's just as much of a pain for me. Honestly, he's already in a right state about Sam Stevens – we are all – and I'd rather call off the interview that have to disturb him again with this *problem*. On such a difficult day as *this*.'

She hangs up. 'Sorted. Two-thirty Thursday as planned. They're emailing over the signed contract now.'

An hour passes. Then two. Nothing from Rick, but I know he'll text the moment there's any news. By five p.m. everyone's drunk so much coffee and is so wound up and wired that I send them all home.

The office is eerily quiet. I turn DCI Sue Fisher's card

over in my fingers. Keep your friends close and your enemies closer. That was always Nan's motto. I dial.

'DCI Fisher? Lola Lovett. I hear my assistant passed on some addresses. I hope they were helpful. Apologies if they were crank calls. I wanted to thank you for your time today.'

She's polite, thanks me for calling. But she sounds distracted. There's a hubbub in the background. Police radios crackling. Says she'll be in touch shortly with any update.

'Thank you. We're all so *worried*. I'm happy to meet anytime, anywhere, if I can be of help.'

The seed is planted. I saw a flicker of desire in her eyes when she first looked at me. Let's see if she takes the bait.

Chapter Ten

TUESDAY

C amber Sands was a couple of hours' drive from Surbiton, and Sue managed it in almost half that. She'd asked the local force to take a look at the bungalow, and they couldn't see anything untoward at all. Neighbours said the place had been auctioned off when the owner died a year earlier, bought by a property developer, and it had been empty ever since. But Tyler had mentioned that Sam liked to walk on the beach at Camber, so it had to be worth a shot.

She'd organised a warrant, and wanted to be there when they broke in. Chances were that this was a dead end, but with little else to go on, and Dev and the rest of the team busy digging through Sam's past while fielding endless hotline sightings, it felt good to be *doing* something. Her instincts told her this was a call that mattered, though she couldn't rationally explain why. Sam had no known links to the area, other than Tyler's comment. Perhaps it was the fact they'd called Lola's agency. Nutters or do-gooders would just get on the hotline for their kicks. So far they'd had sightings of him all over the country, including a bookie's in Brighton, sleeping rough in a hostel in Camden – they had checked that one out – and about ten in Shoreditch. It was the bloody beard that did it. Every poor sod with one was a target.

The M25 was fairly clear, and she used the time to put a call in to Soozie Lightwater.

'Sue! How lovely to hear from you. Though I'm guessing it's about Sam Stevens. I saw it on the news.'

'Correct. But I've been meaning to call you for ages. I'm in the car. How are you? And Star?'

'She's almost twenty. Can you believe it? Out of rehab and got her own place in Clapham. Simon, her dad, pays for it. I'm still running the Lightwater Trust. Star works for me. Feels good to help runaway kids, you know. Therapeutic. I'll never get over Sky's death but at least I feel I'm making a difference. And for Star, losing a twin…but she's getting there.'

'I can imagine.'

'How's your lad? Tom?'

'Typical teenager. Off to uni soon.' She paused. There were so many questions Sue wanted to ask Soozie about coping with teenagers, but this wasn't the time, and Soozie sensed it.

'So, I'm guessing you've met Lola Lovett,' Soozie went on breezily. 'Quite a piece of work. We were at Oxford together. St Hilda's College. She was a couple of years below me. Shafted me good and proper. Took Sam and ended up buying my agency.'

'She told me.'

'Typical Lola. I bet she didn't have a good word to say about me.'

'She wasn't unkind, actually. But can I trust her, Soozie? Is there a chance this is all a big PR stunt and she's in on it?'

'I wouldn't put anything past her. She's anorexic, you know. Control freak. Never admitted it, but I could tell. I asked her once and she flatly denied it. But she looked rattled.'

'Interesting.' Mentioning that might be a way through Lola's defences.

'So bloody self-possessed at uni. No fun. Busy working and downing Diet Coke and salad while we were all drinking, scoffing pizza and sneaking boys into college. But I guess her work ethic's still the same.'

'I'd say so. But I didn't know about that. The anorexia.'

'Well, she was. Might have had a ton of therapy to deal with it, but from what I've read I think it's like any addiction. Never goes away. She grew up poor, you know. Never said much about her early life, other than mentioning a childhood friend, Rick, and getting pregnant at fourteen, which she sorted out. Her mum was a drinker, I think.'

'Alcoholic?'

'Probably, from the little she said. Lola had developed that ability to shut her emotions out, to compartmentalise everything. It meant she could completely focus on success. She's so talented, Sue. I knew it the moment I met her, and when she came to work for me – much as I hate to admit it – she was brilliant. Sam Stevens would be nothing without Lola. She's the one who made him famous. For me he was just another jobbing actor with a pretty face.'

'She seems to think he might just be off on retreat somewhere. Is that likely?'

'Possible, I suppose. Celebs do have a habit of wanting to go off-grid. But they almost always stay in touch with their personal publicists when they do it. That's a co-dependent relationship that's hard to break. So if she's telling the truth and she really hasn't heard from him, that's an alarm bell.'

'What was Sam like when you knew him?'

'Self-obsessed. Ambitious. Drugs. Drink. Much the same as most of the talent who walked through my doors. I didn't think he was particularly gifted as an actor. Pretty, though. Had a rough childhood in Wales, hated his parents, especially his dad, and was living in a grotty flat in Camden. Liked men *and* women, if memory serves. Anyone with a pretty face. Lola seemed to adore him.'

'Could there have been anything going on between them?'

'I seriously doubt it. "Don't touch the talent" is the motto. Always ends badly. Most of his relationships were with men. He used to cruise up on Hampstead Heath when he first came to London. I warned him to stop. Lola's too smart to do anything that would risk her career. She's probably the most ambitious person I've ever met. And I've met a *lot*.'

'Did you ever see Sam when he made it big and moved to Cobshott?'

'I knew he'd bought a place there, but I never saw him. He'd betrayed me by going with Lola's agency, and by then I was out of the celebrity PR world anyway. I had no interest in him, though I did wonder if I'd ever see him in the coffee shop or the nail bar, but I never did. My whole life revolved around Sky and Star, and the other school mums. And finding out who Simon was shagging behind my back.'

'How about Lola? Did you speak to her after she bought your agency?'

Soozie paused. 'I tried, once. When the girls were older. I was lonely, missed my old life. Thought she might give me a job, or at least some freelance work. But she didn't want to know. I was no use to her any more. She uses people. But then we all did. That's what PR is all about.'

The line crackled and Sue knew she was about to lose the connection. 'Look, Soozie, if you think of anything, anything at all, do call me. I'm still on this number.'

'I will. And how are *you*, Sue? I know it's been four years, but losing Rob must still be hard.'

'It is.' She paused. 'Do call me, Soozie. Even the tiniest lead or memory can help. And give my best wishes to Star.'

'I will. Take care.'

Sue turned off the motorway. The drive took her through beautiful Sussex countryside, dipping briefly in and out of Kent. Rolling green pastures and apple orchards were dotted with oast houses, their witch's hat tops silhouetted against the backdrop of the clear blue sky. Soozie was right. Losing Rob still ate away at her soul every single day. She remembered staying in an oast house with him, not long after they'd started dating. They'd met in the local pub, when Sue was a constable working the Kingston beat, and Rob was a self-employed locksmith. The attraction had been instant. Sue had always laughed at talk of being struck by a lightning bolt, but when she first saw Rob, that was it. They'd only been together for a couple of weeks when Rob treated them to a weekend away, and they'd cosied up in front of a log fire, drunk red wine and had the kind of sex that left you feeling utterly intoxicated. The kind she missed. She'd only felt that spark when she looked at someone twice in her life. The first was with Rob. The second, much as she tried to ignore it, was today.

Sue pushed the thoughts from her mind and turned on Radio 4, feigning interest in a science documentary. She drove past the outskirts of Rye onto the flat plain that led to Camber. It reminded her of driving along the Acle Straight to Great Yarmouth in the Medford case. The land – clearly reclaimed from the sea – was as flat as a pancake, its thick green pasture dotted with sheep.

'Control, ETA five minutes,' she said briskly into her radio.

'Received.'

The flat lands gave way to largely run-down bungalows, a bookies, a grim-looking launderette and a takeaway proudly declaring 'We sell pies'. She drove past the entrance to Pontins, a riot of colour aimed at disguising the fact the 'apartments' were ugly, low-rise blocks with all the charm of a 1960s council estate. If Sam had decided to hole up somewhere, Sue thought, it was a clever choice, as Camber was probably the last place you'd look.

Third Avenue was off a tiny, sandy lane that led to the beach, and Sue turned her Vauxhall Corsa into it. There were about ten bungalows spread out on each side, mostly shabby, with faded whitewashed pebbledash, though a couple had been refurbished with clapboards to give them more of a beach vibe. One set of net curtains was twitching furiously, and two squad cars were parked outside Seashore Cottage, which was roped off with police tape. It was a tired-looking bungalow with an overgrown front garden and a dilapidated old lean-to carport on its right. Sue pulled on her bulletproof vest and got out of the car.

'DCI Sue Fisher.'

'Afternoon, ma'am. DI Bill Watts. No reply, and roller blinds are down on all the windows, so we can't see in, but there's been no activity at all. Dead quiet. I've got officers stationed in the back garden, keeping watch. We're ready to enter when you are. Cheap cylinder lock by the look of it, so access will be easy.'

'What's the word from the neighbours?'

'The place has been empty for a year or so. Old couple lived here. One died, the other went into a home briefly and then passed away too. Auctioned off to a local developer a few months ago, and Mrs Gantry who lives on her own in the next bungalow' – he gestured to a slightly less decrepit house on the left – 'said that apart from a few people in suits going in and out around that time, it's been empty. They were expecting it to have a big refurb like those two poshed-up houses, but nothing's happened. We checked and no planning applications have been submitted.'

'Is that unusual in this area?'

'Not really. Developers tend to snap them up and sit on them.' Sergeant Watts lowered his voice. 'Might even be waiting for a couple more neighbours to pop their clogs, so they've got a bigger plot. Won't have long to wait.'

Sue nodded. 'And the developers who own it?'

'Ron Briggs & Son. Effectively a one-man band. Local chap. Hasn't actually *got* a son, as far as we know. He's at his villa in Spain at the moment, according to his neighbours. Costa del Sol. Spends a lot of the year out there, apparently. We're still trying to get hold of him.'

'Anyone seen anything unusual at all?'

Sergeant Watts flicked through his notebook. 'No. Most of the neighbours are elderly and pretty deaf. Go to bed early, get up late. Mrs Gantry says the two posh bungalows and the one to the right of this are rented out on Airbnb, so they're used to strangers and cleaners coming and going at all hours. That's something she's *not* happy about. But it's gone on for a couple of years now so they just try and ignore them. A few deliveries – Amazon and Sainsbury's vans, takeaway pizzas, new wheelie bins, but nothing out of the ordinary. Most holidaymakers order deliveries in, as our big supermarket is about half an hour's drive away.'

'Do we know who was staying in the rented places?'

'The older one was empty. End of the school holidays.

But she'd noticed two young men staying in the closest posh one, and saw lights on in the other, with a white van parked outside it. She'd said "Good morning" to one of the men in the corner shop yesterday and he said hello "in a Russian accent". I don't think she's a linguistics expert. So he could be from anywhere in Eastern Europe.'

'And no signs of a break-in?'

'No, But like I say, the lock is flimsy as hell. Be quick and easy to force. Slipping a credit card in the crack would do it.'

'Good work. Thanks. Let's look inside first. Like I say, this is probably a crank call, but I want to be sure.'

Sue walked across the weed-strewn gravel and knocked loudly on the door with her fist.

'Police. DCI Sue Fisher. Open the door. We have a warrant to enter these premises.'

No reply. Sue gestured to the officer standing ready with a battering ram. The door burst open after two sharp bangs and four other officers surged inside, with Sue and Watts behind them.

The smell. She knew it straightaway.

'In here,' called one of the officers.

A man's body lay face down on the bedroom floor. His excrement and blood had soaked into the cream-coloured carpet, forming a stinking black patch around him. Pulling a surgical mask from her pocket, Sue ordered everyone to stay back.

'House is clear, ma'am,' reported the lead officer. 'Garage, too. No one else here. Just…this.'

'Thank you. Call it in, Watts, and get everyone out of the house,' she snapped, looping the mask over her ears. 'This is a major crime scene. No one is to touch *anything*. Get a forensics team in.'

DI Watts didn't move. He stood rooted to the spot, staring at the body. The man was naked from the waist up. But it was the sight of his back that made both Watts and Sue want to vomit. His chalk-white skin had been carefully peeled away in the shape of huge letters, exposing the raw flesh underneath. It spelled out: DEAD 2 ME.

'Watts!' Sue barked.

He forced his gaze away from the man's back and met Sue's eyes, his face a sickly pale. She'd been in situations like this before and clear, sharp orders usually worked best.

'DI Watts. I need your help. Call it in and keep everyone out. We need Forensics. Now. You got that?'

'Ma'am.'

Watts left the room and, seconds later, Sue heard him retching outside.

Taking a pair of blue surgical gloves from her pocket, Sue crouched down beside the man. His bloated face was twisted sideways and his lifeless eyes stared blindly ahead. Late sixties, Sue guessed. Whoever this was, it wasn't Sam Stevens. His trousers were thin grey polyester, and his watch a cheap Timex.

The woman was on the bed, fully clothed but clearly dead, her blackening hands on her chest as if in prayer.

～

The local pathologist was quickly on the scene, along with far too many police. Sue guessed they didn't get a lot of exciting cases in Camber. Luckily, DI Watts had recovered his composure and was dealing with logistics quickly and efficiently, blocking off the entire street and fending off questions from anxious neighbours about 'madmen on the loose'. Dev was due to arrive within the hour.

Outside, Sue changed into full protective gear, pulling the white disposable jumpsuit over her clothes and slipping into some overshoes. Unlike some pathologists she'd come across, who were as user-friendly as a plank of wood, and found detectives intensely irritating, Dr Emily Drakos was a jolly young woman who didn't seem to mind Sue asking questions while she worked.

'Been dead for three or four days, I'd say,' Emily explained, the young woman's camera whirring with each photograph as she examined the dead man. 'No obvious signs of a cause, and no ID in his pocket. If he'd been strangled, I'd expect to see petechiae – tiny haemorrhages – especially after this amount of time. But I had a domestic violence case just last week where the woman's broken neck only showed up when I dissected it.' She paused. 'Sorry, too much information. These injuries to his back were made post-mortem. No firm evidence of sexual assault. The anus is dilated but that can happen during rigor mortis. There are some small, round, older bruises near the anus which indicate fairly recent sexual activity, likely made by a penis or a sex toy, but again I'll need to carry out tests. I haven't examined the woman yet.'

'Could she have killed him and then taken an overdose?'

'Unlikely. Look at the position of her body. Especially the hands. It's too neat. Someone must have placed them like that, again after death. Even the blanket looks tidily arranged over her legs. No obvious blood on her hands or clothes, either. Whoever carved his back would have got pretty messy. Even doing it post mortem. It looks like they used a scalpel.'

Sue watched as the pathologist carefully worked her way around the dead man's body, marvelling at the sensitivity and respect which she showed it. She needed answers, and decided to push the pathologist for her best guess.

'Do you reckon they were killed in this room?'

'From my observations, I can't rule it out. But I suspect – as far as the man is concerned at least – he was killed elsewhere and brought here. I'll know much more once we get them back to the lab and run toxicology tests. There are two needle marks on his arm, and no evidence they were drug addicts. They both appear well-nourished. So if you were to *push* me,' Dr Drakos looked up and smiled, her eyes crinkling behind the mask, 'I'd say he was injected with something. And that happened somewhere else. There are vomit stains on his chin, likely a reaction to whatever he was jabbed with, but no pile of vomitus. Apart from DI Watts's unfortunate upchuck outside the front door.'

Sue nodded, lost in thought, when a sharp, clear voice sliced through the room.

'DCI Mark Brancombe. You must be DCI Fisher.'

Even through the protective suit and mask, Sue instantly had the measure of him. She'd met plenty of Brancombes over the years – local coppers with puffed-up egos who didn't like London types treading on their patch. Let alone ones dealing with a missing celebrity.

'Sir.' She stood up and addressed him politely, even though they were the same rank. Getting pompous Brancombe on side from the off would make her life so much easier. 'Any help your teams here in Sussex can give us will be much appreciated. We don't know who these people are, or even if they're connected to the missing person case. If they're not, I'll be straight out of your hair.'

'Of course. I've got my best men, sorry, *people*, on it. We've spoken to Ron Briggs, the owner. The super knows him from the Rotary. And the golf club. Decent chap, does a lot for charity. They had dinner just last week. Ron's out in Spain, staying at his villa with Mandy, his wife. There's only one set of keys, and Ron's got them. We're sure he's got absolutely nothing to do with this.'

'That's good to know.' Sue made a mental note to check Ron Briggs out very carefully. 'I'm guessing he'll make a statement in Spain. Just to cross the Ts and dot the Is, so to speak.'

'Indeed. I'll check the Spanish Guardia are taking one for us. Grim, business, eh?' He looked down at the bodies, where Dr Drakos was carefully rolling the man on to his side, unleashing a stench that burst straight through Sue's protective mask.

The man's chest was black and bloated, and livid red

streaks ran down his side. 'Well, must get on,' Brancombe said, beads of sweat peppering his forehead. 'We'll let you have a copy of the pathology report the moment we receive it.'

'Thank you, sir.' Of course you bloody will, Sue thought. Or Chief Biller will be on you and your Super like a heat-seeking missile.

He disappeared out of the house, and Dr Drakos's eyes crinkled into a smile. 'I hope for your sake the deceased are nothing to do with your case,' she said quietly. 'Dealing with DCI Brancombe can be quite a challenge. Full of himself. Oh, and as a heads-up, he's one of the funny handshake brigade. My partner's seen him and the super going into the Masonic Lodge together.'

'Good to know.'

'Bear with. I'm going to change into fresh PPE and examine the woman.'

While she waited for Dr Drakos to return, Sue looked at the dead woman's body. She'd been to so many crime scenes over the years, and was used to dealing in a matter-of-fact way with whatever she found, but there was something utterly heartbreaking about these two not-quite-elderly people ending their lives like this. She hadn't felt so moved by a crime scene, so utterly determined to find the killer, since the Medford case.

Unlike the butchered man, the woman looked almost serene as she lay on the bed. She was of similar age to him, mid-sixties, with long grey hair arranged neatly over one shoulder, and a chalk-white face. Her eyes were open, but

Sue knew that death could do that, so whoever had placed her there may have closed them. Judging by her clothes, she was working-class, conservative and traditional in her tastes, in a knee-length dark-brown skirt and round-necked top, with a small, rectangular gold locket around her neck. A blanket lay over her thighs and her feet poked out from under it, bloated and bunioned. The killer had taken care with her body, treated it with some kind of perverted respect.

Dr Drakos returned with the news that DCI Brancombe had added to the vomit pile, and began photographing the woman.

'What about the locket?' Sue asked. 'There might be something inside it?'

'Let's look.' Taking the locket in her gloved hand, she unclipped it from the woman's body. 'All furred up. Looks like it hasn't been opened for years.'

Slipping on fresh gloves, Sue tried to prise it open, eventually using one of Dr Drakos' sterile tools on it. Suddenly the locket sprung apart. Inside was a tiny photo of a newborn baby's face. The sight of it triggered unwanted memories for Sue, who quickly snapped it shut and sealed it inside an evidence bag.

'She's got similar needle marks on her arm,' Dr Drakos said, carefully placing the woman's bloated arm by her side. 'Likely injected with something, too. Though again I can't say if that's what killed her. No immediate signs of sexual assault, or that she's been restrained in any way.'

'Can I check the man's watch?' Sue asked, pulling on a

fresh pair of gloves. 'It's a cheap one, but you never know. We might get lucky. God knows, we need a break in this case.'

'Worth a try, be my guest.'

The man's body was still on his side, making it easy for Sue to unclasp the watch, though it came away with a revoltingly thick chunk of black skin attached to it. Taking a deep breath, Sue turned it over and scraped off the flesh.

'Bingo!'

On the back of the watch, in neat letters, was an engraving. 'To Dafydd. With all my love. Gwen.'

Dafydd. Gwen. Sue realised she was staring at the dead bodies of Sam's parents.

Chapter Eleven

LOLA

I'm back in my apartment, sitting on the balcony with a single gin and slimline tonic. Eighty-five calories. Six hundred calories today so far, so I can afford it. The River Thames is sparkling in the sunset, and the light makes the steel-and-glass skyscrapers across the river glow red and gold, but I barely notice the beauty, lost in thought.

By the time Rick had arrived in Camber, the local police had taped it off. It was live coverage on the news. A big crowd of locals had gathered at the end of the street, along with half of Pontins. A double murder. One of the victims had to be Sam. I thought I'd be overwhelmed with relief. I didn't know who'd killed him, or why, and I told myself it didn't matter. His death would protect my life and the world I'd built.

But when the first body bag came out, an agonising, terrible despair rose up in my chest and I could hardly breathe. Our lives had been intertwined, woven together so tightly for so long, and *needing* him dead didn't meant I *wanted* it. I'd heard it said that the opposite of love isn't hate, it's indifference. Somehow all the love I'd felt for Sam had twisted into hate, but, in that moment, I knew I still loved him.

I pour another drink, a double this time despite the calories, trying not to remember that night in Paris. Or the time he was shooting in Greece, and I flew out at the end with his latest boyfriend, Pedro, so we could party in Paros, the three of us dancing in a bar in Naoussa before wending our way back to the hotel arm-in-arm at dawn along the whitewashed cobbles. Sitting on the beach at sunset, the sand soft and warm, sipping wine as we gazed out across the endless, brilliant-blue sea. Sam and I could have slept together again – I sensed Pedro would have welcomed a threesome – but we both knew that being lovers would make our relationship too complicated. It would open the door to jealousy, to possession, to ruining what we had, and neither of us wanted that.

The gin isn't numbing the pain, it's making it worse. I stop drinking, and switch off the TV. So far the press haven't connected the murders to Sam. Perhaps it isn't him. Perhaps the dead people were his captors, and he's escaped. Or perhaps this case is nothing to do with him at all.

I've spent most of my career shielding Sam, and that's what started this unholy mess. Lee Soldwell was the first. Sam wasn't A-list then, but I knew he was going to be. He was living in Camden back then, in a tiny flat above The Jolly Cobbler shoe shop, and Lee – 'a money-grabbing fat shit', as Rick called him – was his landlord. A huge man with three chins that always had beads of sweat between them, Soldwell rented out the shabby flat for a small fortune, and Sam paid it because he liked Camden's buzz. Unfortunately he also liked the ease with which he could occasionally pick up coke on Inverness Street and its proximity to the rent boys who frequented Hampstead Heath.

Sam's flat was on the very top floor, up a narrow, steep, staircase, and Soldwell, who ran Lee's Second-Hand Records on the high street, lived just below, so he saw and heard all the comings and goings. He'd bought the run-down flat in the 1980s, when he worked as a minor A&R man for a record label, and when mortgage rates rocketed, converted the cramped loft into a studio flat, with a Baby Belling cooker top and a chemical toilet that constantly smelled. Sam filled it with scented candles and colourful prints, but the 'British Airways Bog' whiff, as he called it, still lingered. Soozie Lightwater was his agent back then, but I was given the day-to-day task of managing him, as although he was fairly well known, in her head he was a B-lister at most, cannon fodder who could bring in cash for the agency with minimal input. I thought differently. Far from being a jobbing actor whose face was familiar from yet another BBC or ITV crime drama, Sam could make it in films, I was sure of it. Hollywood. I was planning to start my own agency and I wanted Sam to be my first client.

But Soldwell became a big problem. I called round to see Sam on the off-chance after a meeting at Channel 5 in

Camden, and, hearing me on the stairs, Soldwell popped his head out of the door. 'Can I have a word?'

I'd met him a couple of times in passing, and Sam had introduced me as his agent. 'I'm worried about the lad,' Soldwell began, ushering me inside his flat, where the thick smell of curry, bad breath and sweaty socks made me want to retch. The room was large and musty, and looked untouched since the 1980s, with a tatty black leather sofa, faded Athena prints on the walls and piles of vinyl records everywhere. A half-eaten plate of baked beans on toast sat solidifying on a side table. His voice dropped to a whisper. 'He brings home a *lot* of rent boys. Sometimes two at once.' He gestured to the ceiling. 'I can *hear* what they're up to. Thin walls, you know.'

'It's not really my business, Mr Soldwell,' I replied. 'I'm sure Sam can take care of himself. If he wants to enjoy the company of sex workers, that's his choice. But if the noise is bothering you, I can ask him to keep it down.'

Soldwell smiled, revealing surprisingly even but deeply nicotine-stained teeth. I realised for the first time that before he'd ballooned and rotted, before he morphed into *this*, he would have been reasonably good-looking.

'The thing is,' he went on, 'I've got a friend on the *Daily News*. I've got *a video*. Of what he does on Hampstead Heath.'

'What do you mean, a video?'

He reddened. 'Night-vision bodycam. Picked it up on Tottenham Court Road.'

I snorted. 'So you went up there and joined in so you

could film him? That's *perverted*. And totally inadmissible in court.'

Soldwell looked offended. 'I'm not a *poof*. I just hung around to see what – and *who* – he was doing. And he did a lot. He's like a fucking Jack Russell when he gets going. Not going to do him any favours in the court of *public opinion*, is it.'

'Let's see it then. This footage.'

He turned on his computer and played it back. 'You've been ripped off with the bodycam,' I laughed. 'That could be anyone.'

'True. But *this guy*' – he pointed to a young, skinny man bent over a fallen tree trunk – 'plies his trade in Inverness Street outside my shop, and he'll do anything for a bag of smack. Including talk to the press. I've seen him going in Sam's flat a few times. Charges by the hour. I hear Sam's got quite a distinctive manhood, with a piercing and a birthmark he'll describe in hideous detail.'

He meant business. 'No one will believe a smackhead,' I said firmly. But deep down I was cornered, and Soldwell knew it. Sam was my great hope, the one I knew could propel us both to fame and fortune. Sure, there would be others. But I'd invested everything in him and I couldn't lose it now.

'Forty thousand,' Soldwell hissed. 'Cash. Or you can find out the hard way who the papers will believe.'

I laughed. 'Are you out of your mind? Sam doesn't have that kind of cash. Besides, the *Daily News* won't pay much for that video and a few sordid details from an unreliable rent-boy who'll say anything for money.'

'True. But the *Daily News* will pay a lot more when it comes with an exclusive, tell-all interview with me, the horrified landlord who had to endure his perverted ways. I can spill on how Sam Stevens likes a bit of BDSM and water sports. What he likes to do on the glass coffee table. I've heard it *all*. How the esteemed Soozie Lightwater Agency must have known all about his habits and covered them up. And the fact he's noshed off a junior minister a few times on the Heath who had a doting wife and kids at home. I've seen the minister going in and out of his flat, too. Andrew Netherington. Tory MP from the Cotswolds. Could have broken up a happy *family*.'

My mind raced. Exposing Sam's penchant for rent boys was career-wrecking enough, but throw a junior minister into that mix and it would be totally unsalvageable. He'd forever be known for it. *Only* for it. I'd spent months lining him up for a major role in a new BBC political drama, and that would vanish like a puff of fucking *smoke*. Not to mention the drugs. Sam Stevens, the coke-head. Drug-fuelled orgies with a minister. The headlines were burning into my brain.

Soldwell ignored my question. He stood there, expectantly, in his sagging tracksuit bottoms and disgusting grey top stained with baked bean juice.

'You're a sick fuck,' I snapped.

He grinned. 'Just looking after myself. You'd do the same.'

'No I wouldn't.'

'Don't get all holier-than-thou with me, lady. You're using him to make money, too.'

'I'm not fucking snooping around the Heath with a camera, interfering in people's private lives and blackmailing them.'

'Needs must.' He took out his phone. 'I can call the *Daily News* right now, if you like.'

'All right. Ten thousand. And not a penny more. But you'll have to give me time.'

'Twenty.'

'Ten. Cash. I'll need at least forty-eight hours. And you don't discuss this with Sam. Ever. Leave me to do that.'

He nodded and opened the door. 'Deal. Forty-eight hours.'

I went up to Sam's flat, desperately trying to keep a lid on the rage that was burning in every single pore. 'Come in, Loles,' he said, as bright and breezy as ever, dressed in skinny black jeans and pink flip-flops. 'How was Channel 5?'

'Fine.' I smiled. 'Listen, hon, can we get some air? Go for a walk over Regent's Park? I need to fill you in on all the exciting stuff coming up.'

I didn't tell him then. We sat on a bench by London Zoo as the green glow of summer faded from the chestnut trees, and chatted about the BBC role, about his upcoming shoot in India. And when we parted I took out a burner phone and texted Rick. He'd know what to do.

Twenty-four hours later, Lee Soldwell was found

floating in the Regent's Canal. He'd been hit in the face with an 'unknown blunt instrument', according to the coroner, fallen in unconscious and drowned. There were no witnesses. I knew Rick wouldn't let me down.

The papers revealed Soldwell had served time for sex with an underage girl ten years earlier, and filthy images were found on his computer, including child porn and grainy, unidentifiable footage of an outdoor orgy. After rounding up some of Camden's flotsam and jetsam, the police discovered he had a wealth of dodgy connections, people he'd pissed off and reasons to get whacked round the head. But no one really cared what happened to Soldwell, and as more pressing crimes stretched their limited manpower, the case joined the pile marked 'unsolved' and everyone forgot about it. Except me.

I didn't lose a single night's sleep over it, especially when his sordid past came out. Getting rid of him made me feel invincible. And I made a beeline for the *Daily News'* editor at the next press events, turning on the charm until the uncontrollable, long-forgotten urges from his middle-aged, dried-up husk of a body outweighed his sense of duty to his wife. To my surprise, Tim Thacker turned out to be a quality fuck. Witty and entertaining, too. We'd been friends with terrific benefits – including his refusal to run any stories about my clients' private lives – ever since.

So when Sam said he didn't want to take the risk of leaving Soozie's agency to join my new one, I had leverage. 'I totally understand,' I told him. 'But what Soozie won't do is go the extra mile. And sometimes, that's what stands between you and success. Remember your old landlord, Lee Soldwell? The one found dead in the canal? He had a video of you with an MP on the Heath, and a rent boy ready to go public.'

'Oh my God.'

'If he'd done it, you wouldn't be starring in *The Power of Parliament* now and hobnobbing with A-listers. You'd have been tainted for life, a washed-up has-been with a penchant for perverted gay sex and details of your intimate birthmark spread across the papers.'

Sam stared at me, too shocked to speak.

'So I took care of it. I've got contacts who can help in these situations. That's how far I'll go to protect you, Sam.'

Telling him was a risk, but my gut told me it was the right thing to do. Sam was self-obsessed. Any morals would always take a back seat to that.

'So you arranged for—'

'Yes.'

He paused, the shocked look in his eyes eclipsed by adoration.

'You did that for *me*?'

That's when I knew we'd make millions together.

I'm in my bedroom checking emails on my laptop when phone rings.

'Ms Lovett? DCI Sue Fisher. I'm on my way back to the office but I have some news linked to the Sam Stevens case.'

'My God. Is it him? I saw the news about the bodies in Camber – that's one of the addresses Olivia passed on to you, isn't it? They're saying they've been dead a few days.' My head spins and I feel I'm going to vomit at what Sue is about to tell me. All I can hear is Sam's voice, his laugh, all I can see is his smile, and suddenly all that morphs into a sickening image of his body, bloated and blackened.

'We're waiting for the bodies to be formally identified, but we believe they are Sam's parents.'

'His *parents*? So Sam is still *alive*?'

My mind is in overdrive, filled with a thousand questions and feelings, a confusing, unholy mix of fear and utter relief.

'I don't know. But we hope so.'

'Why on earth has someone killed his parents?' I blurt out. 'Sam hadn't seen them for years.'

'I know this will be a shock,' DCI Fisher says. 'But we have to consider the possibility that Sam might be responsible.'

For a moment, I'm completely lost for words. Rick is convinced Sam was abducted in that Jaguar. It couldn't be him. Sam isn't a killer. And left that life behind long ago.

'You really think *he* killed them?'

'We're keeping an open mind. That's why I'm calling. To give you a heads-up that we might have to switch the focus from missing person to murderer.'

I'm struggling to think straight. Closing the laptop, I take a deep breath. I have to treat this like any other emergency. Plan how I want it to play out. Switch into my usual clear-headed crisis mode.

'But surely whoever killed them is holding Sam? They've got to be the prime suspect.'

'It's possible. We've told his boyfriend, Tyler, that we suspect the bodies are Sam's parents, but haven't said anything else as yet,' Sue went on. 'DI Basu's looking for next of kin. But the press will get wind and connect the two cases, you can be sure of it.'

If the police tell the public Sam's wanted for murder, his reputation – and mine – will be trashed. Finding him dead at his house from an accidental overdose, as I'd planned, wouldn't have done that. People would still have loved him, watched his movies. He wouldn't have been *soiled*. With my help, they'd have overlooked the drugs, understood he'd just taken them to cope after a long shoot. But being labelled a murderer – and on my books – that's something that neither of our reputations would recover from. The public would be sure I must have known. I need to try and persuade Sue Fisher to keep treating Sam as missing.

'I just can't see Sam killing his parents, DCI Fisher. He'd moved on years ago. Barely even mentioned them. Accepted they were homophobic and the kind of people he didn't need in his life. He wasn't walking round with a massive grudge, wishing them dead. If he had been, I'm sure I'd have known. I still think it's possible he's gone off-grid for a break and is oblivious to all this.'

'Like I say, we're keeping an open mind. It's still

possible. I can't go into details. There are aspects to the murder which indicate Sam could be responsible. I can't divulge them.'

'What about an obsessive fan? He's had some weird letters over the years. Couple of people regularly sending him used knickers. My assistant, Olivia, has long made sure she's wearing latex gloves to open any of his fan mail.'

'Would you have any of the letters?'

'Good God, no. They go straight in the bin. But I can check if she kept a record of the postmark, or the names if the creeps put their names and addresses in. You'd be surprised. Some do.'

She's somewhere on the M25 and the signal keeps breaking up. 'I really think we have to be careful,' I add. 'Sam's an international star, and if we officially put it out there that he's suspected of murder, his reputation will be ruined. Mud sticks. And that could prove very costly for the police if he decided to sue. It would be dreadful publicity for the force if it turns out he's been kidnapped by some nutter like Kathy Bates in *Misery*, or being held in dreadful conditions by an international gang. Or he's just taking a break.'

There's a pause as the signal reconnects. 'Why don't I come straight to meet you?' she suggests. 'I can't hear properly on the phone and I need as much info as you've got about his relationship with his mum and dad. And on those nutters with the knickers.'

'Sure,' I reply, smiling. 'I'm at home. I'll text you the address.'

I drain the last of the G&T, and text Peter to cancel our plans for the night.

Sorry, hon, obvs had hell of a day with all the Sam stuff. Going to bed. Will call tomorrow x.

He's ten years younger than me, a wannabe film director who seems to think sleeping with me will boost his career. Maybe it will. All I care about is having sex on tap when I want it, as lately Tim's been spending time with his wife. Ovarian cancer, apparently.

Twenty minutes later I'm showered, perfumed and dressed in a casual black wraparound skirt with a soft cream shirt, unbuttoned a little too much, just enough to glimpse my pretty white lace bra. My blonde hair tumbles over my shoulders, and I paint on a slick of red lipstick. Sam is alive, I can *feel* it, and I need DCI Fisher on side. I'll do whatever it takes.

Chapter Twelve

TUESDAY

The beach at Camber was one of the deepest Sue had ever seen. The tide was out so far that you could hardly see it, and a shimmering expanse of silver-gold sand swept towards the horizon, as seagulls swooped and a handful of dog walkers dotted the landscape. There were two large, cheap seaside cafés built at the back of the beach and the staff were closing them up for the evening, having had a sudden surge of nosey people wanting takeaway coffees as news spread about the murders.

Sue took off her shoes and walked out on the beach, across the soft powder and past the tide line, her feet sinking slightly in the wet sand. She needed a moment to clear her head. Dev would be here soon, keen to take a look at the crime scene.

The wind was light, barely there, and Sue stooped to pick up a pink shell, one of thousands washed up as the tide retreated. She remembered holidays in Cornwall with

Rob and Tom, holding her son's chubby little hand under an azure-blue sky as they stepped across rock pools, Tom poking them with his net in the hope he'd find a crab or a fish, just to look at before he let them go again. The memory brought back a rush of emotions. Tom, sweet Tom, back when he loved her. When he thought she was a good mum. What was he doing now, locked away in his room, alone and afraid?

Then she thought of Rob, handing her a heart-shaped stone he fished from a glistening rock pool. Even though Rob had been cruel and violent, at times he'd also made her feel like the most-loved woman in the world, and having put several domestic abusers away for years, she knew just how fucked up that was.

Sue pushed the memories from her mind and tried to focus on the case. Behind the beach was a high bank of grassy sand dunes, blocking out the view of the houses – including the crime scene – and tapering down towards the cafés. The whole of Camber was tired and run-down, but then, quite unexpectedly, to the right of the cafés was a row of around fifteen multi-million-pound beach houses. Each was individually designed, all glass and soft, faded wood, with huge windows overlooking the sea. There was a path running along the front of them and Sue walked along it, noticing that almost every house had a notice outside advertising that it was for rent. Some of the houses were huge, like you'd expect to see on Malibu beach, the kind of place that rich families – or even celebrities like Sam – might stay at.

She turned and saw Dev walking towards her.

'They said you'd come down here. I've just met DI Watts at the house. Forensics are still knee-deep swabbing everything, but they're bagging up the bodies now. What do you think happened there, boss?'

'The pathologist says she thinks they were killed elsewhere and dumped there. Actually, that's the wrong word. They were *staged*. The woman had been arranged with her hands in prayer, and, like I told you, the guy's back had been carved. "DEAD 2 ME". That's what Sam's parents told him when they threw him out.' She paused. 'But he's got absolutely no form. Penchant for rent boys, but no evidence of being violent at all. What's the word from the set of that thing he was filming and the director, Simon Omeria?'

'I spoke to Omeria, the producer and several of the cast over the phone,' Dev replied. 'Most of them – including Omeria – said the shoot was a bloody nightmare. *Murder in the Lakes*. Snappy title.' He took out his notebook. 'Pissed down with rain the whole time, and a farmer kicked off and wouldn't allow any of the production trucks to cross his land. Apparently Omeria was having a few personal problems and he's aware he vented his substantial spleen at the cast and crew. Not at Sam, though. He seems to have been spared the brunt of it. But they did have a wrap party of sorts on the Thursday afternoon and everyone says Sam was in good spirits. It sounds like they were just all glad to get it over with.'

'Where's Omeria now?'

'Started a new shoot on Monday. In the Cotswolds. Some period drama series. *Young Lovers*, I think it's called. He's staying at a B&B with the rest of the crew but coming back in the next day or two as the rest of it is being shot at Pinewood Studios in Buckinghamshire. I didn't say anything about him getting handsy with the young actor, Stephen Merryweather, or Sam confronting him about "touching the talent", as Tyler put it.'

Sue nodded. 'Good. I want to keep that quiet for now. He's certainly got a motive to want Sam out of the picture. But killing and mutilating Sam's parents? I can't see how Omeria fits into that. What about Merryweather?'

'Nice lad. Didn't say much, though. He only had a small part and praised the rest of the cast and crew to high heaven. Said Sam was really kind to him and made him feel welcome on set. Clearly worried that if he speaks out against Omeria, his career will be in ruins.'

'Did Sam tell any of them what his plans were?'

'Seeing his boyfriend Tyler, mainly. Everyone said he was madly in love. One of the drivers on set, John Fowey, took him home to Cobshott. I spoke to him. They left around five p.m. and the journey took just over six hours, so they arrived at Cobshott just after eleven p.m. He said Sam slept for most of it, but did chat a little when they stopped at a service station for a drive-through Costa and seemed happy to be going home.'

'What did the driver do after dropping him off?'

'He lives in Brentford with his wife and kids. Works as a driver on a lot of film sets, usually Pinewood Studios, but he does travel around the UK when he needs to. He says he drove straight home, and his wife confirmed it. The team's reviewing ANPR cameras to double-check.'

They walked along in silence for a moment, back towards the cafés, as the setting sun leaked orange through the low clouds, each thinking through the possibilities.

'What about the paparazzo who took the shot of Tyler arriving at Sam's house? Did you trace him?'

'Aussie guy. Freelance stringer. Known as "Jim L" by the other paps. Gets paid in cash by the agency and gave them a false name – Border Force have no record of an Australian citizen known as Jim L or James L entering the UK. Hasn't turned up at his regular patch today, but probably made enough money out of that Tyler shot to take a few days off. He's not been in the country long. Gave the same name to the cheap hotel where he's staying. Again, he pays cash. Hasn't been seen there today, but Uniform are going to check again later.'

'Good. He's definitely worth checking out. Oh, and I rang Lola Lovett a few minutes ago, to warn her Sam might be a murder suspect. She's convinced he's been abducted or is just taking a few days' break. Insists there's no reason to kill his parents, that he'd put them behind him years ago.' She looked at Dev. 'I know, she *would* say that. Can't accept the truth blah blah. But I sensed she really meant it. And I wondered if she knows more than she's letting on.'

'What do you mean, boss?'

'I can't be sure. Perhaps she just doesn't want the negative publicity from him being labelled a killer. But I would have thought that her first priority would be for us to find him. If he's had a breakdown and done that to his parents, he must be in a terrible mental state and at risk of suicide. Finding him has never been more urgent. She didn't even seem to consider that. I'm going to go and talk to her on the way home.'

'Do you want me to come?'

Sue smiled. 'No. And stop fangirling. Or fanboying or whatever it is. You'll need to liaise with South Wales police and find out who's next of kin other than Sam as he's an only child. If Dafydd and Gwen had brothers and sisters, they'll need to be informed. Could be the whole family is a target. Best station officers outside their houses. Just in case.'

They'd reached the wooden beach cafés, where a young woman with spiky pink hair and a rainbow apron was pulling down the last shutter. 'Did you hear about them murders?' she said, giving their smart clothes the once-over. 'Are you the police?'

Sue nodded. 'Have you given a statement to the uniformed officers? They were due to talk to everyone in the cafés.'

'I did. Not that I know anything. They asked if I'd seen an elderly couple in here but I told them, I seen loads. Lots of retired people walk their dogs down here. One elderly man comes down every day and walks up and down for hours. He's almost bent double.' She paused. 'I seen you on the news earlier. You're looking for Sam Stevens.'

'We are. But we work on a lot of cases.' Sue didn't want

her to connect the two. 'Have you ever seen Sam Stevens down here?'

'I don't think so. I'm sure I would have recognised him. There's them posh houses on the front but people who stay in there don't usually come in here. But then I saw the picture of him with a beard and I do serve hundreds of people with beards like that. He looked so... *normal*. Not like a film star.'

Sue took a card from her pocket. 'That's my number. I know lots of people use this café. If you overhear or see anything unusual, send me a text or call.'

The girl slipped it inside her apron. 'Will do. I'm Belinda. Look, I'm just locking up but there's coffee inside. Do you want one to take away? We don't have that posh stuff. People always come in asking for lattes and oat milk, but we just have coffee. Or tea. I can do you a cuppa.'

Sue smiled. She rather liked Belinda.

'Two teas would be great,' she replied. 'Milky. Two sugars. Actually, make it one. I'm trying to lose a bit of weight. Dev doesn't have any sugar.'

They walked on towards the crime scene, takeaway teas in hand. 'Worth a shot,' Sue told Dev. 'She must hear all the goings-on in there.'

Back at Seashore Cottage, two ambulance drivers were wheeling one of the body bags into the back of the van. The large crowd standing behind the tape at the start of the road hadn't dissipated, and the sight of the body bag led to a surge of camera phones in the air.

Dr Emily Drakos came out with one of the forensic team and began pulling off her protective gear.

'Christ, it's hot in there,' she said, beads of sweat pricking her forehead. 'This is Dr Jim Taylor, in charge of Forensics on site.'

'DCI Sue Fisher. Is there anything more you can tell me right now?' Sue asked. 'If you're got a hunch, I'd love to hear it.'

'No blood traces detected anywhere else in the house,' Jim said thickly, through his mask. 'Likely scenario is that this isn't the murder location. They were brought here. There's a lot of sand on the carpets, but that could have been from officers' shoes when you executed the warrant. One of the lads detected four stripes of dirt running up the hallway. Barely visible to the naked eye, but they're there. My guess is they're wheel marks. If I was a betting man, I'd say the bodies came in via two wheeled cases.'

'Did we find any bags or suitcases? Plastic sheeting?'

'No. So if my theory is correct, they were taken away by the killer. I suspect the bodies had been well wrapped inside, as there are no drops of body fluid in the hall, though we did pick up a few hairs, which we'll test.'

'Thank you,' Sue replied. 'I know you'll make a full report, but, in the interim, anything you can tell me will be so helpful.'

'The wheelie bins are clean too,' Dr Taylor added. 'Newly delivered by the council. Unused. We've collected various samples in the hallway and in the kitchen. They should tell us more and we can run them against the DNA database.'

'Any clue as to how the killer got in?' Dev asked.

'No signs of a break-in, or fingerprints. Forcing the lock is most likely. There are a few fingerprints about the place – we need to compare them to the owner's – but none around the body. I suspect the killer was wearing gloves. In my view, whoever did this wanted you to find the body – why else go to the trouble of mutilating it? – but without them leaving a trace.'

'Could one person have done it?' Sue asked. 'Moved the bodies, I mean.'

'They'd have to be pretty strong to lift the cases but yes, it could be done.' He paused. 'I'd better get back in there.'

'Of course. Thanks, Dr Taylor.'

Emily Drakos stuffed her used protective suit into a bin liner and Sue got a good look at her for the first time. She was slightly older than Sue expected – late thirties, at a guess – with bobbed hair the colour of creamy chocolate and a warm, cheery smile that seemed at odds with a life spent dealing with dead people.

'Did you notice anything else that might be useful, Dr Drakos?'

She nodded. 'The woman's hands were bound together at the wrist to keep them in the prayer position. My guess is that the killer planned it meticulously. They'd brought what looks like fishing line to hold them in place. It was obviously very important to them that she was left like that. We'll analyse the line, see what we can glean from it.'

'What about the man?' Dev asked. 'Any ideas why he's on the floor, not the bed?'

'Couple of possibilities,' Dr Drakos replied. 'Rigor mortis had set in, and his body was still stiff, so when the killer or whoever brought him here got him out of the case he was rigid and difficult to handle. Or he was deliberately placed in that position so they easily could do what they did to his back. The woman had likely been through rigor mortis – the time it lasts in everybody is different – and was pliable enough to be laid on the bed.'

'No sign of the scalpel,' Sue added.

Dr Drakos paused, taking a swig of water from a plastic bottle. 'Got to admire their forward-planning skills. Whoever you're looking for is efficient, organised, meticulous. Also, I'm no psychologist, but the position of the man makes him look humbled. Sorry for what he's done. Whatever that is.'

Lola's apartment was almost exactly how Sue had imagined it; grand and spacious, interior designed to the hilt. She took the lift to the twentieth floor, stepping out into a smart corridor, carpeted in dark blue, with thin uplights casting a cool glow along the walls. The door to number 65 was open, and Lola stood in the entrance, holding what looked like a gin and tonic.

'Sue. Thanks for coming, Please, come in.'

Sue followed her down a long white corridor, glancing at the framed pictures along it. Each was a film poster presumably starring one of Lola's clients, and she recognised Sam on three of them including his first big hit, *The Last Star*. She'd seen it at the cinema in Kingston with Rob, before Tom was born. Pushing the memory away, she turned her attention to Lola, noticing how her long, delicately curled blonde hair swayed as she walked. And how thin she was. The kind of thin that meant a lifetime on a diet. Anorexia made sense. No one's genes were that good.

The corridor led into the living room, a huge space with floor-to-ceiling windows that framed the twinkling lights of London at night. It was a breathtaking sight, and Sue instinctively walked towards the open door that led to the balcony, fenced with a clear glass balustrade.

'That's some view,' she said, stepping outside. Lola's black cat followed and rubbed against her legs. Sue bent down to stroke her.

'Hello, you,' she said, as the cat began to purr.

'That's Cleopatra.' Lola smiled. 'She likes you. That's rare.'

'Cats usually do,' Sue replied, tickling Cleopatra's chin. 'I don't know why.'

'They're like humans. They can tell when someone is worth getting to know better.'

In spite of herself, Sue blushed slightly. She stood up and gazed at the view. To the right lay the warm amber glow of Big Ben and the Houses of Parliament, with the River Thames running black and deep beside them. A few boats were sailing up and down, party ones with flickering coloured disco lights. The London Eye dominated the south side of the river, a giant bicycle wheel tastefully lit in red and blue as it slowly rotated, revealing the stunning skyline to its passengers. Beyond it, the Shard's point stood boldly against the night sky, and the skyscrapers in the City glowed green, like Oz.

'I know,' Lola said, with a smile. 'Stunning. I never tire of it. Can I get you a drink? G&T? You must have had one hell of a day.'

'Normally, I'd say no. But I'm officially off the clock, so yes, a small G&T would be lovely. Driving, you know.'

Lola disappeared back inside, and Sue snapped a few photos of the view to show Mike, trying to ignore the unwanted, uninvited desire that welled up every time she was near this woman. It had hit her from the moment Lola had walked into the police station – a desperate need, an urgency that she hadn't felt since Rob. She forced her attention back to the skyline. Living here must make you feel on top of the world, Sue thought. A permanent reminder of your success. And one hell of a daily confidence boost. It was a far cry from her patchy lawn and shed.

'Here you go.' Lola handed Sue the drink, and they stood side by side, Lola leaning slightly forwards over the stainless-steel rail. Sue glimpsed her breast, softly cupped in a beautiful white lace bra, warm and inviting. She'd been with a couple of girls before Rob, so the feeling wasn't new, but the sudden intensity of it took her by complete surprise.

Lola's iPhone buzzed and she glanced down at it. 'I've got those names and addresses for you,' she said. 'People who sent Sam weird stuff. Well, the ones who identified themselves, anyway. My assistant Olivia has made a list and just emailed it over.' She scrolled down. 'There's about twenty, by the looks of it. I'll forward her email to you.'

Sue had hardly eaten anything all day, apart from a deeply unpleasant, watery, lukewarm veggie pasty in the service station on the M25, and the gin was going straight to her head.

'You're sure this is a single? I have to drive.'

'Of course. I wouldn't want you to get into *trouble*.'

She noticed Lola's plump red lips resting softly on her glass, leaving a trace of lipstick. The way her hair brushed against her breast. Her perfume. A moment of escape from the horrors she'd seen that day.

Back to business, Sue, she told herself harshly. *You're here to do a job. You've got two dead people and a murder suspect. For God's sake, Sue, get on it.*

'What can you tell me about Sam's parents? I need to know it all.'

Lola nodded. 'While I was waiting for you, I went over and over everything I could remember. They're from Tonyrefail in South Wales, like I said. The dad was a miner until the pit closed a couple of years after the miners' strike, around 1986. Unemployed ever since. His mum was a housewife.'

'They must have been pretty skint.'

'They were. Sam remembered the strike – he was just a kid. They lived on food parcels and had baths next door once a week because the gas was cut off. And the whole community marching to the pit when they were forced back to work. Lot of wounded pride.'

Sue nodded. 'So the dad was a hard-working, no-nonsense sort.'

'Exactly. To be fair, until Sam's sexuality became a problem for them, they seemed to have done their best. Sam had a tough time growing up – he was bullied at school, called "gay boy", had his head flushed down the toilet, but he didn't say a word about it to them. So – and I told him this several times – they can't be blamed for that.'

'*Did* he blame them?'

'No. Not for the bullying. Not deep down. Though he wished he'd been able to tell them. His dad used to take him fishing, and "down the Legion"' – Lola said it in a perfect Welsh accent – 'some kind of working men's club. Trying to "man him up", I think. He hated it. But his mum seemed a caring sort. Sam didn't talk about her much, but after a few drinks he'd recall sweet little things, like her baking him iced buns for after school, and them watching *The Sound of Music* together.'

'Was his dad violent?'

'If he was, Sam never mentioned it. Not even when he found gay porn under his bed. He'd gone in there rummaging around for Sam's fishing rod, apparently. Got quite the shock when a stack of well-thumbed *Playguy* magazines fell out. I did wonder if the dad was looking for them, though Sam could never entertain the idea. I mean, who rummages under a teenage boy's bed? Sam said he was sure he'd tucked them between the base and the mattress. But Sam and his mum came back from the shops to find them laid out all over the bed, and his dad apoplectic. Told Sam to pack his stuff and never come back. He was sixteen.'

'What did his mum say about it?'

'Sam said she was crying. He tried to reason with his dad, but he just said: "You're dead to me." Those words hurt him more than anyone can ever know. He went upstairs to pack a rucksack, and his mum went up to hug him. All she kept saying was "I'm so sorry". She was in bits. But she didn't stand up to the dad.'

Lola sipped her drink and they stood in silence for a moment or two, gazing at the view. 'Sam's not a killer, Sue,' Lola said softly. 'I *know* him. I'm not saying that as his agent, I'm saying that as his friend.'

'What makes you so sure?'

'Because underneath it all, he never gave up hope of reconciling with them. Especially his mum. I'm not saying he didn't have a lot of anger about what happened – that's partly what fuelled his desire for success. But killing them? No. So I think you need to look for other suspects.'

The gin was really going to Sue's head now, and her elbow slipped off the rail. 'Sorry,' she said, steadying herself, as Lola caught her.

'My God, what kind of host am I?' Lola said. 'I bet you

haven't eaten all day. How about a pizza?' She took out her phone. 'I'm ordering one in. I've already eaten but I'm sure I could squeeze in a slice. Veggie feast OK?'

'Wonderful.'

Twenty minutes later, Sue and Lola were sitting beside each other on the sofa, with a plate of pizza slices between them, and an unspoken desire ready to explode.

Chapter Thirteen

LOLA

S he's exhausted and emotional, I can feel it the moment she walks in the door. Whatever she's seen in Camber has had a pretty big impact. Her suit is creased from the journey and there's a faint smell of sweat. I pour her a triple G&T with plenty of ice, and we stand on the balcony to talk. Sam's alive. All I need to do is find him before the police do, talk to him, tell him how I feel, persuade him to keep quiet about me. Sam and I can find a way through this, I know it.

The view is impressive at the best of times, but on this warm autumn night, with London's sparkle stretching out in front of us, it's truly magical. She's made friends with Cleopatra, too. I'm sticking to tonic water on ice now, though she doesn't know it. I've got to stay focused. Persuade her that Sam just wouldn't have killed his parents. Push her to look for other suspects. That part is easy. He wouldn't have the balls to do it. Not himself, anyway. He knew I'd had Lee Soldwell silenced. And I'd had Rick deal with Des

Lethbridge, too. That lunatic Aussie backpacker. They stood in the way of his success, and at the time Sam was happy for the problems to disappear. But getting his own hands dirty wasn't Sam's style. And his parents were no threat to him.

She's drinking the gin pretty fast, and I can see it's making her tipsy. There's been more than one glance at my boobs. I need to get as much detail as I can about the investigation, and Camber. Whoever killed his parents is likely the same person who has Sam, and Rick needs to find them before Sue does. That unwanted, unexpected moment of relief that burst through when I heard Sam's body *wasn't* in Camber is slightly muted by fear. He still has the power to ruin me, but if we find him first, I'm sure he won't use it.

She tells me the man's body was mutilated, with 'Dead 2 Me' carved with a scalpel. Christ. The woman positioned in prayer, though they haven't released those details to anyone. No signs of foul play at Cobshott, and Tyler's story about helping a friend move house on Sunday night checks out, though she's looking into his past. I tell her Sam repeated the 'dead to me' story to anyone who'd listen, often several times when drunk, so that didn't label him a killer in my book. I'm convinced it wasn't Sam, and I tell her so. Whoever did this is seriously sick in the head. And that's not Sam. They're sending a message. But who are they sending it to?

I'm nibbling on a slice of pizza. One thousand four hundred calories today. I'm on the absolute limit so I can't eat more than a fraction of this piece. Sue's gobbling it down like she hasn't eaten for weeks, and talking about her son, Tom. She's very tipsy and slightly tearful when she mentions him, says he's distant and disengaged. I can tell she's worried about him.

She asks if I wanted kids when I was younger, and I shake my head, saying I was always career-driven. She'll believe that. And it's true. I don't mention getting pregnant at fourteen, or my alcoholic mother who barely even noticed me. I'd sorted that pregnancy out myself. Playing Happy Families was never on my agenda.

I lean back on the sofa and cross my legs, letting my wraparound skirt fall open up to the middle of my thigh. I'm tanned from my recent trip to Santorini, my go-to paradise, a three-day feast of beautiful pink sunsets and sunbathing by an infinity pool, gazing out at the sea, deep blue and limitless, as cruise ships sparkled in the deep volcanic caldera and Peter rubbed lemon-scented sun cream on my back.

Two glances at my thighs. I move a little closer. I'm wet now from the spell I'm weaving, the power that I'm holding over her. She doesn't *want* this, she *needs* it. I twist my hair around my fingers sensually, and uncross my legs, my skirt now falling open enough for her to glimpse my pants. White, lacy.

We're close now, so close, and my fingers curl around the back of her head, stroking her hair, pulling her towards me. My phone buzzes but I ignore it and our lips meet, soft at first, then deep and hungry. Her body is soft and plump against mine, and I unbutton her trousers, my fingers sliding between her legs. She moans.

'W-we shouldn't be doing this,' she gasps.

'I know,' I whisper. 'And that's what makes it so fucking amazing.'

We're curled up together on the sofa, Sue's legs wrapped around mine. Cleopatra jumps up beside me. 'That was beautiful, baby,' I say, stroking Sue's hair. 'I've wanted that ever since I first saw you.'

She's rapidly sobering up, and her body feels tense. 'Lola, I…' she begins, but her words tail off.

'It's OK. This was just…something that we needed. Something we couldn't control. We don't have to mention it again. Unless…' I run my fingers ever-so-softly over her nipple. 'You want to go again?'

Her body is yielding, but this time Sue resists. 'I really must go,' she says, distracted, pulling on her trousers. 'I have a partner, Mike. He will be wondering where the hell I am. I told him I was coming to see you.'

'Then you'll just have to tell him we had a *very* long chat.' I smile. 'Baby, it's OK. Don't worry. I've got a boyfriend, too. Sometimes things like this just happen. And I'm so glad it did.'

'Me too,' she replies, and she means it, though there's fear in her eyes. I've got DCI Fisher right where I want her. What she did with me is a sackable offence. She'd be shamed, discredited, her career would be over if this ever came out. She knows it. And she knows *I* know it.

She's dressed now and skittish, anxiously looking round for her keys. I button up my shirt. 'I won't tell a soul,' I say. 'This stays between us.'

'Thank you.'

'And let me know if there's any more news of Sam. Or who killed his poor parents. Anything at all.'

'I will.'

The front door clicks shut and she's gone, so I pick up my phone and swipe across to an app. Every single glorious moment is there, recorded by the hidden camera in my smoke alarm above us. Audio, too. This is my insurance policy. If DCI Fisher starts poking around in my past, getting too close to me or Rick, this video should silence her.

There are a few slices of pizza left on the plate. I'm mentally, physically and emotionally strung out. And I'm starving. I stuff them into my mouth, barely chewing each piece before I swallow it and force in another, and another, any taste and pleasure overwhelmed by hateful guilt. I'm weak, useless, pathetic. There must be a thousand calories here, and when the pizza is gone I rip open the dip, drinking it greedily. But the binge leave me anxious, adrift, and suddenly the world feels unsafe, unpredictable. Controlling my food is what keeps me stable and sane. It's been *months* since this happened. My restraint rarely slips.

I rush to the bathroom and force a toothbrush down my throat, doubled over as the acid contents of my stomach burn my throat and fill up the toilet bowl. When it's finally all out, I have one last go with the toothbrush to make absolutely sure, and slump, exhausted, on the black bathmat.

Most of the pizza is there. Focus on the numbers, Lola. I calculate that I absorbed maybe a hundred calories, so all is not lost. I flush the loo, loathing myself for my moment of weakness, turn the shower on full and stand under it, still wearing my shirt, waiting for the world to be right again.

Chapter Fourteen

WEDNESDAY

The lights were on at Sue's house, even though it was well past midnight. Mike had parked on the road as usual, leaving her the space on the tiny driveway. He'd been on a late shift and, having been promoted to DCI after the Medford case, was knee-deep in a complex investigation into drug trafficking by Albanian gangs.

Sue was late, but Mike wasn't too worried. They'd worked together for long enough in the past for him to know she was a meticulous detective, and on a high-profile case like the Sam Stevens one, she'd be totally consumed by it. The last text he'd had was around seven p.m., saying she was en route to Vauxhall to talk to Sam's agent. She was stressed about the case, that's why she'd snapped at him, Mike told himself. She didn't mean it.

With Tom out God knows where, he'd shoved a curry ready meal in the microwave and dozed off with a beer in front of the football. Neither of them were big on cooking –

a career spent working unpredictable hours meant they'd both got used to relying on microwaveable meals and pizzas out of the freezer.

Mike was glad to be back working on the drug squad. He still had nightmares about his time on the SGU safeguarding unit and the vile, sickening child pornography cases he'd worked on. Looking back, he'd had post-traumatic stress, and his ex-wife had divorced him over it, saying he didn't love her. He *had* loved her. He'd just locked all his emotions away to help him deal with it. And he wasn't going to make that mistake with Sue. They needed to talk. She seemed so distant, so uninterested in him and anything he had to say. And after her saying he wasn't Tom's real dad, Mike feared that Rob's ghost was wrecking their relationship.

If only she knew what he knew. He'd kept it secret from her during the Medford case, to spare her pain, to save her career. But he'd found evidence that Rob was somehow linked to the Mayfair child sex ring. 114b Onslow Avenue. He didn't know how, but he'd found the address on Rob's phone. Onslow Avenue still burned into his brain, after the horror of what they found there. Maybe, just maybe, now was the time to tell her. To make her see what a bastard Rob really was.

The sound of a key in the lock woke him with a start. 'Hello, love,' he said sleepily. 'That you?'

'Iss me,' slurred Tom, walking in to the living room with a bag of McDonalds. He was so drunk he could barely stand up. 'Got an Uber.'

'Had a good night?' Mike asked.

'Yeah.'

'Where d'you go?'

'Out.'

Tom's clothes stank of weed, and his eyes were hazy, unfocused. He slumped on to the sofa and was asleep in seconds, the McDonald's on his lap, untouched.

Mike knew he'd have to talk to him, but this wasn't the time. Getting any sense out of him would be impossible and the last thing Sue needed was to come in from a shift and find Tom in this state. She was already worried sick about him.

Turning Tom gently on to his side – he'd seen enough dead teenagers who'd choked on their own vomit – he rummaged under the sink for a bucket and placed it on the floor by his head. Quietly, though Mike was sure Tom was dead to the world, he took a blanket from the airing cupboard at the top of the stairs, stepping carefully around the creaky floorboards, and tucked it round him. He turned off the living room light and left the door slightly ajar so he could hear if Tom stirred.

With no more news from Sue, Mike decided to go to bed. She'd be exhausted when she came in, and at that point no copper wanted twenty questions about their day or the case. Usually she'd have grabbed a burger on the way home, and would creep in quietly so as not to disturb anyone, coming straight up the stairs to bed. Mike hoped she'd do that today, and be spared the sight of Tom in that state. He pondered carrying the lad up to bed but feared he might start vomiting. Or turn aggressive. Like his father.

The lad had been through a tough time, no doubt about that, Mike thought. Violent, abusive father, his mum being attacked in the Medford case. Tom had always seen *him* as a father figure, but maybe when he actually got together with Sue and moved in it was a step too far. Maybe it was all of those things. Maybe he was just being a typical teenager. Losing his dad couldn't have been easy. Even though Rob had been a bastard, and, in Mike's view, deserved to be dead, he was still Tom's dad.

Mike padded quietly back up the stairs and turned off the upstairs light. Tom's bedroom was at the front of the house, and the light was on, glowing under the door. If Sue saw it, she'd go in there and try to make conversation, try and engage with the son she felt she'd lost. So he grasped the handle to open the door, just to turn it off.

The door was locked. Each of the original 1930s doors had been refitted with lockable handles, which they only secured when going on holiday. Rob, a locksmith, had insisted that if a burglar got in, they'd soon give up and go elsewhere if all the doors were locked. Sue had rolled her eyes when he told her that, pointing out that they didn't have anything worth nicking. But she still locked them dutifully when they went away. Rob had had such a hold over her, and even now, four years on, little things like that told Mike she still, despite everything, loved him. It hurt, he couldn't deny it, but he couldn't share that with Sue. He understood this was Tom's home, but wished with all his heart that they'd sold up and started afresh. Even if they'd stayed on the same street. But Sue wouldn't hear of it.

Up close, this lock on Tom's room was different. The lad had changed it to a hotel-style one, which automatically locked when you closed it. Tom had to be hiding something.

Mike and Sue's bedroom was a couple of steps across the hallway, at the back of the house, a cream-coloured, bland room with built-in Ikea wardrobes down one wall and their double bed on the other. At least she'd agreed to buy a new one of those. On the right, overlooking the garden, was Sue's dressing table, a mess of make-up, unopened post, old phone chargers, Biros and post-it notes. But Mike quickly found what he was looking for.

He bent open the hairgrip, tugged off the plastic pieces with his teeth and poked one end into Tom's lock, followed by a second bent hairgrip, wobbling one of them and the handle. Seconds later, the door clicked open.

The room was a tip. It was small, a typical teenage room in many ways, with a single, unmade bed in the corner, and walls covered in posters of bands Mike had never heard of. Mike hadn't been in here for months, and as far as he knew, nor had Sue, ever since Tom started demanding 'my space'. He looked around it with a copper's eye, ignoring the rotting pizza boxes, filthy sheets and duvet cover and piles of dirty clothes. On the shelves were Tom's chess books, and Mike sighed deeply as he remembered the sweet young lad he'd taken to chess matches, sometimes hanging around for hours as he finished a game, and the beaming smile as he proudly showed him his medals. Rob had preferred rugby, and hadn't had time for the gentle lad who used his brain rather than brawn. Mike had sat in the room chatting to Tom so many times, and it had always been neat and tidy, which had made him smile and laugh as Sue was the messiest person he knew.

Mike hadn't intended to pry, but now he was in he was damn well going to find out what the hell, if anything, was going on. Someone like Tom – the Tom he thought he knew – naturally kept things spick and span. Not like this. He scanned the room, starting at the top. No false ceiling, so that was clear. The posters were stuck on with Blu Tack and Mike meticulously peeled up a corner on each one, checking behind it. Nothing.

It looked like Tom hadn't put on new sheets for months. Mike hadn't changed since he got home from work, and always carried latex gloves in his pocket. Automatically, he tugged on a pair and felt carefully around the edge of the wooden bed, lifting up the mattress, but apart from a mass of stiff tissues – the lad obviously keeps himself busy in that department, Mike thought – there was nothing suspicious. He felt along the skirting for a loose board, but everything seemed sound. No false back in the chest of drawers. The carpet was nailed down and Mike couldn't see any evidence it had been lifted. Against the wall stood Tom's old battered, wooden toybox, which Sue had bought him when he was first born. Fearing what might be inside, Mike lifted the lid, to be greeted by several stuffed toys, two Buzz Lightyears, Monopoly, Cluedo, a blue lightsabre, a backgammon set and a jigsaw of a map of the world. He checked. Nothing untoward inside them.

Mike opened the bedside cabinet. Inside was a dark wooden box about seven inches long, and an inch deep. He'd seen boxes like this before. Taking a deep breath, he opened it.

No needles, no drug addict's 'works'. Just photo after photo of Tom with his dad. The lad clearly missed his father.

He felt a rush of guilt. Tom was eighteen and entitled to his privacy. Closing the box, Mike stood up and did a last visual sweep of the room.

If only he could get Tom back into chess. He'd loved the game and the friends he made there. None of them came to the house any more. His chess set was on the top shelf with the books. Mike lifted it down, blew the dust off it and picked up one of the pieces, turning it over in his fingers. He'd bought the set for Tom when he was about ten, back when he was 'Uncle' Mike. A couple of the books, too. He remembered writing 'Happy birthday, Tom' and the date in the front of one.

Mike reached up to take one of the books off the shelf. It wouldn't budge. He tugged harder. All the books seemed to be glued together.

Tom's old wooden toybox stood against the wall, under the shelf. He took a second look at it. There were marks on the flat top. Someone had been standing on it.

He stepped on to the toybox and grabbed each end of

the row of chess books. There were about fifteen of them. They slid out as one.

Mike closed his eyes, wishing he could unsee what was in front of him.

The books had all been carefully hollowed out. Inside were three burner phones and four bricks of white powder, which looked exactly like cocaine. If so, its street value would be a couple of hundred thousand pounds.

What the heck had Tom got himself into?

He replaced everything exactly as he had found it, and closed the door quietly behind him.

Sam was thinking of his mother. His mind kept drifting into the past, a brief moment of escape from the filth and the fear, only for the sickening reality of his fate to slice through and smother him. At first he'd tried to busy his mind by counting seconds, trying to keep track of how long he'd been here. But his mind was hazy now, unfocused. Desperately thirsty, he tried sucking the dry hessian bag through his gag. His lips were cracked, and every time he tried to stand up he was so dizzy that he slumped to the concrete floor again.

Memories flashed in and out of his mind. His mother holding his hand, on his first day at school, baking him iced buns and teaching him to play 'pooh sticks' in the river. His first home, their little terraced house back in Tonyrefail, the swing in the garden with the jagged wooden seat, and the strawberry plants she'd tend lovingly by the back door, letting him pick the biggest and best ones for tea. The painting of her he'd done at school, which she proudly pinned up in the kitchen. The miners' strike, being hungry and walking past his dad shouting on the picket lines. Walking behind his nana's coffin as she left her bungalow just outside the village for the last time. And of the magazines under his bed, which his mum must have disturbed when she was hoovering, carefully replaced – but not exactly as he'd left them – as though they were unseen. Until the day his father found them. Being lashed with his belt had hurt. But it was the words 'You're dead to me' that had haunted him ever since.

He thought of his mother, crying, as he packed his rucksack. Handing him the two twenty-pound notes she secretly kept in a tin for 'emergencies' and her necklace, a simple silver cross, so that 'God will always protect you'. But, worst of all, the image of her standing beside his father on the step as he walked away. He was only sixteen. She could have left with him. She could have tried.

He'd spent most of the money on a train to London, and spent the first few hours wandering around Paddington, frightened and alone. It was a sticker in a phone box that saved him. *London Gay and Lesbian Switchboard*. One of the volunteers, a gentle Irish man named Ian, had gone to Paddington to meet him. Ian and his partner David had offered him their spare room for free. They became the caring fathers he never had. Ian helped him write a letter to his mum, giving their address, to let her know he was safe. She didn't write back.

Sam knew that without Ian and David, he'd probably be dead. And when he found work as a wardrobe assistant at the National Theatre, he moved into a flat share. Ian and David had stayed in touch, but kept their distance after two of his parties when he was high on cocaine. Sam had sensed their disapproval. He hadn't invited them after that.

Ever since the day he left Tonyrefail, he'd been determined to 'make it'. To prove he was somebody. To prove to his bastard of a father that the *world* loved him, even if he didn't. And Lola had been a huge part of that. Lee Soldwell had it coming. The world was a better place without a paedo like him and Sam had made his peace with that. He'd gone through too much to have someone like Soldwell trash it. But Des Lethbridge? Des's murder had burned into his conscience for *years*. He hadn't asked her to have Des killed. But she'd done it anyway.

Des was an Aussie backpacker, a twenty-one-year-old from Melbourne with a mop of curly dark-brown hair and a cute grin. He'd worked his way across Europe after his mum died suddenly, and was doing evening shifts in a bar in Mykonos. For Sam, it was just sex. A lot of it. He wasn't quite a household name then, hadn't starred in any movies and Des – whose knowledge of film and TV went no further than *Neighbours* – hadn't even realised he was an actor.

They parted as friends, though Des had tears in his eyes, so Sam gave him his address and phone number, saying they should hook up if he ever made it to London one day.

Des had seemed settled in Mykonos, and had plans to take a boat to Athens at the end of the summer season where he hoped to pick up work as a cab driver. Sam didn't expect to see him again.

Two weeks later, Des turned up on the doorstep. He'd bought a one-way ticket, needed a place to stay, and firmly expected Sam's to be it. Finding Sam partying with two guys he'd just met on the Heath came as a shock. He thought they were *exclusive*. He was in love.

Des spent a fitful night on the sofa, while Sam called Lola in a panic. He wanted Des gone. At first, her plan seemed to work. She gave him cash to pay for a room in Camden's Holiday Inn, and a plane ticket back to Mykonos. But day after day, when Sam arrived home from an audition or a lunch date, Des was waiting. It turned out he was bipolar and refusing to take his meds. Sam tried taking him for a drink, talking, then tough love. Told Des straight that there was no future for them. That's when he threatened suicide. It took Sam all afternoon to talk him down, and he returned to the hotel when Sam promised to take him on a tour of London the next day. Lola said she'd take care of everything.

Sam honestly believed Lola would get Des some help, maybe have him sectioned. But the next morning, walking up Camden High Street towards the hotel, to take Des out as he'd promised, he saw police erecting a forensic tent by an alleyway. Two homeless men, toes poking through their filthy shoes, were watching from behind the blue and white police tape. They looked around fifty, though Sam figured they could be younger.

'What's happened?' Sam asked an officer standing beside them.

'Please move on, sir. Let the officers do their work.'

'Overdose,' one of the homeless men said. 'Another one. Always sad when it's a youngster, eh.'

As the police pulled the tent around the body, Sam glimpsed the tie-dyed T-shirt Des had worn in Mykonos. His death didn't even make the papers, just another druggie in Camden, and the police had no reason – or the energy – to suspect foul play.

Sam did. Des never touched hard drugs. He'd been too paranoid to even take his meds. This was Lola's doing.

He'd confronted her, and she'd denied it. Said her henchman Rick wasn't even in the country, and that she'd been trying to organise a hospital bed for Des. But Sam knew she was lying.

After that, no matter how successful he became, how many lines of coke he snorted, how many films he starred in, how many smiles he painted on, how many rent boys he slept with, Sam was unhappy. He felt empty inside, that there was a big black void that swallowed up his movies, his flashy homes, his money, and spat out this crying little boy, curled up and afraid. Worthless, just like his father had said.

But then he'd met Tyler at an AA meeting. Sam had just come out of a long stint in rehab, hoping that this time it would actually work. Tyler was younger, but persistent.

Pretty, with short dyed-blond hair, almond-shaped blue eyes and an in-your-face job as a climate change campaigner. Vegan. Teetotal. Grown up in care, but like Sam had found his way in the city. The job bothered him, as Tyler was regularly photographed glued to the M25, but as Lola had pointed out, even if the press did run it, global warming was the new starving Africans or AIDS as far as celebs jumping on a cause was concerned.

Being with Tyler helped him stay sober. He'd given up eating meat and dairy. Started meditating. He hadn't been off drink and drugs – or in a relationship – this long for years. Lola had been his muse, his mother, his sister, even his lover. Everything. But the more he meditated, the more he realised how much she controlled and hurt people. She and her henchman, Rick. If she'd had Des killed for him, what was she doing for other clients? It was wrong, and she had to be stopped.

Sam would never have done it. Lola knew too much about him, and if she was going down, she'd pull him down with her. Have him up for conspiracy to murder. Say it was his idea. Even if he was found innocent, the court case would wreck him. The rent boys, the drugs, it would all come out. No. So he'd threatened her. Made her think he planned to go to the police. That he had people watching her. Left her to stew. And then, when she was really rattled, properly freaking out, he was going to say he'd keep her secrets if she promised to stop. Sam was sure Lola would never hurt him. They had too much history. Underneath it all she loved him. And he loved her. But he'd never had the chance to tell her everything was OK, that he wouldn't go through with it. He'd found himself in here.

There was a sudden thud above his head. Dozing and drifting in and out of consciousness, it was the first sound he'd heard. He tried to scream, but no sound came out of his dry throat at all. Another thud. Scratching. Then a very muffled voice. Footsteps.

He rolled over, forcing a wail out of his mouth and kicking the bricks with his tethered feet until they bled. The footsteps began to fade. Wailing louder now, he banged his head into the bricks, willing them to return. Whoever it was, and whatever they planned to do to him, couldn't be worse this this. He hadn't touched done drugs for more than a year, but right now he'd take anything. Even if it killed him. Just to make it *stop*.

He slumped to the floor, blood dripping from the fresh wound on his head, realising that this hellish room was underground.

Chapter Fifteen

LOLA

I'm in the office bright and early, catching up on emails. A small group of paparazzi are huddled outside, probably hoping Sam will show up, or he'll be found dead and they'll want pictures of me, sobbing. Either way, it's a chilly, drizzly day and I need them onside so I've sent them a delivery from Costa. Lattes all round and some chocolate cookies.

Olivia's already in and is making us both a coffee.

'Did those pics appear of April at the Ivy?' Olivia asks. 'I can't see them on the *Mirror* site.'

'No. April's been texting me this morning, moaning there were no paps outside when she got there. I tipped off that new guy, Jim L. Useless fucker. He could have made a few quid out of that.'

'Jim L? The Aussie? He wasn't outside this morning. That's strange. He's been there constantly since Sam went missing. I think he's obsessed with him.'

'What makes you say that?'

'Well, *he* took that shot of Tyler arriving in Cobshott. I checked with the picture agency. But he must have known we normally stop those sort of shots being used, so it could have been a complete waste of time. I mean, how did he know that a snap of Tyler arriving at Sam's would suddenly be worth a small fortune? Unless he knew he was going to disappear.'

'Fair point.'

'And one of the paps said he'd do *anything* for money.' She lowered her voice. 'Rumour is that he also works as a rent boy. He's even been lurking round Sam's shoot in the Lake District. The other paps think he's a bit weird. I asked them.'

'So you think him and Sam…'

Olivia reddened. 'Oh gosh, I don't know. I'm sorry, Lola, I'm sure I'm speaking completely out of turn. I just wondered if I should tell the police?'

Sam and Jim L. I can imagine it. He's certainly pretty enough to pique Sam's interest. Maybe Sam was up to his old ways and met him on the Heath. Maybe Jim L knows where he is, and it's just a matter of time before we get a ransom demand.

Then there's the Heath. Where, according to Lee Soldwell, Sam had had sex with Tory MP Andrew Netherington. Was Sam blackmailing him? Sam wouldn't do it for the money, but since he'd gone all left-wing and found a *conscience* lately, maybe he'd threatened to out Netherington. Especially as the MP recently voted again a bill to improve LBGT rights. That would have wound New Sam right up. It's possible...

I need to stay calm, give no hint that my mind is a mass of contradictions, of possibilities. 'The police have enough to be sifting through, Olivia. They'll have checked to see who took the shot of Tyler, and they'll have talked to the paps. But it's certainly something you and I can check out. Get me a home address for Jim L and his full name.'

'On it.'

I scroll through my emails, still dwelling on what I'd had planned for Sam. The overdose. One injection and he'd have drifted away into a haze of blackness. Forever silenced. But I couldn't ignore the panic I'd felt when I thought he was dead, or the relief that he might be still alive. If Rick could find him, reason with him, save his life, he might agree to save both of us. I'd texted Rick.

New plan. Want Sam alive. ALIVE. LMK if you find him. I need to talk.

The press are already making the link between the dead bodies and Sam. Although they're officially unidentified, word has clearly got out, and gossip website Celebstar is running with *Camber corpses may be Sam Stevens' mum and dad: police intensify search for the star.* If Sam has been kidnapped, survives and plays ball, we could make millions. He could star in a movie of his own life.

Olivia walks back to my desk, staring at her iPad.

'That was quick.'

'Sorry, haven't done it yet. I forgot to say Kym Sylvian has a photoshoot and press call this afternoon. That *Make Bake* cooking show we lined her up with. They're doing round table interviews with journalists. Do we need someone there to oversee her? It's in a studio in Notting Hill.'

I'm struggling to think about anything other than Sam, and how the hell I'm going to help Rick find him. Tyler still has to be the place to start. With last night's pizza purged and zero calories ever since, sharpening my senses, I kick my brain into gear. 'Yep. Message Anastazia and tell her to cover it. She can get any journalists to sign the usual Pieces of Paper. And tell her if anyone mentions Sam, Kym can say how worried she is. Cry a bit. She could do with some sympathetic press. Or any press at all, given most people still don't know who she is.'

Olivia nods, tapping notes into her iPad. '*Mail Online* ran the pics of Georgie Heaven at Mildred's with the headline *Georgie Goes Green*. Mentioned the vegan jacket, too, so everyone's happy,' she says. 'Oh, and John Banion is auditioning for the lead in that Netflix drama about Ukraine. It's a biggie.'

'Good. Schedule me a call with John for this afternoon. And one with the casting director. Milo, isn't it? I might be able to offer him a few of our lesser mortals at cheaper rates if they take John.'

Her inbox pings. Mine too.

'It's the *Sun*. They've got…'

I glance at my screen. 'Video of Michael King dogging in

a woodland car park near his home in Esher. For fuck's sake. How many times have I told him not to shit on his own doorstep.'

'Looks like he stayed in his car,' Olivia went on, watching the clip they'd sent us. 'It's grainy, and he's got a hat on, but you can see it's him.'

'Christ. He's even used his own car. With personalised number plates. The *stupidity*.'

I dial Michael's number, but he doesn't pick up. He's a Premier League footballer, so I call his club's coach.

'I don't care if he's in an ice bath. I need him on the phone, *now*,' I snap. 'Unless you want a *very* damaging video of him wanking in his Tesla splashed across the *Sun Online*.'

Michael's on the phone within thirty seconds.

'Lola? What is it?'

'Does your wife know about the dogging?'

'Jesus. No.'

'Did you go alone?'

'Yes.' He sounds quiet, ashamed. 'I didn't know there would be dogging. I was just out for a drive. I-I just parked there.'

'Shut the fuck up. Eleven p.m. in a car park popular with doggers. No one is buying that, including me. If you want me to help, start talking. Have you done it often?'

'Once or twice.'

'Do you mean ten or twenty?'

'About ten.'

'Always the same car park?'

'No. There's one down the A3 where I usually go. Near Wisley. There are often phone torches on. One must have been a camera.'

'So there could be *other* videos. On different *days*?'

'I suppose so.'

'We can't say you were duped into going if you've been more than once. Why the fuck did you take a car with personalised number plates? And open the window?'

'The wife had the Mini. She'd gone to Zumba. And then out with her mates for dinner. I didn't think anyone would recognise me or look at the plates. I never get out of the car. But it was steaming up so I opened it to, er, get a better look.'

'For fuck's sake, Michael. I need to give them something or they'll splash this. You're going to have to tell your wife. And we'll give them the exclusive on her coming out of the fertility clinic.'

'What fertility clinic?'

'The one she's going to visit in the hope you can start your family. Because you've struggled for so long to fall pregnant.'

'I'm not saying that. People will think there's something wrong with me.'

I laugh. 'Well, they certainly will if they see that video of you pleasuring yourself in the Tesla. And when the baby's born, they get exclusive photos of it.'

'But she isn't having a baby. We don't want kids. I told you that.'

'I know. But they don't know that. We can follow it up with an interview about the tragic early miscarriage.'

Silence.

'Or,' I continue, 'we can let them run the dogging tape, and see how that plays out with your Nike sponsorship deal. Especially as you're promoting youth football. Tell your wife we'll get her on *I'm A Celebrity… Get Me Out Of Here!* Or *Strictly*. After the miscarriage.'

It's sorted, and I tell Olivia to make the arrangements. There's a clinic on Harley Street I've used before. Paying for a fertility test will cost him less than he gets paid per hour.

'How do you know the wife will play ball?' Olivia asks. She grins. 'Sorry about the unintended pun.'

'Because she won't want to give up the lifestyle. Swanning round Esher, buying whatever the fuck she wants and getting her hair done every day. Frankly, I'd rather shoot myself in the head, but the WAGs seem to like it.'

Olivia's hovering around the desk, something she never does.

'Was there something else?' I ask.

'I couldn't sleep last night…' she begins.

I don't want to know. I have absolutely no interest in what Olivia thinks, feels or does, unless it's related to work. She's here to get the job done, and that's that. But her brown eyes suddenly look tearful, and I need her fully on her game.

'I can't stop thinking about Sam,' she goes on.

'I know,' I say gently. 'But we've got to keep Lola Lovett PR running. Do our jobs, no matter how hard it is. It's what

Sam would want. Crying won't help bring him back. And it wrecks your make-up.'

She manages a smile.

'How was your journey in this morning?' I say, eager to change the subject.

'Fine. I got a seat on the Tube. I like to get in early.'

'Me too. Remind me, where it is you live again?' I haven't the foggiest. She could commute in from Edinburgh and I wouldn't know.

'Just off the King's Road.' Olivia was so posh that she didn't even feel the need to say *Chelsea*.

'I need to start paying you less.'

'It's my parents' place.'

'We should get you on *Made in Chelsea*.'

'God, no.' She pauses. 'Anyway, I'd be far too boring.'

'No wayward siblings? Or cheating boyfriend? They love all that kind of stuff.'

She shakes her head. 'Only child. And single.' She's uncomfortable talking about herself, always has been. Very stiff upper lip. 'What do you think happened to Sam, Lola?'

I sip my coffee. 'I don't think we should worry about Sam. He's probably on a wilderness retreat somewhere, with his phone off.'

'Really? Is that what the police think?'

'I saw them last night. They're keeping an open mind.'

'Celebstar is saying those bodies in Camber are his parents.'

'I know. But that doesn't mean Sam is dead.'

She edges from foot to foot, nervously.

'For God's sake, Olivia, *out with it*.'

'I was thinking...and please don't shout me down, but could *Sam* have done it?'

'Sam? Mutilate corpses? Good God, no. Even on drugs and booze, he's never been violent. Let alone to his parents. Whatever had happened in the past, he was over it.'

'Of course. It was just a thought.'

I take another sip of coffee. 'And that's why you'll go far in PR, Olivia. Because you can think the unthinkable. And that means you're always prepared. Also, what do you make of Tyler?'

'Tyler?' She looks shocked. 'You don't think...'

'In this business, Olivia, you learn to expect anything.'

'I don't really know him. I mean, I've chatted to him at a couple of work things. That birthday party a few months ago, at your place. Does a lot of gluing himself to things. Mainly roads.'

'Does he seem like a gold digger to you?'

'Not at all. He's very passionate about *causes*. And they seem to dote on each other. Sam's stayed clean since they got together, so he must be good for him.'

'True.' I pause. 'But text me his address. The flat in Soho. And order me a cab. I think I'll pay Tyler a visit.'

'Sure. Oh, and I got you the deets on Jim L. I'll text those too. His address is Kingsmead Hotel, a seedy dump in King's Cross. I checked with reception. They haven't seen him today, though. Booked under the name James Lethbridge.'

I'm in a cab on my way to Tyler's flat on Charing Cross Road, two floors above a bookshop, my palms sweating and my mind in total overdrive. Lethbridge. Jim L had to be linked to Des, the Aussie backpacker who'd fallen in love with Sam. But why turn up after all these years? Des's cause of death was officially 'overdose' and the Australian embassy had informed his family, according to my police contacts. Jim would have been a child at the time. Had he grown up hearing how Des fell in love with the now-famous Sam Stevens and died heartbroken in an alleyway? Did he want *revenge*? Had *he* taken Sam?

I left Olivia with instructions to visit the Kingsmead Hotel and find out everything she could about James Lethbridge, before striding out of the front door, telling the paps there was no more news and I'd be back shortly. They didn't follow me, though I'm pretty sure a motorbike is tailing my cab. I glance over my shoulder as I step out and the rider, dressed in black, is parked down a side street.

I have no idea if Tyler is in, but it's only nine a.m., so it's likely. I jab the intercom. No reply, so I press it again, and send him a text.

Tyler. It's Lola Lovett. I know you're there. Open the door.
It's about Sam.

It's a gamble, but the buzzer sounds and the blue door unlocks. I push it open. The stairs are steep and narrow, dimly lit, not the most inviting of entrances, and Tyler leans over the wooden banister, topless.

'Lola? Up here.'

He's jittery, strung out and, to my surprise, clearly high. 'W-what is it?' he stammers. 'Have they found him?'

I gesture to the door. Tyler's short, and I'm just under six foot tall in heels, so I tower over him, my black Chanel suit in sharp contrast to his grubby shorts and espadrilles.

'Shall we go inside,' I say firmly. It isn't a question.

Tyler nods and practically runs into the apartment, a compact studio room, where he starts clearing up McDonald's wrappers and trying to hide a glass pipe, which, judging by the plasticky smell in the room, had just featured crystal meth. He seems almost afraid of me. 'Does that say *cheeseburger*?' I venture, ignoring the drugs. 'I thought you were vegan.'

'I am.' He's clearly rattled, his eyes darting around the room and avoiding my gaze. 'I'm just, you know, *struggling*.'

'Don't worry. Your secrets are safe with me.'

Something's clearly not right. Tyler's on edge and I wonder if Sam is secretly using again. He's never taken meth, as far as I know.

Tyler tips the wrappers into the bin. 'What is it? Is he, you know, *dead*?'

'I don't know. I spent yesterday evening with the police. They're doing a forensic sweep of Cobshott. The Hampstead flat, too. Full forensics in white suits. So if there's anything, they'll find it.'

I'm toying with him. If he's got *anything* to do with this, I want to know about it. Being high is a bonus. He's more likely to crack.

'Have you heard anything from the police?' I continue.

'I had a call. From that FLO lady, Serena. She said two people had been found dead and they could be Sam's parents. That was it. No details. Didn't even say where they were. I saw it on the news, too.'

'Anything you tell me stays between us, Tyler. Think of me as a lawyer. I'm not going to say a word to the police. I just want to find Sam.' I pause. 'They're going to dig into everything. So if there are secrets you'd better tell me. Fast. Was Sam using again?'

He nods, speaking so quickly his words run into each other. 'He'd got himself into a right mess with drugs. When he was on set in Ullswater he got stressed and started drinking. Rang me up a few times, pissed. Cocaine, too.'

'Really?' I eye him suspiciously. 'But he was getting up at six a.m. Wasn't late on set or I'd have heard about it. And I spoke to him some evenings. He sounded fine.'

'Well, he wasn't. He'd got all worked up about his parents.'

'His *parents*?'

'Yeah.' Tyler was warming to his theme now, the drugs loosening his tongue and boosting his confidence. 'You know, the stuff they'd done to him in the past. Bad stuff. He wanted them dead.'

'How do you know that?'

'He *told* me. Said they deserved it.'

'Well, his wish has come true.'

Tyler doesn't even look surprised. 'I read about it online. It's got to be Sam. He's killed them. Sliced them up like the homophobic shits they are. Now *they're* dead to *him*.'

I think back to yesterday's press conference, when Tyler was sobbing into the cameras, pleading with Sam to come home and for anyone who knew anything to come forward. The tears seemed genuine enough. Now here he is, twenty-four hours later, convinced his boyfriend is a killer. Is it some drug-induced paranoid fantasy? Possibly.

'What about James Lethbridge? The paparazzo. Jim L. Do you know him?'

'I dunno. Who is he? There are so many.'

'You'd better not be lying to me, Tyler.'

I take out my phone. 'What about this guy?' I snap, showing him a picture of Andrew Netherington MP. 'Ever seen him with Sam?'

'No.' He's defensive now. 'And I don't know who *he* is either. He looks like a right *tool*.'

Could Sam really have done it? If he'd got into meth, then I have to admit it's possible. Perhaps that was what was behind the threats to me. Sam had never forgiven me for Des Lethbridge. Maybe he just wanted to even old scores. Maybe the Jaguar leaving the house wasn't a kidnapping after all. Maybe Sam was totally mixed up in this.

'Well, if he did kill his parents,' I say, 'he's going to be in a bad way. We've got to find him before the police do. We need to get him lawyered up and get his story straight.

Otherwise all this…' I waft my hand in the air. 'All the money, all the houses, the flash holidays, will be gone. And he'll be locked up for life. You'll be back in the gutter where you came from. Do you understand me, Tyler?'

Tyler lights a cigarette, the intense hit from the meth clearly waning, his eyes hazy.

'Listen. If I'm round here talking to you, the police can't be far behind. I know they've taken a statement but finding those bodies is going to escalate things. You need to get your shit together. For *Sam's* sake.' I pick up the bong. 'Get me a carrier bag. I want you to put all the drugs in it. *All* of them.' He does as he's told, throwing in a small bag of crystal meth, a wrap of cocaine and a big bag of weed. 'The Rizlas, too. All of it. Now, if the police call you in, you say *nothing* about any of this. Not a word.'

I rummage under the sink for a bottle of spray bleach and hand it to him with a kitchen roll. 'Wipe down the surfaces with this. Empty the bins. And open the fucking window.'

Ten minutes later, the carrier bag is dumped in a bin on Charing Cross Road, and I'm walking back to the office, well aware of the black-suited motorcyclist following at a distance behind me.

Chapter Sixteen

WEDNESDAY

The satnav was showing two and a half hours to Hampstead, so Sue decided to take the train in to London. She wanted to look around Sam's flat there, see what she could learn about him. Appletree Lodge was too sterile, too manicured to give any insight into what Sam was really like.

She'd also arranged to meet Tyler at his flat in Soho. CCTV on the trains and cell site analysis of his phone confirmed his story – he'd arrived in Cobshott on Saturday lunchtime and returned to London on Sunday afternoon, taking the train to Waterloo and the Tube to Borough. She didn't want to rely on the paparazzi shot – that could easily have been taken at any time.

Sue's gut told her there was more to learn about Tyler. She'd left Dev at the station, digging into his past. One of the other DIs could have done it, but Sue also wanted a bit of time alone, to think.

She was utterly ashamed of what she'd done with Lola and yet completely elated by it. Sleeping with her broke almost every rule in the book. If it ever came out, she would be sacked for it. But she missed sex with Rob so much, or maybe it wasn't sex with Rob but sex that was driven by pure lust, something that felt wrong and was yet so right. She'd *needed* Lola from the moment she first saw her. Being bisexual was something she'd never felt the need to broadcast, and Mike had no idea about it, though Rob had thoroughly enjoyed her descriptions of what she'd got up to with a girl at school.

The guilt was starting to kick in now, and as the train came to a halt at Vauxhall she gazed out at the shimmering skyscrapers and wondered which one was Lola's apartment. Last night had been quite simply incredible, but she knew it was a one-off that could never be repeated. Sue spent her whole life doing the right thing, hunting down rapists and murderers, taking people who hurt others off the streets. Trying to be a good mum to Tom, even though she felt such a failure. Not drinking too much, never touching drugs – though she'd smoked a few joints in her teens – and getting her mum and dad's shopping in for them every few days. Taking them to hospital appointments, making sure the carers who went in twice a day were doing what they should. Saint bloody Sue. Trying to be a good partner to Mike, even though she knew in her heart they should have stayed friends. For once, just once, she wanted to let go of the reins. And with Lola, she had.

At home, Mike had seemed stressed, brushing his teeth

without Abba, or indeed any singing at all. Apart from asking if she wanted a cuppa, he'd been out the door sharpish. Sue was sure he didn't know about Lola. There was no reason for him to suspect, or for Lola to tell him.

She knew she should apologise for saying he wasn't Tom's dad. It must have hurt him deeply. But after all, it was the truth. And blaming Mike for Tom's behaviour felt a whole lot easier than facing the fact it might be because she'd stayed with Rob.

Besides, Sue told herself, it wasn't the right time to talk. He'd got enough on his plate with the big drugs case he was working on. Mike was chasing the middle-men distributors, the people who used kids to move drugs through ghastly county lines networks, but was repeatedly hitting a brick wall.

It was just after ten a.m. when Sue arrived at Waterloo, the wide, glass-topped concourse its usual whirl of announcements, commuters, lost tourists and too many wheelie bags. At this time of day, travelling into London was generally a breeze, unless there was a strike or South West trains had one of its regular signal failures. Sadly, suicides also happened all too often on the fast line to London, and Sue had attended several at Surbiton early in her career.

It was a cool September day, with a bright-blue sky, and Sue decided to walk across the Hungerford footbridge over the Thames towards Tyler's flat. Big Ben stood tall and proud to her left – finally free of the scaffolding that had covered it for five years, much to the dismay of tourists and locals alike – and to her right, the dome of St Paul's was silhouetted against the sky, dwarfed by the skyscrapers in the City. Sue loved the view of St Paul's, the way it stood dogged and determined throughout the Blitz, but seeing the Thames always reminded her of Rob, of his final moments, and she kept her gaze above the river. It was a relief when she left it behind and crossed over the Strand to Trafalgar Square, weaving her way through pavement artists' drawings, tourists and an organised group of beggars.

Tyler's flat was much smaller than Sue expected. Since it was paid for by Sam, she'd imagined him putting up his not-quite-toy-boy in some luxurious pad. It was a studio, with a smart but tiny kitchen in one corner of the room and a small bathroom on the left. Tyler looked like he hadn't slept for days, and there was a hint of a sickly, plastic-type smell, which Sue recognised instantly as crystal meth.

'I just wanted to see how you're doing,' Sue began.

'Not too good.' Tyler lit a cigarette. His hands were trembling slightly, and huge black circles framed his red eyes. 'Started smoking again. For the nerves.'

'I think Serena the FLO has been in touch with you? We've had it confirmed now. The couple found murdered in Camber are Sam's mum and dad.' Sue paused. 'I need to ask you about Sam's relationship with them.'

Tyler shook his head. 'He didn't have one. When he left, they told him he was dead to them. Well, the dad did, anyway.'

'Did he have any contact with them?'

'None.'

Sue pushed away an image of Tom leaving and never seeing him again.

'And what were his feelings towards them?'

Tyler hesitated, and Sue took his hand. 'Whatever has happened, Tyler, we must find him. He could be a danger to himself. You need to tell me the truth.'

'He was still very angry with them. Especially his dad. And especially after a drink.'

'I thought he was teetotal.'

'He was, when we first met at AA. But things hadn't gone too well on his latest film. *Murder in the Lakes*. Simon Omeria had made everyone's lives hell. He'd started using again, too. Drugs. Cocaine, crystal meth, whatever he could get his hands on.'

'That can't have been easy in Ullswater. Sourcing crystal meth in the middle of the Lake District.'

'You'd be surprised. Sam's got plenty of money. He'd pay people to drive from London if he needed to score.' He snorted. 'So much for saving the planet.'

'So what was he saying about his parents?'

'He wanted them dead. Wished all kinds of ill on them. Even sending them into the fires of Hell wouldn't have been good enough. He blamed them for his unhappiness.' He paused. 'Because no matter how rich Sam was, or how many parties he went to, it was never enough.' Tyler pointed to his chest. 'Sam was just sad. In here.'

'Do you think he could have hurt them?'

Tyler burst into tears, and nodded. 'If he was high, then yes.'

Sue walked over to the kitchen and poured Tyler a glass of water. 'Drink this,' she said gently. 'I want you to stay here and call me immediately if Sam turns up. He might do.'

'D-do you think he's killed himself?' Tyler stammered.

'Let's focus on finding Sam,' Sue replied.

Tyler watched from his window as Sue crossed the street. He took out a burner phone and started typing.

Can't do this anymore. Can't leave him there. We have to let him go.

The reply was immediate.

No. We had a deal. U get to do the parents, I get him. Police need to think he did it. Then case closed. Keep your fucking nerve.

Tyler typed quickly.

They deserved it. He doesn't.

Yes he does.

Sue headed straight for the Northern Line, the escalator taking her down into the bowels of London, past brightly coloured digital ads for West End shows, and took a seat in a carriage at the far end of a train.

There was no wi-fi in the tunnels, only at stations, so Sue checked her messages intermittently. She'd already called Dev after leaving Tyler, saying they should consider Sam a suspect in the Dafydd and Gwen Morgan murders. 'Re-check the hospital morgues,' Sue told him. 'Any unidentified bodies. Especially in areas where suicides are common. He could have killed them and taken his own life.'

The Tube rattled its noisy way up to Hampstead, disgorging a noisy group of Italian tourists wearing identical Union Jack backpacks at Camden, giving Sue time to think. She stepped off the train at Hampstead and took the lift to ground level, remembering the time she'd taken Tom to London Zoo on a day trip, and they'd *had* to make a detour to come here because it was the deepest Tube lift in London. He'd loved facts and figures like that, his quick mind gathering information, sorting it, classifying it, rather like hers did on a case.

What had happened to that thoughtful, intelligent boy, who planned their trips with train timetables and held her hand on the escalator in case she fell? Thick tears welled up in Sue's eyes as she thought of him locked away in his room, out of reach, held prisoner by emotions that she didn't understand.

The lift doors opened and Sue stepped out into the

sunlight, flicking the tears away with her fingers. She had a job to do. Sam's flat was in the heart of Hampstead Village, an olde worlde maze of little streets and Georgian houses. A uniformed officer stood outside the entrance, and Sue showed him her ID, which he studied carefully. She was glad Dev wasn't here to point out she wasn't so well known in these parts.

The flat had its own entrance, little more than a red door in a wall, which opened into a beautiful walled garden. It was the ground floor of a large Georgian house, and everything that Cobshott wasn't. This was clearly Sam's home, a place where he could be himself, without the painted-on glitz and glamour of showbiz. An old Chesterfield-style sofa and two cosy armchairs stood in front of an open fire, the grate still laden with half-burned, cold coals. Framed photographs of Sam stood on the mantlepiece, mostly funny snapshots with friends, though there was one with Tyler on a boat, and one of Sam as a little boy, standing in front of a tiny terraced house.

There were wellies by the front door and raincoats in the hall. Even the kitchen had a homely feel, with unmatching pots and pans, and a row of kitsch nick-nacks on the window sill, which he must have collected on his travels – a snow globe saying 'Las Vegas', a rough plaster model of Paris's Montmartre, and an ashtray with a painting of a red-domed Greek house saying 'Mykonos'. The cupboards and fridge were well stocked, all vegan food, including plant-based pizzas and burgers, and animal-free products in the bathroom. His vegan lifestyle clearly wasn't just for the press.

Sue checked the case file. According to neighbours, he didn't have a cleaner here, and kept a low profile, though in the past they'd seen him arrive back with three or four male 'friends', and until recently he'd often had male callers. Discreetly.

She pushed open the door into the bedroom, where Forensics had taken away the duvet cover and sheets. The bed filled most of the room, and the entire ceiling was tiled with mirrors. Unlike the rest of the flat, the bedroom felt colder, with sliding black wardrobes down one wall. The bedside drawer was open, where – according to the notes – Forensics had removed a large number of sex toys for analysis.

The lead forensic officer for the Hampstead flat was Dr Rita Hall, whom Sue knew well from previous cases. Rita blew hot and cold. Sometimes she'd accept being pressed for her suspicions, other times she'd snap, 'Wait for my report.' Sue had a copy of her preliminary one, but she wanted to talk it through.

Sue dialled. 'Rita? Sue Fisher. I'm on the Sam Stevens case and at the Hampstead flat right now. I know you're still working on the evidence, but I'd really appreciate five minutes to chat through what we know.'

'Go on.'

'The bedclothes. In the flat.'

'Been washed. They'd been newly put on the bed. We took them just in case. But we've got a mass of semen stains on the carpet, including his. Only in the bedroom. We're running tests now but you're looking at multiple men in there. Thirty or forty over a period of time, I'd say.'

'Can you tell how old the stains are?'

'Not officially. But there's an experimental test that can. Probably wouldn't stand up in court, but I ran it anyway. They all seem to be between a year and three years old. I'm guessing that's when he last had the carpet cleaned. So no indications of recent orgies in there. Not without careful use of condoms.'

'What about drugs? Any sign?'

'Still none so far. Wei Zhao hasn't found any in his team's sweep of the Cobshott house, either. We're working through the samples, though.' She paused. 'I heard about the bodies in Camber. Is Stevens a suspect?'

'Confidentially, yes. His boyfriend says he was back into drugs and booze.'

'I'm not saying he *wasn't*,' Rita chose her words carefully, 'but if he was, I would have expected to find some evidence of that. Drug paraphernalia, bottles of booze – possibly hidden, if he was ashamed and trying to delude himself. Obviously we went through the bins. Only empty bottles were sparkling water, lime cordial and posh ketchup.'

'Can you give me an educated guess?'

'Did he kill his parents? No idea,' Rita said brusquely. 'I've just been looking at Emily Drakos' prelim report. Carving words into the skin, eh? Interesting.' There was a pause, and Sue sensed a tinge of professional jealousy that Dr Drakos was working on a far more forensically thrilling part of the case. 'Was he using drugs and booze around the time he disappeared? Not in his own homes. And for someone as famous as him, home is where you'd be most likely to do it.'

Outside the flat, Sue called Dev. 'Bring Tyler in. He should be at his Soho flat. We need to question him under caution. Get him to come in voluntarily. He's lying about Sam using drugs, and I want to know why.'

'Do you want me to arrest him if he won't play ball?'

'Yes. I can't risk him doing a runner if he's spooked. Conspiracy to pervert the course of justice. I don't have enough to formally link him to Sam's disappearance. But something's not right.'

'On it. We've traced the people who were staying in the rented bungalows in Camber. A Croatian man on holiday – the mysterious "Russian", no doubt – recalls hearing a car engine start sometime in the early hours of Saturday morning. And we've just had a breakthrough on CCTV. DS Howe noticed a big black car driving into Cobshott's Crown Estate around ten p.m. on Sunday and out again around forty-five minutes later.'

'Nothing usual about that.'

'Exactly. We just made a note of it, along with all the other cars. But the thing is, she's found a similar car on CCTV from the off licence in Tonyrefail going towards the bungalow around noon on Friday, and away from it at half-past one. So we just checked Camber. Similar black car goes past the chip shop at eleven p.m. on Friday night, and in the other direction two hours later.'

'Tell me you can read the plates.'

'Too grainy. But we're getting the images enhanced and the vehicle examiners to take a look. Hopefully they can at least identify the make.'

Sue thought for a moment. 'Tyler said Sam couldn't drive. So did Lola. I checked and neither Tyler nor Sam has a licence. We need to find out who was driving that car.'

Chapter Seventeen

LOLA

I 've no idea who the motorcyclist is that's following me, but it's starting to really freak me out. I text Rick. He's in Soho, and says he'll handle it. Probably just a paparazzo, but I'm starting to get jumpy.

Could it be Jim L? Rick hasn't found him yet. And if he's got Sam, will he play ball in letting him go? Everyone has a price.

I mull over what Tyler said. If Sam was back on the drugs, that Jaguar Rick saw leaving his place could have been a dealer. Or his abductor. Or maybe, after all, Sam's just gone off to clear his head.

It's noon and Olivia's back, carrying my usual order – avocado baby sushi rolls from Itsu. 346 calories. She's a good girl, Olivia, she gets my order exactly right every single time. Not like the unpaid intern I had before her, who was dispatched to buy a *specific* tuna sandwich and returned with some gigantic beast she'd had made for me in the local deli 'as a treat', laden with extra mayo and a distressingly unknown number of calories. She didn't do that again. I let her go.

I was eleven when I started counting them. After Nan died. Losing her and starting at the grammar school, where I just didn't fit with all the posh girls and their money and their ways, stressed me out. I've read enough about it since to know that focusing on my body, how fat I was, was just a distraction. Stopping myself from eating became as addictive for me as red wine was for Mum.

That's when I became friends with Rick. I don't know how I'd have got through school without him. He was always there to talk to, to confide in. We were the only ones from the council estate, despised for our unironed clothes and second-hand shoes. I look the others up on Facebook sometimes. Most of them are married with kids, living comfortable, boring middle-class lives as solicitors or dentists.

I was never very good at it, the not-eating. In my teens I kept my weight around six stone, though I wished I could go lower. The not-eating never completely engulfed me, as it has done to others, the addiction dragging them down. I don't use its name because I hate the label. Once you're slapped with that, that's all people see you as, searching the web for photos to see how thin you became.

It's always been my crutch, a way of focusing my mind, sharpening it, blocking out pain. I still hate my body, and see fat bits when I look in the mirror, even though, rationally, I know I'm thin. But I don't weight myself hourly any more, have thrown out the scales, and focus on sticking to 1,600 calories a day. It keeps me sharp, and it's enough for me to fully function, provided I don't do too much exercise. Not-eating is about control – obviously of your body, but really of your mind.

I'm still trying not to think about last night's binge. Zero calories today so far, but I am desperately hungry. Olivia won't be long. She's far too ambitious to take long breaks, in case she misses something. Almost all the other agents are out on jobs with clients, including Anastazia, who was thrilled to be in the thick of it, fending off journalists' questions about Sam even if it did mean shepherding Kym Sylvian through tiresome interviews about the dreadful *Make Bake*.

I've barely given Sue Fisher a thought. I did what I needed to do, enjoyed it. Much more than I expected. I hadn't had to fake a thing. But I think of her now, wondering if she's been to see Tyler yet. So long as he keeps his trap shut about Sam being back on drugs, all should be well. I hadn't seen that coming at all. Sam had seemed totally committed to the whole clean living thing. That last session of rehab had really seemed to work. But I guess once a junkie, always a junkie. Like Tyler. That little money-grabbing bastard had got Sam back into drugs, I was sure of it.

That's when I remember his words. 'Sliced them up like the homophobic shits they are. Now *they're* dead to *him*.' So bitter. So knowing.

The police hadn't released any details about the

mutilation of the bodies. It was Sue who had told me. Even the gossip sites weren't even alluding to it.

Sliced them up. Dead 2 Me.

Tyler has to be in on this. And he must know where Sam is.

Olivia's coming through the door with a big bag of Itsu as I sweep out of it.

'Still no sign of James Lethbridge,' she says. 'The hotel where he's staying is so grim, Lola. Rents rooms by the hour. The greasy guy on reception said he's been living there about a month. Pays cash. I really think we should focus on him.'

'Good work. Now clear my diary for this afternoon,' I snap.

'Oh my God. Have you found Sam?'

'No. Just a few personal things to take care of. Private matters. I'll be on my mobile. For emergencies only.'

A black cab will be quicker than an Uber. There are plenty driving up Tottenham Court Road. I flag one down and I'm at Tyler's flat in minutes. Rick meets me outside.

'If Tyler did it, he's carved up a body, Lola. This could get messy.'

'Not as messy as the police getting to him first. We need him alive. He's our best hope of finding Sam. So we need to do whatever it takes.'

'Got a needle in my pocket. Just in case.'

'Be careful. He was off his head on meth when I saw him this morning. We can't risk him ODing. He's our only lead.'

Outside, I text Tyler, using my burner.

It's L. Dead 2 Me. I KNOW. U need to let me in. I'm the only person who can get u out of this. No police.

The door buzzes and we enter the dreary hallway. Rick goes first, bounding up the stairs. Tyler's door is slightly open. He's sitting on the floor, whimpering and rocking like a baby. The crystal meth has worn off, and without any weed to take the edge off, he's crashing. There are two phones beside him, one iPhone, one burner.

'Look at me, Tyler.' Rick's controlled, cool. 'Is Sam alive?'

He nods. 'I-I think so.'

'And you know where he is?'

He nods again.

'Where the fuck is he, Tyler?' I snap.

'In the Cotswolds.'

'The *Cotswolds*? What the fuck he is doing there?'

'Address?' Rick's focused, professional.

'The Gables. Near a village called Winchborough.'

'Which road?'

'Long Lane, I think.'

'Is Sam in on this *charade*?' I hiss. 'Did *he* put you up to this? Is he holed up there, off his head?'

'No, no, *no*.' He's getting agitated, and Rick gives me a sharp look, warning me to keep him calm. 'But we have to hurry. He…he might be dead already.' More thick tears well up in his eyes. 'I was high when I did it. The parents, too. They had it coming. *He*…didn't.'

'What have you done to him, Tyler?'

'Hidden him. Tied him up. They paid me to do it.'

'Who paid you?'

'Some guy. I don't know his name.' He began to sob harder.

'What guy? Is it James Lethbridge? Andrew Netherington?'

'I-I don't know his name.'

'We're going to take a drive, Tyler,' Rick says calmly. 'And you're coming. Because I don't trust you. And because you can tell us *everything*. Don't even *think* of making a bolt for it. Or shouting out. We're going to walk calmly to the car. And you're going to take us to where Sam is. Do you understand?'

Tyler nods. 'I don't know if he's—'

'Dead?' I glare at him. 'Still there? We're about to find out.'

Rick's car is in the underground car park in Chinatown, a couple of minutes' walk away. He pulls Tyler roughly to his feet, takes his arm and leads him down the stairs. The streets are busy, but we make our way through the tourists and office workers, the air thick with the smell of cheap Chinese, burgers and diesel fumes. Tyler seems broken, almost *relieved*, and he gets in the car obediently. Rick puts him in the back, and once the door is closed, zip-ties his hands and feet together and gags him with a piece of cloth, all behind the blackout windows. He tips one of the back seats forward, revealing the car's boot.

'Get in,' he orders, snapping the seat back into place behind him.

I tap 'Winchborough' into the satnav. Three hours. Then I scroll through Tyler's burner. All the messages are deleted, except for one. Unread. Received a few minutes ago.

Get out of there. They're coming.

Chapter Eighteen

WEDNESDAY

C haring Cross Road was at a standstill. Dev and DS Fiona Howe crawled along it in their unmarked car, turning right into a side street opposite Tyler's flat. Dev parked on the double yellow lines, and a traffic warden on a scooter appeared out of nowhere, walked up to the car and started examining it.

'Police,' Dev said, showing the woman his badge.

The traffic warden held out her hand expectantly, so Dev handed it to her, and she made a point of examining it in detail before handing it back. Just doing her job, Dev told himself, getting more irritated by the second.

'Law still applies to you.' The traffic warden, a dark-haired woman in her thirties, with an Eastern European accent, seemed to be taking particular pleasure in winding him up. 'Unless it is a clear *emergency*.'

'Of course,' Dev replied patiently. 'But this *is* an emergency. We're working on a major crime.'

The warden grinned, and gestured to Charing Cross Road. 'If it's the man from the TV appeal you are looking for, he's not home.'

'How do you know?'

'This *my* patch,' she said, puffing up with a sense of pride that Dev could only marvel at. 'I know *everything* that go on here. He left a few minutes ago. I saw him outside flat. Walked off that way to Chinatown.'

'Was he alone?'

'I not know.' The warden was enjoying every second of her moment of glory. 'The street was busy. Lunchtime. I only saw through crowds.'

'I'll need to take your details,' Dev replied. 'What's your name?'

'Kovalenko. Daniela Kovalenko.'

'I might need you to make a statement, Ms Kovalenko. Have you seen anything else in the past few days?'

'He come and go a *lot*. Day and night. There is a dealer who work the corner of Litchfield Street. He buy his drugs there.'

'What about visitors?'

'An older woman earlier. I not see her come out. But no others. I not look all the time, though.' Her chest swelled with importance. 'Pretty big patch to cover.'

'Had you seen Sam Stevens at the flat before?' Fiona said.

'Yes. Before he go missing. Not since then. I recognise him from films. He very famous in Ukraine.'

Dev noted down the woman's details and handed her a

card. 'If you see or hear anything, please text me. Ever thought of becoming a police officer?'

The woman sighed. 'I *was* police officer. One of first women inspector. People took selfie with me when women finally allowed to join Ukraine police. I not have right visa to join police here. Maybe one day. But I enjoy my work.'

'Thank you, Ms Kovalenko.'

'Makes me feel lucky,' Fiona said, as they crossed the road to Tyler's flat. 'Imagine finally being allowed to join the force, then getting displaced by war and ending up a traffic warden.'

Dev nodded. 'Though some days on this job I'd rather be a traffic warden. I was a junior officer on the Medford case. It was bloody *grim*. Being berated by Porsche drivers raging that you've given them a sixty quid ticket would be a breeze compared to that.'

They stopped outside the main entrance to Tyler's flat and knocked on the blue front door. No reply. Dev called his mobile, but Tyler didn't answer that either, so he rang Sue. 'Traffic warden saw him leaving the flat a few minutes ago, after a visit from a woman. She didn't know if he was alone. Do you want us to check Chinatown? He could be in one of the restaurants.'

'No harm in looking. Check the sex clubs in Soho, too. He wasn't in a good way when I left him. Really tearful. Strange smell in there too, crystal meth if I'm not mistaken.'

'Makes sense. The warden said she'd seen him scoring on the street corner.'

'See if you can trace his dealer. But I don't want to spook

Tyler, Dev. Ask Uniform to help you look too, but keep it all low-key. He's unstable, unpredictable. The last thing we need is him doing a runner or topping himself.'

'Will do. Are you heading back to the office, boss?'

'Not yet. I've just arranged to meet Julia Peace, Sam's co-star in *Murder in the Lakes*. She lives in Belsize Park, just a walk away. I'll talk to Julia, then I need to get back. I've got a couple of things to take care of.'

The message from Mike had arrived just as Sue was leaving the Hampstead flat.

Hope case going OK. Know you're busy, but need advice on this drugs bust. Are you in office this pm? Got some evidence I need you to look at.

Why was he messaging her in the middle of a murder case? These days pretty much everything Mike did irritated her beyond belief. She sent an abrupt text back.

In Hampstead. Back later.

As she walked down Hampstead Hill towards Belsize Park, she thought about Tom. She'd always expected – and secretly hoped – that he'd stay reasonably local. Southampton was only an hour's drive away, and when he'd received his conditional offer back in March, she was thrilled for him. Tom chatted about how they'd need to get all his stuff together, how he'd come home some weekends with his laundry.

It was soon after that that Tom began to change. He stopped going to chess club, where he tutored the younger players. Flatly refused to go, and wouldn't say why. Just that he had 'gone off it'. Didn't see many of his usual friends, either, and spent a lot of time in his room. He'd never really gone through the typical teenage phase, so Sue had put it down to that. Perhaps he was nervous about leaving home for the first time. He'd always been so protective of her when Rob was alive, but now he barely noticed if she was there, and if she was, seemed to find her presence repellent. At least he'd passed his A levels and kept his uni place, though not with the flying colours he was predicted.

No matter how hard she tried, Sue couldn't shake the feeling that she was to blame. She'd stayed in that abusive relationship with Rob, and Tom had heard and seen things that no child should. Maybe Tom now hated her for that. Maybe growing up had given him a new perspective and he saw her as weak, someone who didn't even deserve pity, or kindness. She'd always told herself she'd walk out if Rob ever laid a finger on Tom. He never had. But Sue now realised that the scars from the emotional impact of growing up in an abusive home – even if you weren't the one being used as a punchbag – ran horribly deep, no matter how much she'd tried to shield him.

Even Mike didn't seem to be able to get through to him

either, though Tom seemed less guarded towards him, which hurt and irritated Sue in equal measure. After the Medford case, her emotions had been so raw that she'd waded straight into a relationship with Mike. It had seemed so *easy*. Mike was already a big part of her life, and of Tom's too. When he'd made the first move to kiss her, as they sat in the park sharing a bottle of wine, she'd been slightly surprised, but kissed him back.

These days she found herself irritated by Mike's predictability, as the things she'd loved about him as a friend became stifling, suffocating, in a relationship. She didn't want to sleepwalk through life, having curry every Thursday, to be handed an umbrella at the door if it was going to rain. She wanted to run outside and dance in it.

That spark, which for so long had been hidden, had suddenly burst through with Lola. She shouldn't have done it, Sue knew that. But did she regret it? No. Because when Lola had caressed her, kissed her in ways that no one had since Rob, she'd felt *alive* for the first time in years.

Now Mike was bothering her with some nonsense about his drugs case. Whatever it was, he certainly didn't need her input on it. He had a whole drugs squad of officers to talk to. This had to be a ruse, a way to get her attention, and that wound her up even more. She had enough on her plate with Tom. And with the case. He should know better.

Julia's house was a pretty, three-storey, semi-detached villa just off Haverstock Hill. Even though she was a well-known actress, much of her work was in the theatre, so there was no way she could afford it on her salary. Sue had already researched her and the money came from her husband, Bill, who ran a hugely successful internet lettings agency, Bounce!, which rivalled Airbnb.

'Please, come in,' Julia said cheerily, opening the front door. She was in her mid-thirties, with a wide smile and a warm personality, her hair neatly braided in dreadlocks. The house was tastefully decorated in pastel colours, and an elderly ginger cat dozed on a chair in the hall, who opened his eyes briefly to look at Sue, assessed her as acceptable and then closed them again.

'Thanks for seeing me,' Sue replied, stroking the cat as she passed. 'Like I said on the phone, it's just procedure. I know you've already spoken to my colleague Dev, but I just need to find out all I can about Sam's state of mind before he went missing.'

'Sure. I've got a few minutes before I pick the kids up from school. I like to collect them when I'm between jobs. Just finished a long stint in the Lake District. Didn't see them for a month.'

Julia led her through into a large kitchen, which ran the full width of the house. Beyond it bifold doors led to a small garden. Sue was beginning to develop a deep, irrational hatred for bifold doors, just as she loathed coffee chains. Just another middle-class trophy. She'd rather have her old-fashioned, draughty French windows any day.

They took a seat at the wooden kitchen table, where Julia was icing home-made fairy cakes in pink and green. 'I've got two.' She smiled, wiping her hands on a tea towel. 'Liam and Lena. Liam loves green. Do you have any kids?'

'One.' Sue smiled. 'Typical teenager at the moment, I'm afraid. He's eighteen and off to uni soon.'

'Empty nest, eh? I can't wait.'

'You might not feel like that when it happens,' Sue said wistfully.

'True. I bet it only seems like yesterday you were dreading World Book Day. Those themed outfits. The *endless* competition. We've got mothers at school who spent *months* planning them. These cakes are for tomorrow's cake sale. Normally I send them in with a packet of Mini Rolls and scrabble for some round glasses to make Liam look like Harry Potter.'

Sue smiled. 'Same here.'

'So, what can I tell you about Sam? We'd worked together a few years ago on *The Moment*. He was quite different back then.'

'In what ways?'

'Self-obsessed, late on set, doing drink and drugs. In short, an absolute pain in the arse. I almost didn't take this job when they told me he'd been cast as the lead. But he's really changed. Teetotal, no drugs, even gone vegan. It wasn't the easiest of shoots, but Sam acted like a buffer between the cast and the god-awful director. Simon Omeria.'

'His boyfriend Tyler mentioned there were problems.' Sue paused. 'The director getting a bit too hands-on. I'm not here to investigate that. But anything you can tell me, just to help me understand how Sam was feeling, would really help.'

Julia nodded. 'I saw one of the younger actors, Stephen Merryweather, coming out of Simon's trailer. He looked pretty shaken up. We went for a walk and Stephen confessed Simon had tried to touch him up. Promising him a bigger part in his next film if he went along with it.'

'Christ.'

'Yeah, I know. I was going to challenge Omeria myself but when I confided in Sam, he said he'd do it. He went in Omeria's trailer and read him the riot act.'

'Did Omeria deny it?'

'No. Apparently he started crying. Said his wife had left him for the guy from Virgin Media who came to mend their broadband – seriously, she had – and he was going through a few personal problems. Sam told him that if he ever touched Stephen again, or anyone without their consent, the whole cast would walk off set.'

'How was Omeria after that?'

'A lot less difficult with the cast. He didn't lay a finger on Stephen again. Sam also threatened to expose him in the press if he ever heard allegations in the future.'

'And you're sure Sam was off the drugs?'

'Positive. He's a really lovely guy when he's clean.' Tears welled up in Julia's eyes. 'I really hope he's OK. I saw the news. About his parents. I know he didn't have any time for them but he'll be completely devastated by what's happened. He was telling me he's been studying a lot of Buddhism lately, finding it in his heart to forgive them. What was it he said? Every night he meditated and imagined sending them "metta" or universal love. And something about holding on to resentment is like picking up a burning coal.' She glanced at the kitchen clock. 'Goodness, I must go. The kids will be out shortly.'

'Of course. Thank you again, Julia. Just one quick question – Simon Omeria. Do you sense he's in any way mixed up in this?'

'Good god, no. Pervy and handsy, but that's about it. And he's far from alone in the film and TV industry, though #MeToo has helped.'

Sue walked down the hill towards Chalk Farm tube station, pondering the case. Tyler was definitely lying about Sam being back on drugs, but why? Was he trying to frame him for his parents' murder? She checked in with Dev, but still no sign of Tyler, so they agreed to put a check on all ports and airports.

The Tube was packed and by the time Sue had navigated Waterloo and endured a delayed train to Kingston, she arrived back at the police station feeling stressed, hot and irritable.

A group of paparazzi were still gathered outside.

'Sue? Any news on Sam?'

'Nothing further to add,' she replied, stepping briskly into the station. 'We'll update you as soon as we can.'

Mike was in the reception area, talking to the custody sergeant. 'Ah, Sue,' he said brightly. 'Know you're busy, but I've got some documents for you. Can I have a minute?'

'Sure. My office?' Sue had the distinct feeling he'd been waiting for her. They walked through the incident room, where the initial manic buzz of the investigation had settled into a quieter, more focused air.

'Briefing in ten minutes,' Sue snapped, ushering Mike into her office and closing the door behind her. To her surprise, he pulled down the roller blinds.

'What's up, Mike? I've got a lot on. Dev, Fiona and Uniform are out trying to pick up Stevens' boyfriend as a suspect.'

'I know you're busy, love. But this can't wait.' There was a worried look in his eyes, which Sue didn't like.

'This isn't about your investigation, is it? Look, if it's about our relationship I really don't want to talk about it now.'

'It's Tom.'

Sue paled. 'Tom? Is he all right?'

'Yes. Nothing like that. No accidents or anything. I found cocaine in his room.'

'*Cocaine*?' Sue could hardly believe what she was hearing. 'But he's always been so anti-drugs.' She paused, trying to take it in. Tom and *drugs*?

'Does he know you know?'

'No. I put it back.'

'Well, let's leave it like that. The last thing I need is Tom thinking we've snooped on him. He hates me enough as it is. Kids try stuff, you know that.'

'A *lot* of cocaine,' Mike went on.

Sue ignored him. 'What were you doing in there?'

'He came in last night and I thought he seemed high. So when he passed out I had a look.'

'He *passed out*? Why didn't you tell me?'

'Not literally. Fell into a deep sleep. He was on the sofa. Don't worry, I stayed with him and put him on his side in case he threw up. Then I put him to bed. Before you got home so late,' he added, with a hint of bitterness in his voice.

'Yes, I *was* late home,' she said defensively. 'Because I've got the unenviable task of finding out what the fuck has happened to Sam Stevens. So don't start giving me a hard time, all right?'

'Sorry. It's just you've been, you know, not really *there* lately. Even when you are there, you seem miles away. But that can wait. The cocaine can't.'

'I'll have a word with him. Probably just trying stuff out before he encounters it at uni. Experimenting.'

'It wasn't just a wrap, Sue. I found four kilos of it.'

She laughed. 'Don't be ridiculous.'

'Sue, I'm telling you. He's got four kilos. Stashed inside his chess books, which he's hollowed out.'

'Mike, this is nonsense. You were probably dreaming. Or had too many beers down the Nag's Head after your shift. He'd *never* do that to his books, let alone store four kilos of coke. Did you actually double-check when you'd sobered up?'

Sue just couldn't accept it. She'd brought Tom up to understand the dangers of drugs, that at least six people die to make every kilo of cocaine, that anyone who buys or sells it has blood on their hands. She'd told him horror stories of the crack dens she'd raided when on the drug squad, shown him photos of dead addicts, their bodies and lives ravaged and ripped apart. And now he was *dealing*? It didn't make sense.

'I know it's hard, love,' Mike said patiently. 'But sticking your head in the sand won't help Tom. He's clearly got in way over his head. Which explains his mood swings lately. I'm thinking county lines. Perhaps they're using him to store their gear, knowing there's a drug squad copper and a murder detective in the house. Last place the police would look for four kilos of coke.'

Sue picked up a file. 'Look, Mike, you're being ridiculous,' she said abruptly. 'I need to brief my team on the Stevens case. We can talk about it tonight, at home. Tom's sensible. He simply wouldn't have kilos of cocaine in the house. He'd know it would wreck both of our careers if it came out. He wouldn't do it, and that's that. There's clearly been some mistake. You've been so busy tracing county lines that you're imagining them *everywhere*.'

'I'm not, Sue.' His voice was urgent. 'Look at how he's been behaving. We've both seen the change in him. You might not want to face the fact he's a drug dealer, but you *have* to. That's what good parenting is about.'

Sue's eyes were so full of blind rage that Mike automatically took a step backwards. 'Don't *ever* lecture me on good parenting. *You've* never had kids.'

'How can you say that to me, Sue? You know why.'

'Well, maybe you were infertile for a *reason*.'

'What's that supposed to mean?'

'Because you'd make a shit parent. Now just fuck off and take these ridiculous allegations with you.'

She tugged open the roller blinds, opened the door and strode into the incident room. 'Gather round, everyone. I just need to bring you all up to speed on Tyler Tipping.'

Chapter Nineteen

LOLA

Rick drives us out of London along the Westway, the showy skyscrapers and 1970s council tower blocks sharp against the leaden autumnal sky. The traffic is surprisingly light and the road widens into the M40, its green signs turning to motorway blue, and industrial estates giving way to fields and hedgerows as heavy, grey clouds laden with rain thicken overhead. He turns on the windscreen wipers as we approach Oxford, but there's no time to visit my old college, St Hilda's, with its pretty, honey-coloured walls, enclosing draughty old buildings which, for a time, had been my home.

It was a women-only college back then, but I'd often sneaked Rick into my room, which was opposite Soozie Lightwater's. We were both reading English, but unlike Soozie, I worked flat out, determined to get a First. Success was everything to me. She didn't care, especially after she met her boyfriend Simon in her second year. Soozie spent her time in the pub, punting, taking ecstasy or having silent sex with Simon in his tiny room at Worcester College overlooking the quad, while his not-really-asleep room-mate quietly got his kicks, too. I wanted to be more Soozie.

The headmistress at my grammar school was over the moon when she heard I'd been accepted, announcing it in assembly and saying I'd shown just how anyone could turn their life around. The other girls gave me hell after that. But Rick and the not-eating got me through the rest of school, and Oxford too, somewhere else I didn't fit in, with its terrifying formal dinners and high tables laden with calories, chunky girls who got up at six a.m. to go rowing and posh boys playing rugby, swilling champagne and boasting about their latest imaginary conquests. I kept my head down and *worked*. But after we graduated and Soozie asked me to join her new agency, I saw it as a chance to reinvent myself. I modelled myself on her, outwardly at least, creating the hard-nosed agent Lola Lovett that everyone knew and feared. Inside I was still a whirl of calorie-counting, self-loathing and control. But it turned out that I was *better* at it, the managing, the organisation, the dealing with clients, protecting their reputations, and she never forgave me when I started Lola Lovett PR, taking Sam with me. Soozie liked to be in charge, with me as her sidekick, doing the dirty work. I'd created the monster that was Lola Lovett and now I'd become her. The fact I'd wanted Sam dead just proved it.

The motorway skirts around Oxford and we turn off the M40 near Chipping Norton, heading cross-country, deep into the heart of the Cotswolds. As we pass through chocolate-box villages, the sun breaks through a gap in the rainclouds, warming the cottages' golden stone and casting long shadows in the church graveyards.

Could Tyler be telling the truth about the drugs? Possibly. But I'd never trusted Tyler's relationship with him. Always seemed to me he was there for the money. Rick still thought a gang could be involved, though that didn't explain why there had been no ransom demand. Yet. And then there was James Lethbridge. Had he paid Tyler to hurt Sam...or worse?

'You know Andrew Netherington's constituency is about twenty miles from Winchborough,' Rick says, glancing in his rear-view mirror.

'I know. But I can't believe he'd shit on his own doorstep.'

'He might. If he was confident he wouldn't get caught.'

'You think Sam might have blackmailed Netherington? Who then used Tyler to kidnap him?'

'It's possible.'

'Are we being followed? Any sign of that motorbike?'

'No. But listen, we don't know who's in this house, Lola. You'd better stay in the car. Let me handle this.'

The Gables is outside the village, a secluded old farmhouse standing in acres of land. Sheep are grazing in the fields in front of it. Rick drives straight past and parks further up the lane. I yank down the back seat, revealing the boot, where Tyler is tied up and curled in the foetal position.

'Wake up,' I hiss. 'Where *exactly* is Sam in the house?'

He squints in the bright light. 'Not in the house. In the garden. Right at the end. Old air-raid shelter.'

I slam the seat back up. 'Wait here,' Rick orders, handing me the keys. He's pulled on a protective hooded black coverall, gloves and mask.

'No chance.' I tug off my heels and pull on a pair of flats from my bag.

'Then you'll need this.' He hands me a fresh coverall. It's baggy, but I pull it on over my clothes.

'Gloves, too,' he says. 'And mask. We don't want to leave any traces here.'

'Do you believe Tyler?' I ask.

'I don't know. There's a stile back down the road,' Rick says. 'Must be a footpath. Let's see if it goes behind the house.'

I lock the car. We climb over the stile and walk quickly along the narrow footpath, well-worn and lined with tangled raspberry bushes. My heart is thumping, my breath quick. If Sam is here, there's a chance to save him. To put this whole ghastly mess between us right again. And to make money.

As we near the house, the path veers off to the right. Rick strides into a small wooded area. I can see the back of the house, a couple of hundred feet away. There's no sound, no sign anyone is there. A thin piece of rusting barbed wire in the woodland serves as boundary, but there are gaps here and there, and flattened grass where what look like wild animals – or dogs – have pushed their way through.

We crawl under the wire to take a look at the garden. It's huge and overgrown, a jumble of weeds and swaying grasses a couple of feet tall, with a rusty children's swing rising up out of it. Ivy is spreading up the back of the house. The whole place looks abandoned, unlived in, left for nature to reclaim it.

Rick takes out a small pair of binoculars. 'The curtains are closed,' he says.

'Can you see a bunker?'

He shakes his head. 'Too overgrown. I'll have to go in.'

Rick crawls forward. I follow. Staying low, hidden by the grasses, we check the end of the garden.

That's when I see it.

'Over here! Quick.'

The ground rises up slightly in a shallow mound, and when I tap it with my hand, it's solid. A roof.

We feel our way around it. The roof is small, maybe twelve feet long and five feet wide. It's some kind of metal, covered in moss and grasses. I'm longing to call out, to bang on it, to let Sam know I'm there, but it's too dangerous. There could be a sniper in the house. Or inside it.

'I can't find a door, Rick,' I whisper.

'It's here.'

He's standing on overgrown steps at the far end. In front of him is a large, rusting metal door, secured with a new padlock. Rick takes a hairgrip from his pocket and picks the lock in seconds.

The metal door creaks open.

We're staring at a brick wall.

'They've *bricked him in*?' I hiss. 'Jesus Christ. Sam, can you hear me?'

Silence.

I'm starting to panic now, but Rick stays calm. He goes back to the car to get a crowbar and a hammer. Working quickly, and as quietly as he can, he chips away at the mortar in the middle.

'Hurry up,' I urge.

The wall is a couple of feet inside the door. Whoever forced Sam in here didn't want him to get out.

The first brick is loose. Rick jabs it with the crowbar and it falls inside the shelter. The stench almost makes me retch.

I grab my iPhone from the pocket in my coveralls and shine the torch in the gap, holding my nose through the mask to stop myself vomiting. Part of me doesn't want to look, to see the horror that I now know must lie there.

Sam is in the far corner, curled up, unmoving. His jogging trousers are filthy, and he's surrounded by congealed vomit and faeces.

'My God.'

I don't want to shine the torch on his face, to see his dead eyes staring back at me, but I move the beam slowly up his body. His hands and feet are zip-tied together and his head is covered with some kind of hessian sack. As the light touches the sack, he moves slightly.

'He's alive, Rick. Get that fucking wall down.'

Rick hammers at the bricks and I claw at them with my bare hands. The hole widens, brick by brick, just enough for me to crawl through. I don't care about the filth, I just want

Sam. To make sure he'll keep my secrets. To put this right. To make sure he knows it wasn't me. And to find out the name of the bastard who did this to him.

'Sam. Sam, wake up. It's over. I'm here.'

There's enough light breaking through for me to see the sack is tied tightly round his neck with a cord. I pick it apart and the cord comes loose, releasing a flood of congealing vomit. His eyes are rolling, unfocused, and his mouth is gagged. Taking his limp body in my arms, I tug at the vomit-stained gag, amazed he hasn't choked to death.

'Sam, Sam! Look at me. It's Lola. I'm here. You're safe now.'

'We need to get him back to London,' Rick says. 'There are doctors there who will take care of him, no questions asked.'

I look down at Sam. For a moment, his eyes focus on mine. His voice is barely a whisper. 'Lola. I-I knew you'd come.'

He doesn't hear my reply, doesn't feel me shaking him.

His eyes are still blue, brilliant blue. But they're vacant, unseeing.

I'd dreamed of his death, tried to make it happen. To silence him. To punish him for wanting to tell the world what a monster I'd become. To stop him doing it. To save myself, my career, my life. But this wasn't quick or painless. He's died right here in agony; tortured, tormented and afraid.

A wave rushes through my body, a wild whirling rush of every emotions – fear, anger, sadness, despair. Relief, too. I let go of Sam's lifeless body and feel my hands starting to shake uncontrollably.

'He's gone, Lola,' Rick says, his voice matter-of-fact.

'I know.'

Focus, Lola. Four hundred and fifty calories so far today. I'm on track. Focus on the counting. Not on Sam, not here, not this stinking room. The trembling subsides, and the wave recedes, rushing deep, deep inside me, into the darkness. I'm calm, controlled.

Now Sam is just another problem that needs to be solved.

Chapter Twenty

WEDNESDAY

Sue turned the Corsa out of Kingston Police Station and drove through the town centre, on her way to Richmond. Simon Omeria had to be worth a visit. His assistant said he'd been on location in the Cotswolds since Monday, but would be home around six p.m. and happy to chat to her, before his next block of filming at Pinewood Studios started the next day. Dev was still in town, trying to track down Tyler, so Sue decided to go alone.

It was the rush hour, but Sue didn't care. She didn't want to go home, didn't want to think about Mike or that nonsense he'd confronted her with. Tom simply wouldn't deal drugs, and as for hollowing out his chess books... Mike was either making it up for attention or dreamed it. Besides, Sue told herself, Sam had been missing for three days now. She was running out of time. Finding Sam had to be her priority.

The traffic crawled around the one-way system, past the

town's cavernous nightclub, PRYZM, the spelling of which had always irritated Sue immensely. To her, it would always be Options Cinema, where she'd sat in the back row with Rob in the early 1990s, grasping his hand in terror during *Silence of the Lambs*. She'd dreamed of being a detective back then, and even the grisly horrors that Hannibal Lecter unleashed in the movie hadn't put her off. But her career so far had certainly given her unexpected glimpses into hell, and unlike Lecter, what she'd seen was all too real.

She swung the car on to Richmond Road, driving past the family-owned Bevan's Butchers with its giant carcasses of meat displayed like glamorous, bloody coats in its refrigerated, spot-lit window. Sue hadn't touched meat since the Medford case. Flesh was flesh, and she avoided eating anything with bones. Or a mother.

Her phone beeped, and Sue checked the text as she waited at the traffic lights. It was from Emily Drakos.

Prelim results on the Morgans' post-mortem. Heroin and benzodiazepine overdose. Massive amount injected straight into their veins. Would have killed them within minutes. Estimated date of death, Friday.

Sue switched to hands-free and called Dev to tell him. 'Pick up local dealers near the flat. Tyler won't have gone far to score. See if he's bought smack and benzos off them recently. And check with his GP, see what meds he's on.'

'OK, boss. I'm in Soho checking the sex clubs. No sign of him so far. DS Howe's watching the flat.'

'I'm going to see Simon Omeria. I'll keep you posted.'

'Oh, and boss – the footprint outside the utility window in Cobshott matches Stevens'. Looks like he'd locked himself out. We've got a partial ID on that black car, too. Expert says his "best guess" is a Jaguar saloon. Older model. His guesses are pretty accurate.'

'Right, get Uniform to check out dark-coloured Jaguars registered in the Surrey area. Most of Cobshott drives Teslas and 4x4s. We might get lucky.'

The road took her through Ham and snaked back along the Thames into Richmond, where people were gathering in the riverside restaurants to eat and drink. Omeria's house was just off the Green, a quaint terraced cottage in a small row; the kind of beautiful, cosy home that Sue would love to retire to. She pulled into one of the residents' parking bays, feeling more house envy for this cottage than she'd ever felt for any of the sterile mansions in Cobshott.

The bricks were painted white, and fading pink roses rambled around the peach-coloured front door. She tapped the brass knocker firmly. 'DCI Fisher. Come in,' Omeria said, in the kind of commanding voice that was used to being obeyed. He was a short, squat man in his forties, grey but not balding, with trendy thick black glasses. The door opened straight into a small living room, a welcoming hippy hotch-potch of faded sofas covered in patchwork throws, bowls of potpourri and distressed white cabinets. Not what Sue had expected at all.

'Only been here a month,' he said in his upper-class English accent, waving his hand dismissively at the room. 'I was in the Lake District for most of that. This place is rented. Stop-gap. Split up with the wife. Far too girly for my tastes.'

'Sorry to hear about your wife,' Sue replied.

'She's in my house on Richmond Hill,' he added, bitterness oozing from every word. 'With the kids.'

'That must be difficult.'

'You have no idea.' He paused. 'Anyway, you're here about Sam Stevens. Found him yet?'

Omeria's bullish manner was rubbing an already grouchy Sue up the wrong way. 'I can tell you're someone who doesn't like to waste time, Mr Omeria, so I'll get straight to the point. I understand Mr Stevens spoke to you privately about one of the younger cast members, Stephen Merryweather. About what happened in your trailer.'

He paled slightly, but waved his hand again, dismissively. 'It was all a misunderstanding. I thought Stephen was interested. He made it clear that he wasn't and I apologised.'

'So you didn't offer him a role in your next film in return for sexual favours? Because that's what I've been told.'

His overconfident, domineering manner was stalling, Sue could see it in his eyes. 'Not that I recall.' He paused. 'Since Gina – my wife – left, it's been tough, you know.'

He looked at Sue, doe-eyed, manipulatively hunting for sympathy. Aside from the case, her mind was a mixed-up mess of emotions and Omeria was triggering a wave of fury she didn't know she had.

'So your wife running off with the broadband engineer

entitles you to sexually assault a nineteen-year-old, does it?' she snapped.

'No, no, *no*. It wasn't assault.' Omeria buried his head in his hands. 'Do I need a lawyer? Am I being questioned?'

Sue recovered her composure. 'This is not a formal interview. Like I said, Mr Omeria, I'm here to talk about Sam Stevens. Finding him is all I'm focused on at this stage. No formal allegations have been made against you. But I could always visit Stephen Merryweather and see how he feels about *that*.' She paused. 'It's in your interests to cooperate with me. Because it seems that you had a good reason for wanting Sam silenced.'

'My God. You don't think I had anything to do with it?'

'Did you?'

'No.' Omeria was sweating now, beads of it on his brow and fear in his eyes. 'Sam threatened *me*. He said he'd go straight to the police if I ever…made that sort of mistake again. Believe me, I won't.' He paused. 'I did wish him ill for a few hours, and privately called him every name under the sun, but when I calmed down, I realised Sam was right to call me out on it. What I did was wrong, and I told him so.'

'Did he accept that?'

'He apologised for shouting at me, but said his position on going to the police still stood. I promised him I'd never do anything like it ever again. It really was a momentary lapse of judgement.'

Momentary lapse of judgement. The way he dismissed

sexual assault so casually triggered a surge of anger, but she forced herself to let it go. For now.

'How did Sam seem on the shoot? Was he easy to work with? Sober?'

'Totally sober. And very easy. Unlike some of the cast.' He snorted. 'Julia Peace kept trying to rewrite bits of the script, saying her character wouldn't do this or that, and then I had the writers kicking off. Sam stepped in to mediate every time there was a creative *clash*. I didn't see him drinking or using drugs at all.' He paused. 'I saw the news about his parents. He'll be devastated when he finds out.'

'What makes you say that?'

'After the row, he invited me to join him one evening in his hotel room, listening to a Buddhist talk on YouTube. It was all about forgiveness. Wasn't for me. Every time a fucking Virgin Media ad comes on the TV I still want to burn it to the ground. He said it might help me cope with the Gina situation, because Buddhism had helped him forgive his parents. He was going to visit them before he started his next project.'

'Did you get the feeling he'd already spoken to them?'

'He didn't say. But given their age, he didn't want to leave meeting up with them much longer. I think he invited me because he knew I was stressed. We'd had endless rain, I wasn't in the best of moods and, frankly, the shoot was an ordeal. Gina and that fucking broadband guy, probably shacked up in my *house*. In my *bed*. The only blessing was I didn't have that infernal agent of Sam's breathing down my neck every night. Lola Lovett. They'd had some kind of row and she kept her distance. Normally they were joined at the hip.'

'A row? Do you know what it was about?'

'I asked him why she wasn't on the phone every night, or turning up on set to make sure everything was to her – and his – liking. He just said they'd had an argument over the past. She'd done something that he didn't agree with, ethically. I don't know what it was, and when I asked, he didn't say. He talked a lot about ethics and most of it went straight over my head. Even though I read English at Oxford. Lola was pretty different back then, I can tell you.'

'You knew Lola at *Oxford*?' Sue could barely contain her surprise.

'I did. Frankly I find it hilarious that she tries to keep her education quiet. Never gives interviews herself, and edits her Wikipedia page like a hawk. She prefers the "school of hard knocks" narrative, though it is true she's from a council estate in Farnborough. I was at Worcester College, Oxford with Soozie Lightwater's husband, Simon. The two Simons, we were known as. Shared a room with him for a while. Soozie's quite a girl.' He smiled. 'Lola was quiet then, bookish. Not the praying mantis she is today.'

'Were you and Simon an item?'

'Good God, no.' He paused. 'I mean, in the interests of full disclosure, there were a couple of nights when...we were just experimenting. Teenagers, away from home for the first time. Soozie knew nothing about it. She was always trying to set me up on a date with Lola but she really wasn't my type. Thin as a rake and never bloody ate anything. Soozie reckoned Lola was obsessed with her weight after having that baby at fourteen.'

'A baby?'

'Yes. Gymslip mum. She'd confided in Soozie on one of the rare nights she got drunk. Who told Simon. And he told me.'

'What happened to the baby?'

'Adopted at birth. Soozie said Lola didn't even get to hold them. I had a soft spot for Lola after that.'

Farnborough. Sue remembered it from Tyler's first statement. That's where he grew up. In care.

Chapter Twenty-One

LOLA

I'm staring down at Sam's dead body, counting, thinking.

'Lola, we've got to get away from here,' Rick urges.

'Fetch Tyler,' I snap. 'Force that bastard to see what he's done. Then he can tell us why.'

Rick nods, and goes back to the car. I want Tyler to see this, to shock him into telling the truth. It has to be about money. Maybe he's persuaded Sam to change his will. But the horror of what I've found is shattering my thoughts and scattering them in pieces. The counting isn't working. I focus on yesterday, how many calories I had then. And then the day before. *Stay in control, Lola.*

Tyler reveals another way in and Rick opens a hatch in the roof that we'd missed, flooding the chamber with the day's dying light. Now the full horror of what's happened to Sam is there for us to see. The chamber is full of blood and filth, and brown dried bloodstains show he's been clawing at the walls. His head is bruised and the bone on his right arm is broken completely in two, its jagged end poking through his swollen, blood-stained skin.

Pink foam bubbles from Sam's mouth.

Tyler is beside Rick, still gagged and bound, but when he sees Sam he begins to wail.

'This, Tyler, is what you've done. You've tortured him. You've *killed* him. You're a sick fuck of a murderer, Tyler. So you'd better start talking. About Sam and his parents.'

As he opens his mouth to speak, Rick shoves him through the hole.

There's a heavy thud as Tyler lands face-down in the filth.

He gurgles slightly, and his body begins to convulse, twitching and shaking, his eyeballs rolling in his head. Then, suddenly, silence.

'That's the least he deserved,' Rick says simply, checking his pulse to ensure he's dead. 'And, Lola, killing Sam has set you free. Your secret is safe. If he told Tyler, it's dead with him.'

I nod, staring at Tyler's vacant face. He's right.

Six hundred and forty calories.

'We need to go, Lola,' Rick said firmly. 'Lock this place and leave them in it.'

'I can't leave Sam in *here*. Not like this.'

'We don't have a choice. Lola!' Rick's voice is firm, determined. 'Sam's already gone. That's just his body.'

'What about the doctors? The ones who don't ask questions? Can't we get them to pick him up?'

'And do what, Lola? It's a dead fucking body. What do you want to do with it? It isn't Sam any more. If Tyler acted alone, they could be here for years until someone finds them.'

He's right. Sam believed in the afterlife, that once your body is gone you are reborn again. This wasn't *him*. This was just flesh, which would rot and die. Sam isn't here, in this filthy hole.

'Are you sure we can't—'

'Don't be ridiculous. No. We seal up and leave.'

Rick helps me to my feet. I'm dizzy and nauseous, but a survival instinct is kicking in. I have to get out.

I can reach the trapdoor in the roof but it's too high for me to climb through, so I squeeze back through the bricks. Rick and I replace them roughly, balancing them in the hole, and swing the metal door closed. He clicks the padlock shut, and climbs up on to the roof to re-lock the trapdoor. My heart is thumping now, my overwhelmed, confused, foggy brain thinking more clearly. We push our way through the undergrowth and climb in the car, tugging off our coveralls and stuffing them into a plastic bag, which Rick tosses on the back seat.

Soon we're back on the M40, leaving Winchborough and its secrets behind us. We stop at Beaconsfield services for petrol but I'm still too nauseous to face eating or drinking anything, even water.

'You should let it go,' Rick says, chewing loudly on a prawn sandwich. 'Tyler was probably acting alone. Had Sam changed his will lately? Leaving everything to the little shit? He'd have to have waited seven years if the body wasn't found, but he'd have inherited *millions*.'

I gaze out of the tinted window across the car park, a mass of lights under the dark night sky. I haven't told Rick about the unread message on Tyler's burner phone. For once, I want to handle this alone.

'Well, that's my advice, Loles,' he says, screwing the sandwich wrapper into a ball. 'I'm going for a wazz. Back shortly.'

I take out Tyler's burner phone and send a text.

Laying low. But need to talk. Meet me tomorrow, 1pm, South Bank. Under the bridge where the bookstalls are. Be there.

Chapter Twenty-Two

WEDNESDAY

The children's home where Tyler grew up stood jagged against the night sky, a rambling Victorian house with turrets and tall chimneys, ivy creeping unchecked across its face. Some of the windows were smashed, and inside all was dark. It had been five years since the unimaginable suffering that children had endured at Lavington Place had been exposed, and Sue suspected Tyler was one of them.

Sue's contact in social services had accessed the records. They were incomplete, and only went back to his arrival at Lavington, aged ten. Tyler was occasionally fostered for short periods, but the placements never worked out and he was repeatedly sent back to the home. At sixteen, as routine, he was assigned a new social worker, who'd since died. But his first social worker, Margaret Taymar, lived close to Lavington Place and was willing to talk. With Dev back from London, and Tyler still missing, they'd set off. Sue had ordered DS Fiona Howe to keep watch on Lola, who hadn't yet returned to her apartment, while Uniform were still watching Jim L's hotel.

'Haven't been here for years,' Margaret said breathlessly, climbing slowly out of her old Micra, which she'd parked beside Sue's. She was in her sixties, heavily overweight, with swollen legs, the skin stretched so tight it looked ready to burst. 'Dreadful place. If only we'd know what the children were going through.'

You should *have done,* Sue thought. 'Thanks for coming, Mrs Taymar,' she said briskly.

'I thought it was best to meet here,' Margaret said. 'My husband, he doesn't like any talk at home about Lavington Place. It was hard, you know, when the truth came out.' She looked up at the house, tears in her eyes. 'Some people thought I should have known. I wish I had. But children can be very good at hiding things, especially from those who care.'

Sue thought of Tom, of the cocaine, the mood swings. Of how she'd hidden the truth about Rob's violence for so long. Maybe Mike hadn't been lying. Maybe Tom was in trouble.

'We're concerned for Tyler's safety,' Dev said. 'So any background you can give us, anything you can remember, would be helpful.'

'He was a troubled lad,' Margaret replied. 'Very troubled. Even before he arrived here when he was ten.'

'Where was he before that?' Sue asked.

'Lymebrook House. He'd been in and out of foster care

from the age of one as his parents were kids themselves. Lot of different social workers. We had a high turnover of staff back then, and Tyler was shoved from pillar to post. I remember reading it in his notes. God knows where those notes are now. The boss here, Jack McMurdo, randomly shredded a lot of stuff when he realised things would come *out*.'

'CAIT – the child abuse team – are checking through the archive now,' Dev said. 'There are still enough boxes on Lavington Place to fill a room, so we might get lucky. We do know that Tyler was never one of the men who came forward in court with allegations of abuse.'

Margaret nodded. 'I'm not surprised. It takes a lot of courage to speak out, to go through a court case. Only a few of them found it.'

'Did he have *any* contact with his birth parents?' Sue asked. 'Over the years?'

'With the father, yes. The mother, no. I remember it because he was an unusual case. Not many of the kids on my books had any contact at all. But the notes said the father had turned up at Lymebrook House and his foster homes quite a few times, keen to stay in touch, even though the staff hadn't actively encouraged it. Tyler was blond, blue-eyed, and they'd hoped someone would go on to adopt him. But every time they arranged a placement it went wrong.'

'Because of his behaviour?' Dev asked.

'Sometimes. He was a challenging child. That's one of the reasons he was assigned to me. I often got given the difficult cases. But sometimes things just don't work out. I remember one prospective family early on had spent a fair bit of time with Tyler, but the wife fell pregnant naturally and they didn't go ahead. Sometimes it's just rotten luck. He certainly had plenty of that.'

'What happened to his birth father?'

'Tyler said he suddenly stopped coming when he was about four. I don't know why. But I do know Tyler was very upset about it, even though he tried not to show it.'

'How was he difficult, when you met him?' Sue asked.

'Sullen, uncooperative. I was used to that. I'd had teenagers of my own. But Tyler had this terrible anger inside him. He'd hit things, act on impulse and be sorry later. The longer he stayed at Lavington Place, the worse he got.' She sighed. 'Now, we probably know why.'

Sue nodded. 'When did you last see him?'

'Must have been at the handover. Just before he was sixteen. It was just routine. We changed all the kids round at sixteen, so they had a fresh face to help them navigate out of the care system and into adulthood. Wean them off us, though Tyler was never with a social worker long enough to become dependent. Paula Ugwu took him on. I saw her around from time to time. She seemed to get on OK with him at first. But the courts kept turning down his request to leave the care system. She said he was deeply unhappy about that. I remember her saying he walked out of Lavington Place on his eighteenth birthday, the date he could legally do so, and never went back.'

'What happened to Paula?' Dev asked.

'Suicide.' Margaret shook her head. 'She didn't leave a note. But it was the guilt, you know. The not seeing the abuse that was going on right under your nose. It was during the Lavington Place court case. The papers and TV were all over it, the public was baying for blood. She took an overdose.' Margaret took a deep breath. 'Paracetamol. I saw her in the hospital. Took her two days to die.'

Sue thought back to the Medford case, the lives ruined and lost through abuse. They stood together in silence for a moment. 'Do you want to look inside?' Margaret added. 'It's due for demolition soon. The lock on the back door was always easy to force, if anyone was locked out. Probably rusted through now.'

Margaret was right. The back door opened and she stepped inside, followed by Sue and Dev. Sue wasn't religious, or interested in the spirit world at all, but even she could feel a ghastly, intense atmosphere in the house, as if all the bad things that had happened there were leaking out of its very fabric.

They were standing in a large, moonlit kitchen, where deserted worktops and pots and pans, still left on the shelves, gathered dust. Cobwebs were strung from every corner, and a dark corridor stretched away from it, disappearing into the blackness.

Dev took a mini torch from his pocket and shone it up the corridor, sending three rats scurrying away.

'That room at the end, that was McMurdo's office,' Margaret said. 'Where most of the abuse happened.'

Part of Sue wanted to recoil, to run out of the building

and never return. But if she truly wanted to understand what had happened to Tyler, walking down that corridor would help. No matter how unpleasant, how scary it was, the children who had lived here had endured far, far worse.

She followed Dev down the wood-panelled corridor. Doors led off it on both sides, some standing open, revealing small bedrooms with stripped metal beds and no mattresses. 'They took everything,' Margaret said. 'Your lot. The police. For testing. Even the carpets.'

'Where was Tyler's room?' Dev asked.

'One of these. Ground floor. I can't remember which. And that's the living area. The youngsters would hang out in it.'

Dev flashed his torch around the room, a wide space with patio doors opening into what, in the blackness, was probably the garden. There were several old sofas, and mice or rats had chewed into the seats, so the filling spilled on to the floor. A table tennis table had been smashed up, and PEDO BASTARDS was sprayed in red on one of the walls.

The door to the office was slightly ajar, and Dev pushed it open. No moonlight reached here, so Dev swung the torch around. It was a large, imposing room, with empty bookshelves covered in dust, and a large, leather-topped desk, its drawers gaping open. An old-fashioned wooden hatstand stood in the corner. Two rats sitting on the desk froze in the narrow beam of light. Behind the desk, there was a fireplace with a mantlepiece and framed print above it, a large, old-fashioned painting of a hunt, with white jodhpurs, black hats and red jackets streaking across a countryside landscape.

'My God.'

'What is it, boss?'

'That painting. I've seen one just like it before. In the Medford case. Crime scene photos taken at Onslow Avenue, Mayfair. Where the paedophile ring was active.'

'Where you found the missing girl?'

'Yes. We uncovered a lot of footage of orgies too on a laptop, of young girls and boys being abused there. This picture often appeared in the background. CAIT thought it was all shot at Onslow Avenue, but I suspect some of it was here. McMurdo must have had links to it.'

The carpet around the desk had been taken up and Sue shuddered at what they must have found on it, and thought of the poor children who had stared helplessly at that painting as their childhood and their lives were stripped from them.

'I've seen enough,' she said suddenly. 'I'll alert CAIT, get them to check the footage, see if they can identify this room. They're still investigating that ring, so it might help catch anyone else who got away with it.'

'McMurdo didn't get what *he* deserved,' Margaret said bitterly. 'Pleading not guilty forced those brave kids into the witness box. And then dying of a heart attack before the end of the trial meant they didn't get the closure they wanted. Even though the inquiry believed them.'

Sue, Dev and Margaret walked back down the dark

corridor, overwhelmed and haunted by what they had seen and felt.

'Come on, Dev. Let's get out of here. The best thing that can happen to this place is that it's razed to the ground. The sooner the better.'

Back at the car, Sue thanked Margaret for her help. 'We may need a formal statement. If we do, I'll be in touch.'

She called DCI Lauren Brown, the new head of CAIT, who'd helped on the Medford case. Lauren was mid-thirties, ex public school, a high-flyer with a mind like a steel trap who took no nonsense from anyone, and who'd stepped in to cover for Sue after the Cobshott attack. Sue had a lot of respect for her. 'Lauren? I'm at Lavington Place. There's a print on the walls we've seen before. The hunt. Same as the one at Onslow Avenue.'

'Good God. I'll get the team on it. Might be some leads. That paedophile ring was much bigger than the few people we caught at the time. I have my suspicions it goes right up to some senior MPs in Parliament. Those poor kids.'

'Anything in the Lavington Place files?'

'We're going through them. Biller's seconded me temporarily to the case. I've called officers in and some of your team is here, but there are literally thousands of original papers, some of them in completely random order.'

'See if you can find anything on Tyler. Birth certificate, parents' names, any evidence or statements he gave about the abuse at Lavington, which weren't used. We can get a copy of his birth certificate first thing in the morning, but I'm guessing the father's name isn't on it.'

'Hold on.' Sue could hear Lauren speaking to one of the team. 'There's a statement here from Tyler, filed under "not actioned".' She paused. 'Christ, it's grim reading. Looks like he reported being abused at Lavington in 2008, but nothing came of it. And there's a couple of pages from old records. This one's from somewhere called Lymebrook House. Notes about organising parental visits.'

Sue held her breath. 'What does it say?'

'The child's father, Martyn Tipping, is to be permitted supervised access once a month, at Lymebrook House.'

'Please tell me there's an address.'

Lauren paused. 'You're in luck. It says a social worker visited his father's home at 26 Magdalen Mews, Bluebell Court, Farnborough, to carry out a risk assessment. They decided any visits must be held at the children's home.'

'Lauren, you're wonderful.'

'Hang on, I'll check who's living there now.' She tapped the computer. 'No Martyn Tipping on the electoral roll, but there's a Harry Tipping. Could be a relative?'

The chances of Tyler being in Magdalen Mews were low. But there *was* a chance.

'I'll go round there now,' Sue said.

She radioed it in. 'I'll need back-up.'

Magdalen Mews was a run-down street on Farnborough's Bluebell Court council estate, a maze of shabby, uncut lawns, dumped sofas and barking dogs. A handful of houses, dotted here and there, had been cared for, with pretty hanging baskets and brightly painted front doors, but number 26 wasn't one of them.

DS Fiona Howe had just reported Lola arriving home. 'Keep watching the flat,' Sue ordered. 'If she leaves, follow her. I want to know where she goes.'

Sue parked round the corner from Magdalen Mews, and a squad car pulled in behind her. It was eleven p.m., but a light was on in the front room, shining through what looked like an old dirty tablecloth pinned up as a curtain.

'DCI Sue Fisher,' she told the local officers in the squad car. 'We're on a murder inquiry, so I need you to watch the front and back of the house, in case anyone makes a run for it. DI Basu's done a recce and there's a yard leading into an alleyway. I very much doubt the suspect is inside, but you never know.'

'Do we need armed response?' The young officer looked nervous.

'Not at this stage. I don't want to go in heavy-handed unless I have to.' She gestured to a wall where 'kill the pigs' was spray-painted. 'I imagine we're already not too popular round here.'

'Yes, ma'am. There are some lock-ups a couple of streets away that the locals guard with their lives. Mostly small-time drugs, counterfeit goods.'

Drugs. Sue thought of Tom.

'Ma'am? You OK?'

'Of course.' She snapped back into work mode. 'One of you go round the back.'

He nodded and made his way around the back of the terrace. Sue walked round the corner to the front door and knocked gently on it, keen not to rouse the entire street. No reply, so she knocked again.

A man opened the door just a couple of inches. He was, Sue guessed, in his sixties but drink had taken its toll. Thin and bald, he was dressed in dirty grey jogging bottoms and green socks with a hole in one toe. He was topless, revealing a skinny, sunken chest and track marks on his arms.

'DCI Sue Fisher…' she began.

'I ain't using.' He held up a half-empty bottle of Tesco vodka. 'Keeping it legal, see.'

'Mr Harry Tipping?'

He eyed Sue and Dev suspiciously.

'We're not here about the, er, *using*,' Sue added. 'I need to talk to you about Martyn.'

'*Martyn?* Why?'

'Can we come in?' Dev asked.

Harry shifted from foot to foot.

'We just want to talk,' Sue said. 'I won't be looking for anything else.'

He opened the door a little wider and they stepped into the hallway. The place was a mess, with bare lightbulbs and a stained beige carpet covered in dog hairs. Harry bent down and picked up some of the letters and junk mail that covered the mat.

'Haven't had a chance to tidy up,' he said, adding the post to the unopened pile on a shelf.

The filthy living room was a 1970s time warp, with a

flowery carpet and fake brown leather sofa. A coffee table littered with empty drug wraps, Rizlas and burned spoons stood in the middle of the room, with a large dog basket beside it and a lump of uneaten dog food tipped directly on to the carpet. A copy of yesterday's *Sun* lay open on the racing pages, with certain horses carefully circled.

'Lost my Ginny today,' he said, taking another swig of the vodka and gesturing at the empty basket. 'Vet said there was no more he could do. Alsatian. Had her for ten years.'

'I'm so sorry,' Sue said.

He nodded. 'Do you want to sit down? I'd make you some tea but I've run out.' He held up the bottle meekly. 'Vodka? I can get us glasses?'

One glance at the sofa told her it was probably harbouring needles. 'No, but thank you,' she said kindly. The man seemed gentle and lonely, even *glad* of the company. 'I'm trying to get in touch with Martyn. Are you related?'

'I'm his dad.'

'It's about his son.'

Harry looked at her, puzzled.

'Tyler?' Sue went on.

His hazy blue eyes sharpened. 'Tyler? I ain't seen him for years.' He paused. 'Is he the lad that was on the news? He was a Tyler. Sam Stevens' boyfriend? I saw the appeal.'

'We believe so.'

'So he done well then, the lad. I'm glad. Martyn adored him.' He paused. 'I always worried Tyler might have been in Lavington Place children's home. Local place. Terrible abuse. Lot of the kids later took their own lives, you know.'

'When did you last see Tyler?'

'A few years ago now. He turned up on the doorstep, just like you. Wanted to see his dad.'

'Do you know where Martyn is?'

'Like I told Tyler, the cemetery. With my wife.' His eyes were filling with tears.

'They must both have been very young,' Sue said gently.

'Rosie, my wife, was thirty-three. Leukaemia. She died a few months after Tyler was born. Lost our Martyn four years later. He was just nineteen.' Seeing the burned spoons and wraps on the coffee table, he picked up the newspaper and placed it on top. 'Sorry. You don't want to see that. Every day's been a battle ever since.'

Sue liked this man, a broken soul who'd offered her all he had – his vodka, and the truth. She'd had a warmer, more genuine welcome in this house than she'd ever received anywhere in Cobshott.

Harry took another swig of vodka. 'I blame the social. Martyn was already in bits over his mum. Seeing her die slowly like that, it was terrible. Martyn and me, we had baby Tyler here for a while, but with Rosie and everything, they took the baby away. Said we weren't *coping*.'

'What about Tyler's mum?' Dev asked.

'She lived here for a bit. Alison. Local girl. They were just kids, both fourteen when Tyler was born. No idea how to look after a baby. I did most of it. But I had my wife to look after, too. Until the end.' He took a faded book of photographs from the shelf and flicked through it. 'That's my Rosie.'

Sue looked at the photo, a young woman, stocky, blonde and full of life, sitting on a Ferris wheel.

'Is Tyler's mum Alison still on the estate?'

'Yeah. Lives on Lavender Road. She's a grandma now. Went on to have more kids. I see her down the shops sometimes. Nice girl. Always asks after me.' He pointed to another photo. 'That's Martyn.'

Harry was right. Martyn was little more than a child, but he held the newborn baby proudly, with tears in his eyes.

'It all went wrong when he had the *other* baby.'

'He had *two* children?'

'Yeah.' He took out a pouch of tobacco and began rolling a cigarette. 'I told Tyler how his dad tried to keep contact with him, visiting him at foster places every now and then. Tyler remembered that. Martyn always hoped we'd get Tyler back. But then, when Tyler was four, Martyn got his *new* girlfriend pregnant. Turned out she was fourteen, not sixteen like she'd said. Underage. The social took the baby away.'

'Can you remember the girlfriend's name?'

'Lulu? Lolla? Something like that. Went to the grammar school, but she wasn't posh at all. Martyn was head over heels for her. When she got pregnant she tried to hide it, until it was too late. She dumped him and said she was having the baby adopted. That broke his heart. But she phoned here when she went into labour. Said her mum was drunk and she had no one else to turn to. Martyn went straight round and she had the baby twenty minutes later on the bathroom floor. He called her Rosie. After his mum.'

Could it be *Lola's* baby? Sue remembered Simon Omeria's words. *Soozie reckoned Lola was obsessed with her weight after having that baby at fourteen...gymslip mum... adopted at birth.*

Harry held out the photo. 'That's baby Rosie in the bathroom. The ambulance driver snapped it. But when they got to the hospital, the social took the baby straight out of Martyn's arms. His girlfriend wouldn't even look at the baby. Wanted nothing to do with it. Martyn tried to fight it, but the social said he didn't stand a chance. The adoption was already legally arranged, and if he knew what was best for his kids, he'd *want* to stay out of their lives. They'd be adopted by *proper* families. The social even threatened to *prosecute* him. Like a *paedo*. Said they planned to have Tyler adopted too. It broke him.'

He lit the roll-up and took another deep swig of vodka.

'I'm sorry to ask,' Sue said gently, 'but what happened to Martyn?'

A thin tear rolled slowly down his cheek. 'He'd lost his mum, his children, his girlfriend. I was a waste of space, drunk most of the time, trying to cope. He went to the cemetery to see his mum, put flowers on her grave. Pink ones. And a note, which washed away in the rain. The he climbed over the fence by the railway, waited for a fast train and jumped.'

~

Outside the house, Sue gestured to the two uniformed officers to stand down.

'If it's Lola's baby, Tyler has a half-sister,' she told Dev. 'She could be in on this. Maybe they both want money.'

She dialled Soozie Lightwater's number.

Chapter Twenty-Three

LOLA

I t's lunchtime, and the South Bank is busy, which will make it easier for me to blend into the crowd. My hair is tied back, and I'm dressed in black trousers, a loose black sweater and trainers. Whoever it is that Tyler's been working for, who warned him to get out of his flat, replied OK on his burner to meeting 'him', so here I am at one p.m., walking towards the bookshops under the bridge, trying to spot someone who might want Sam dead.

I caved and told Rick about the phone and the meeting. He was furious. Said we should have thought it through, made a proper plan. Still, he promised to shadow me, make sure I'm protected. Just like he always does. The angel on my shoulder.

I'm on three black coffees and almost zero calories today but my mind is slightly fuzzy and unfocused. Last night, when I got back from Winchborough, was a bad one. I bought two dozen Krispy Kreme donuts in the garage and ate until I didn't even need to *make* myself sick. My throat is sore today, my head a mess. I can't unsee Sam in that bunker, can't get rid of the stench, no matter how many times I shower, can't stop going over and over the hell he endured. And I can't stop regretting I'd ever wanted him dead, while being relieved that he is. It's fucked up. I can see the monster I've become, and I hate it.

I made it into the office first thing this morning, even took some calls and agreed a couple of castings for clients. Rick insists that acting normal is crucial. No one must suspect I'm traumatised, or whatever the hell else I'm feeling, having seen someone I loved left to rot in their own fucking *filth*.

I'm angry in a way I've never felt before. Usually if I'm wound up, I can stay cool, controlled, rely on the counting to keep me calm. But today even that's not enough to suppress the rage that's erupting inside me. It's blocking out *everything*. Whoever Tyler was working for has to *pay*. They *owe* me.

The cab drops me near the Royal Festival Hall so I walk down the steps to the riverside walkway, past the skateboarders, their wheels whirring and scraping over the concrete in the graffitied underpass they've made their home. A man dressed in a bright-blue suit leans against the river's railings, playing a jazz tune I don't recognise on a battered dull-brass saxophone, his instrument case folded open in front of him. There's a pound coin in my pocket, so I toss it into the velvet-lined case and he smiles with his eyes. The melody is haunting, sweet, and Sam would have loved it.

Waterloo Bridge is ahead of me, and underneath, the booksellers have laid out their wares on long rows of trestle tables at the South Bank book market. It's a London tradition to sell second-hand and new books here, everything from cookbooks to crime, attracting tourists and locals who browse up and down the rows, whisked away into a new world each time they open a different book.

J&G Books is my favourite. The owners, Josh and Gemma, are a friendly couple in their twenties whose grandparents started the market back in 1982 with a couple of boxes. Their stall isn't open today, so I head for the next one along and mingle with the customers, pretending to peruse the books.

Rick was right. This isn't going to work. There are too many people here, and any one of them could be expecting to meet Tyler. Young bearded guys in jeans with rucksacks and caps, older men with greying hair and polo shirts, young women with babies in prams. I can't even rule out the tourists with selfie sticks. Anyone capable of kidnapping and killing one of the country's biggest stars had got to be a master of disguise.

That's when I see her. About my age, business suit, short dark-brown bob. She's looking at the books but seems distracted, keeps glancing over her shoulder. Scanning the crowd. Running my fingers over the books, I move closer. Tyler's burner phone in my pocket buzzes.

Lola. I know it's you. Where is Tyler? Text back the
address or you'll never see Sam again.

They've seen me. They must be here. And they don't
know about the carnage that's unfolded in Winchborough.
The woman with the bob is looking at her phone.
Impulsively, I grab it.

'What the fuck are you doing?' she snaps.

I hand to back to her. 'I'm so sorry,' I reply. 'I thought
you were about to drop it.'

She gives me a filthy look but I've seen the text.

Sorry I'm late, honey. Are you by the books? We can grab
some dinner. Love you x

I scan round, checking who else is on their phone. Half
the people on South Bank are staring at their screens while
the world happens around them.

I take out the burner phone. Time to call their bluff.

I know who you are. If you want Tyler back, you need to
start talking.

Chapter Twenty-Four

THURSDAY

S oozie called Sue back within minutes.

'Sue? Sorry I missed your call. Have you found Sam?'

'Not yet. I need to ask you about Lola's baby.'

'Has she had one?'

'No. The one she had at fourteen.'

'Oh gosh, yes. She had it adopted. Baby girl. I thought you'd know all about that. Never had any contact, or wanted it. But that was almost thirty years ago. Surely that can't be anything to do with the case?'

'I can't go into details, Soozie. But I need to hear everything you know.'

'She got drunk at Oxford one night, which was rare, and told me she'd been seeing a guy on the estate in Farnborough. He was older, maybe eighteen. Mark or Martin, as I recall. He already had a little boy with someone else.'

'Did she mean to get pregnant?'

'No. But she said she thought he did it on purpose because he wanted another child. I think the first one was in care. Promised to "pull out" and didn't. More than once. Lola tried to abort it late on with a coat hanger. Grim. She didn't want to be a mother. Ever.'

'Why didn't she have a proper abortion?'

'She left it too late. It sounded like she was in complete denial for the first few months. Lola tried to hide it from her mum, and herself. Then she had it on the bathroom floor, and social services took it away.'

'How did Lola feel about the baby?'

'Angry that the dad had "done it" to her. She didn't feel anything for the kid, as far as I could tell. Just wanted rid. I remember being very drunk hearing the story and shocked that someone could be so ice-cold. We didn't mention it again.'

'Listen, Soozie, you've been a huge help. I can't say any more right now. But I'll be in touch.'

'No problem. And, Sue, be careful. I saw the news reports on Sam's parents.'

'Don't worry, I will.'

Sue was sure of it now. Lola's baby was Tyler's half-sister.

~

Mike was snoring in bed when Sue finally made it home from Farnborough at two a.m., and Tom's door was closed, though a faint light shone under it. She paused outside his door, wondering whether to knock, but as she did so the light snapped off. He must have heard her on the stairs. Definitely wanted to be left alone.

She thought of Lola's baby, unwanted and unloved, and for a second couldn't imagine how anyone could reject a child. She'd do anything for Tom, anything, even give her own life. But then she thought of Lola, so loving, so caring, so giving, that night in her apartment. Wasn't it true that when people had sex, you saw their real souls? And then she thought of Lola as a fourteen-year-old girl, afraid and giving birth in a bathroom on the rough estate, marvelling at how she'd gone on to make something of her life. Hopefully her baby had done the same.

Shattered, strung-out and stressed, Sue crept into the bedroom and laid her trouser suit carefully over the chair – it would stand another day's wear – dropped the cream shirt in the laundry basket and eased herself carefully into bed, trying not to wake him. Sometimes, on a complex case, Sue would toss and turn, but she was so exhausted that she was asleep within seconds.

Her alarm went off at 6:30 a.m. and she rolled over to speak to Mike, hoping to tell him about the case as a way of clearing the air after yesterday's row. She still couldn't believe the nonsense about Tom, but she knew they needed to talk about it. But she regretted what she'd said. Mike always had Tom's best interests at heart, and the guilt over the hurt she'd caused him burned in her mind, filling Sue with a self-loathing she hadn't felt since staring at the bruises Rob had given her.

The bedclothes were pushed back, the bed was cold and there was a faint smell of toothpaste wafting from the bathroom. Mike had gone. Not *gone* gone, but he was clearly avoiding her too. A sadness settled on her like thick black treacle, seeping through her pores and blotting out the blue sky, which leaked through the gap in the curtains.

She slid her legs out of bed, reached for her dressing gown and opened the curtains wide. The sun was still low in the sky, but it was a real blue-sky day, with just wisps of white cloud streaked here and there. Mrs Martin next door was already up and pottering in her greenhouse, emerging with a trug of bright-green tomatoes, which she placed on her wrought-iron garden table.

There was something safe about Berrylands, about suburbia, a surface predictability that Sue found comforting, an antidote to her work. This wasn't a place where people dealt drugs on street corners, or had their kids taken into care, though she knew all too well that behind every neat set of curtains, every mowed lawn, every car that was washed on a Sunday, could lie horrific abuse, alcoholism and violence. Here in suburbia – unlike the Bluebell Court estate – it was hidden, and people who probably should have their kids taken away, didn't.

Mike hadn't made her a cuppa, but she wasn't

surprised. If they'd had a breakthrough, an early call, he'd have gone straight in. Or maybe he was properly upset. She walked past Tom's closed door and down to the kitchen where she made a cup of tea, glancing briefly at their empty wall planner. Gone were the days of parents' evenings, of chess matches, of sports days. Tom would be leaving soon, but in so many ways it felt like he'd left already.

The pain and emptiness she felt gnawed at her soul, dragging her down into despair. When she'd felt like this with Rob, on the darkest days, she'd focused on caring for Tom. Now all she had left was work, and she turned her mind to it.

Twenty minutes later, Sue opened the front door and walked out to the car. Mrs Martin was in the front garden now, carefully deadheading her dahlias.

'Morning, Sue,' she said brightly. 'Got some lovely raspberries off the bushes this morning. I'll make your Tom some jam. He can take it with him to uni.'

'Thanks.' Sue wasn't in the mood for one of Mrs Martin's chats, but she knew the lady was lonely, so she gave her a warm smile. 'You're up early today.'

'Didn't sleep too well. Car doors slamming always wake me up.'

Sue sighed. 'That might have been me.' Mrs Martin knew exactly how to get her point across.

'Don't worry, love. Oh, and thank you for getting Tom to

keep that music down. I didn't hear it at all yesterday.'

'You're welcome.' Mike must have had a word.

'And tomatoes. I'm going to make some chutney. I'll give you a jar for Christmas.'

Sue smiled again. 'Thanks, Mrs Martin,' she said, getting into the car.

Mrs Martin lowered her voice to a whisper. 'Any news on Sam Stevens?'

'We're working on it.'

The incident room was surprisingly quiet, with everyone poring over their coffees and computers. At 7:30 a.m. she called the team together for a briefing.

'Hopefully you've all seen the email with the background on Tyler. Still hasn't returned to the flat. Uniform are keeping watch on it, plus Cobshott and Hampstead. We've got an APW out on all ports and airports, and we've also had officers up on Hampstead Heath, targeting the cruising areas, asking if anyone's seen him. At this stage, we have to consider him the prime suspect in the murder of Dafydd and Gwen Morgan, and in Sam's disappearance. He could be acting alone, or with others. Motive, I suspect, is money. Dev, what's the latest on Sam Stevens' will?'

'Solicitor says it *was* changed recently, but to benefit his mum. He'd left ten per cent to Tyler. So he'd probably clear over a million. And Stevens has left sizeable gifts to Buddhist centres and LGBTQI+ charities.'

'A million pounds is enough of a motive for me,' Sue replied. 'There's also Lola's adopted child. She's likely nothing to do with the case, but I'm sure she's Tyler's half-sister so he might seek her out, or have done so already, and we need to find her. He might be staying there. Fiona, Dev, get on to the adoption agencies. We need her birth certificate, to know who adopted her, and where they are now, or if she was left in a children's home, like Tyler. The Lavington Place records are incomplete, so it's possible she was there, too. She might be a victim of abuse. DCI Lauren Brown and her team are going through those. I'll approach Lola Lovett myself when we know more. It's unclear if she knows anything about the child.'

She turned to Dev. 'What have we got on Tyler's recent background? Other people he associated with?'

'Sketchy. He had a range of jobs before meeting Sam a year ago and lived in a flat share in Wandsworth. Uniform have spoken to his two flatmates, who are still there. They say he lived there for about three months in their box room after they advertised for a flatmate online, and kept himself to himself. He worked at McDonald's in Charing Cross when he first moved in, often the late shifts, and they were working in the City so they barely saw him. Said he occasionally had guys back, and didn't touch drink or drugs, as far as they knew. If they offered him a beer he always said no. They thought perhaps he was in recovery. He didn't talk about his past.'

'What about the latest job, with Climate Crisis charity? What do we know about that?'

Dev checked his notes. 'Started it not long before he met Sam. They were advertising for activists willing to join in direct action, lying down in the road, that kind of thing. The director said he was reasonably reliable and passionate about people's rights, especially LBGTQI ones. Had a few sick days, but nothing out of the ordinary. Way before that, he was on benefits, but he stopped claiming about a year before he met Sam. I'm guessing he did a lot of cash-in-hand, whatever it was, as there's no record of him paying tax in that period.'

'And how about Lola Lovett? What are her movements?'

'Got back last night about ten p.m. Alone. Went in carrying two large boxes of what looked like Krispy Kreme donuts.'

'Anyone else in or out?' Sue asked. 'That's a lot of donuts.' Especially for an anorexic. Sue hadn't shared that with the team, though she didn't really know why. It felt too personal, a part of Lola that they didn't need to know. 'Unless she was taking them to work today.'

'No,' Fiona replied. 'Could be for a work event, though. DI Jeff Greene took over from me, and he said she left in her car about seven a.m., alone. They followed. She parked in the underground NCP car park in Chinatown and walked to her office. Hasn't left since. Unfortunately he didn't notice if she had the donuts.'

'And where are we on Jim L, the paparazzo? PC Evans, you're on that, aren't you?'

'I am. Still hasn't been back to his hotel. We're trying to locate him.'

'Good. Fiona, did you bring Tyler's drug dealer in?'

'We did. Temporarily overlooking the stash he had in his pockets quickly got him talking. Tyler's bought pretty much everything off him for months, and recently asked for large amounts of benzodiazepines and heroin. He couldn't be specific about when. To be honest, the guy doesn't even know what day it is. So Tyler hasn't suddenly relapsed. He's been on drugs for a while. The dealer hadn't seen him for a day or two, though. And he said he hasn't sold anything to Sam Stevens for more than a year.'

Sue nodded. 'From what Julia Peace and Simon Omeria told me, Sam was definitely clean. It seems Tyler was doing drugs behind his back – or at least Sam wasn't joining in.'

'The dealer added that he'd seen a motorbike around lately. Rider dressed in black leather. Often parked near Tyler's. He's used to seeing couriers but was wary of this one in case they were undercover police. I checked with the drugs squad but they don't have any operatives in that area right now.'

The incident room door opened and Mike walked in. He caught Sue's eye, clearly eager to talk.

'OK, everyone, let's get on it. Sam Stevens is depending on us.'

She gestured to Mike to join her in the office, and he closed the door behind them.

'Up early this morning...' she began.

'Sue.' His voice was worried, urgent. 'It's Tom. He didn't come home last night.'

'He was there when I got home,' Sue replied sharply. 'I saw his light go off. I was standing right outside it. For God's sake, Mike, you're becoming *obsessed*.'

'Did you actually *see* him?'

'No, but—'

'I've just texted his mates, the ones I know, anyway. None of them have seen him.' Mike lowered his voice. 'Remember what I told you yesterday?'

There was a sharp knock on the door, and Chief Biller walked in.

'Sue. Sorry to interrupt. I've got the press breathing down my neck for an update. We're going to have to give them *something*.'

Dev poked his head around the door. 'We've found her, Sue. Lola Lovett's daughter.'

Tom looked out at the sunrise, his thin T-shirt no protection against the chilly wind that blew on the clifftop. He'd taken the train the night before, clear in his mind what he had to do.

He'd spent his life trying to protect and care for his mum. But after his dad's death, that love had been swamped by anger, twisted into a rage that burned away at his very soul. He despised her for staying with Rob, for putting up with the violence, for making his childhood an endless, secret landscape of fear that one day he'd come home and find her not just beaten up but dead.

Every single day, he was glad that his dad was gone. And that, too, ate away at him, piling guilt on top. Every time he looked at his mum, the feelings threatened to overwhelm him, and the safe world he'd created to cope, with his chess and his schoolwork and his 'nice' friends, suddenly felt like a prison. He wanted to walk away from all of it, start again, find a life where he could be *him*, discover who he really was, not the person he'd had to become.

University was coming. That was his way out. But it was months off, and when a new, older friend he met in a pub in Kingston offered him some weed, he tried it. Smoking took the pain away. Soon he was hanging out with a new crowd, smoking, drinking, skipping chess. For once in his life, Tom felt in charge, doing what he wanted, not what he felt he *should*.

But the weed became more frequent, stronger. He tried cocaine too. And when his new friend asked if he could 'look after' some gear 'just for a few days', Tom hesitated. He hadn't done drugs in the house. The shed, yes, and down the playing fields, but not in the house. If he was caught with drugs, it would wreck his mum's career. Mike's too. No matter how much he hated what Sue had done, underneath the toxic mess of emotions, he still adored her.

But the friend was persuasive. So Tom agreed, storing a small bag of cocaine inside a chess book. No one would look there. Then it was burner phones. More cocaine. And more. When he said no, the 'friend' threatened him. Said he wouldn't be safe out drinking in Kingston. Or even in his own home. And they'd need him to 'keep some gear' for them when he got to Southampton uni. Get other students to help, too.

Tom tried to stand his ground. He said he'd return the drugs and the phones, and wanted out. So they threatened to kill his mum. They knew who she was, 'a pig', where they could find her. She'd be found with her throat slit.

His bright future, the new life he longed for, had evaporated. No matter which direction he looked in, Tom saw blackness and pain, not only for himself but for his mum, for Mike, for his old friends who still called to see how he was, for the friends he hadn't met yet, whom he'd be forced to use and abuse.

He'd always been a logical boy, and that logic took over. He was calm, rational, composed when he crumbled the bricks of cocaine into the toilet and flushed it, when he set the timer on the light in his room, when he stepped on the train last night, when he alighted at Eastbourne, and walked to the cliffs to watch his last sunset. No drink, no drugs. Just logic. Knowing what he had to do.

Tom stood up, took a swig from his water bottle, and pulled his rucksack on to his back. He remembered walking this path with Sue, as she held his hand and told him to be careful near the edge, how they'd stopped for a rest and tucked into peanut butter sandwiches, wrapped in tin foil, as the limitless sky stretched over the sea at Beachy Head.

No one saw him walk towards the edge and keep on walking, apart from a seagull, which swooped high above him, towards the pink-tinged horizon.

Having pacified Biller with the promise of updates for the press, Sue told Dev she'd join him in a moment for the latest on Lola's child. She closed the door.

'Mike, I'm sure Tom is fine. He's *eighteen*. You're fussing. I'm right in the middle of something here—'

'I checked the drugs. They've gone. The burner phones, too.'

'Told you it was in your imagination. For fuck's sake, Mike, get a grip.' She opened the door, expecting him to walk out of it, but he slammed it shut, raising eyebrows in the incident room. Dev glanced over, but she nodded to indicate all was well.

'Sue. Listen to me. Tom's got himself in trouble. His chess friends said he spends a lot of time in the Burlington Arms, with a new crowd. Rough lot. They never hear from him.'

'He's just moving on, Mike. From all of us.'

'Maybe. But I don't like it, Sue. Something's not right. His light could be on a timer, the bulb could have blown… Unless you saw him in the flesh, I'm worried.'

'The bulb blew just as I walked up the stairs? Come on, Mike...'

Mike loved Tom, she knew that, and he was a first-class detective, but since Rob died, he could be overprotective. Of both of them.

Then she remembered Mrs Martin's words. *Thank you for getting Tom to keep that music down. I didn't hear it at all yesterday.*

'All right, Mike. You're starting to worry me now. Check out the Burlington Arms. Speak to the landlord, see if he was in last night. Put your mind at rest. And mine,' she added. 'Text me as soon as you hear.'

Dev was lurking outside the office door, partly to check if Sue was OK, and also brimming with news about Lola's baby.

'Everything OK, boss?' he said, as Mike hurried past him.

'Fine,' Sue replied, trying to hide her sense of unease. 'Mike thinks Tom didn't come home last night, that's all. He's going to check the local pub.'

'Do you need to go, boss? We can cover this...'

'No. I'm sure he's fine. I think he *was* at home. And if he wasn't he's probably sleeping off a hangover at a mate's house. We've all done it. What's the news on Lola's daughter?'

'Mary Carter. She was adopted straight away, as a newborn. By a couple in the Cotswolds. Jonathan and Penelope Carter. I've got the address – The Gables, Long Lane, Winchborough. Sounds posh. And all three are listed on the electoral roll.'

'How long will it takes us to get there?'

'Couple of hours. If the M25's clear.'

'Get Uniform to watch the house. Discreetly. See if anyone goes in or out.'

∾

The Gables was, as Sue expected, a large, sand-coloured farmhouse brimming with old money. She pulled the Corsa into the large gravel driveway, as sheep grazed in the fields opposite and a slight chill bit through the autumn air. An old Nissan Micra was parked in the drive.

A large old-fashioned metal bell pull was on the right of the door, and Sue rang it, making a loud clang, which sent the sheep scurrying. She heard footsteps on the tiles inside, and the door opened.

'Can I help you?'

The woman was in her twenties, with dark hair tied back in a ponytail. She was wearing a plastic apron and blue latex gloves.

'DCI Fisher and DI Basu,' Sue said, showing her badge. 'We're here to see Jonathan and Penelope Carter.'

'Come in.'

The young woman led them through the wide, tiled hallway, past painted portraits and a large, old-fashioned display cabinet filled with porcelain china ornaments, which Sue guessed were family heirlooms. She opened a door on the right and went into a square room lined floor to ceiling with books.

'The library,' she said simply. 'Please, wait here.'

Sue walked around the room, marvelling at the display. There were books of all shapes and sizes, everything from the Second World War to Alan Carr's autobiography. One section, behind sliding glass, contained much older books, presumably more valuable.

There were two leather armchairs in the centre of the library, and an unusually tall coffee table, on which stood a vase freshly filled with cut dahlias. The window overlooked a large garden which, like the rest of the house, had seen far better days. The grass was a couple of feet tall, desperately needing a mow, and the flower beds – which had clearly once been someone's pride and joy – were tangled and knotty, though still colourful as their unchecked flowers still bloomed.

Sue heard a sound in the hallway and the young woman returned with a wheelchair. Penelope Carter was a thin, white-haired lady in her seventies, so tiny that she seemed to disappear into the chair, dressed in a long blue skirt and a white shirt with a high collar.

'Mrs Carter, this is DCI Fisher and DI Basu. They've come to see you.'

Penelope looked up, her rheumy pale-blue eyes looking at each of them in turn. 'Tea?' she said brightly. 'Would you like some tea?'

'Yes, please,' Sue replied.

'Sonia will fetch some. Be a dear, Sonia, and make these kind people some tea. Biscuits, too, if we have any.'

The young woman nodded. She'd removed her apron and gloves, and was dressed in a navy blue uniform, with *HomeFromHome Carers* embroidered on the chest.

'Have you come far?' Penelope continued, smiling.

'London,' Sue replied.

'Well, you definitely need tea then. Be a dear, Sonia, and make these kind people some tea. Biscuits, too, if we have any. And bring some for Jonathan. Where is he?'

Sonia gestured to Sue, who followed her out of the room. 'She has dementia. It's been fairly stable, but we lost Jonathan a couple of years ago, and sometimes she's worse than others. She was more confused after that.'

'What about their daughter, Mary?'

'She comes to visit. Usually once a month. I'm Penelope's regular carer, and either me or one of the girls coming in four times a day to see to her gets her up, opens the curtains, makes her meals, puts her to bed about 5:30 p.m. Unless Mary's here. Then she does it all and doesn't need us.'

'When was she last here?'

'Sunday. She phoned on Saturday night to say we didn't need to come in until Monday morning. And to tell her mother not to worry about the garden, not that Penelope had mentioned it. Mary usually does the mowing, but she said she'd get a gardener in. Is she all right?'

'We think she may be able to help us with some

background on an investigation, that's all. Where does she live?'

'London. They have a town house in Linwood Street, Chelsea. She moved there when she went to uni. Probably lives on family money. There's plenty of it.'

'Do you have a photo of her?'

'There's one in the living room. Hang on.'

Sonia returned with a framed graduation photo labelled *University College London*. Mary was pretty, blonde, with brown eyes. Just like Lola's.

'Thank you. Do you mind if we take a look around?'

'Fine with me. And Penelope will just say yes. One thing that's been a godsend is she's become childlike, and generally quite content. I hear she was quite different before. Much more irritable and controlling.'

Back in the living room, Dev was talking to Penelope. 'My daughter, she's wonderful. She's here somewhere. Sonia, can you fetch her? I remember the day I first held her in my arms. A tiny little thing. Her mother didn't want her.'

'Did she know she was adopted?' Sue asked.

'Adopted? Who's adopted?'

'Shall we get you settled in the television room, Penelope?' Sonia interjected. 'We've got yesterday's *Bargain Hunt* to catch up on.'

'Oooh, yes please. Well, it was very nice to meet you. I hope you enjoyed your tea.'

As Sonia wheeled Penelope out of the room, Sue explained to Dev what she'd learned. 'Let's check the house.

The gardens, too. This would be the perfect place for Tyler to lie low.'

Stepping out of the back door reminded Sue of *The Secret Garden*, which she'd read and loved as a child. They'd searched around the house, where most of the upstairs rooms were covered in dust sheets. Photos of Mary were all over, and she had the largest bedroom, decorated in dusty pink with white-painted furniture and throws embroidered with tiny, colourful flowers. On the face of it, this seemed like an idyllic place to grow up, surrounded by wildflower meadows and adoring parents, and a world away from the hell of Lavington Place, but Sue had seen too many perfect worlds shattered by secrets to assume anything.

The garden was wild and overgrown, though not in a way that suggested it had been like it for long. A good mow and some serious pruning would soon sort it out. Someone had loved this garden, that was clear. The once carefully planted flowers in the beds surged and bloomed, now out-competed by weeds, and to the right stood a greenhouse, its windows still intact but the inside rambling and brown, and to the left a potting shed, the door closed and padlocked.

Sue walked the garden's perimeter, which was partly walled, the rest loosely marked by rusting barbed wire tangled in the weeds. An old children's swing stood abandoned, creaking slightly as it swayed in the breeze. Fields, presumably belonging to the house, stretched beyond the low walls to the left and right, and a wooded area lay straight ahead, screening the overgrown public footpath, which Sue had noticed on her first recce of the house.

The springy weeds were slightly flattened here, as if someone had recently walked on them, leading across from the barbed wire to an area in the rear of the garden. As she moved closer, there was a faint smell of sewage, barely there, but enough to make Sue suspect the garden had a cesspit.

That's when she saw it. Hidden in the weeds. A roof.

The top was completely covered in moss, but there was the clear outline of a trapdoor. It had to be an old bunker of some kind, perhaps an air-raid shelter.

She should retreat and call for back-up, she knew that. But she was so close, and hadn't made a sound approaching. The bunker was quiet. The moss had been disturbed around the door. Someone had recently opened it.

Pulling on a hair of latex gloves, Sue grasped the metal handle and opened it.

The stench and the flies flooded out as the light poured in.

'Dev!' she shouted.

He ran across the grass towards her, retching at the smell. Sue shone her torch into the bunker, lighting up every corner.

'Christ.'

One body was leaning against the wall, the other was

sprawled on the concrete, his face twisted to the right. Two men, both clearly dead. Sam Stevens and Tyler Tipping.

Dev stared into the hole, and retched.

'Call it in,' Sue barked.

As Dev radioed for help, she looked down into the pit, swamped by sadness. She'd *failed*. If she'd been quicker, if she'd been sharper, if she hadn't wasted time fucking Lola, then maybe, just maybe, she could have saved him.

She pushed the feeling aside. Two more people were dead and she had a job to do. The trapdoor's inside handle had been removed. Sam's feet and legs appeared to be tied together. His arm was broken and unbandaged, and there was no food or drink. He'd clearly been thrown in here to die. Had Tyler found him, and fallen in? Or had Tyler jumped?

She called DCI Lauren Brown.

'Lauren, it's Sue. We've found two bodies, likely Sam Stevens and Tyler Tipping. Suspect is Mary Carter. Address Linwood Street, Chelsea. She's involved in this somehow. We need to find her urgently. Has she got previous?'

If anyone could find Mary, it was Lauren.

'We'll need to pick up Lola Lovett, too,' she went on. 'Lola may not realise it, but she's Mary's birth mother. This is all going to be a lot for her to take in, so will need careful handling. Keep her at the station until I get there, in case any of this leaks. Take her phone too. I want to be the one to speak to her.'

'On it.' Lauren replied. 'Last report on Lola is she'd been to the South Bank book market. Now back at her office, so she'll be easy to pick up. Let me check on Mary Carter.' She tapped the keyboard. 'Mary is clean. No arrests or convictions. Registered as sole occupant of number 14, Linwood Street. Mary Olivia Carter.'

Olivia. Sue had heard that name.

'Hang on a moment, Lauren.'

Sue searched her emails.

Lola had forwarded it to her, that night in her flat. The list of people who regularly sent Sam strange fan mail.

Forwarded message. From Olivia Carter
oliviacarter@lolalovettpr.com.

Olivia. Lola's assistant.

Chapter Twenty-Five

LOLA

Whoever's got Sam isn't replying to my text. I'm back in the office after my failed trip to the South Bank, on edge, jittery. Most of my agents are at their desks, chatting to each other or on the phone, normal life going on all around me while my mind fragments, shatters. A bleak, black sadness is swamping me in waves, and each time it hits, all I can think of is Sam, in that pit. I haven't eaten, I can't eat. Can't even drink. Counting is the only thing that's keeping me sane.

'You OK, Lola?' Olivia asks, handing me a black coffee. I place it on the desk, untouched.

'Of course.' I'd hoped no one would notice, but Olivia never misses a trick.

'Is there news on Sam?'

'No, nothing.' I turn away from her, terrified she'll see my emotions. Rick had told me to keep things normal, and he was right. I couldn't allow a hint of the horror I'd seen to leak. 'What's the latest on that new casting director, Karen Killick?' I say briskly, taking a deep breath. 'Have you nailed her down to a meeting yet?'

'I chased her this morning,' Olivia replies. Ever efficient. The most organised assistant I've ever had. But right now I want her out of my hair.

'Email her again. She's casting that Amazon space drama set on Jupiter – I mean, *really*, it's made of gas – but I'm hearing Robinson Sinclair Agency is all over it. The last thing I need is them filling up the cast. And what time is the *YourSong* launch tonight?'

'Six o'clock. At the Mayfair Hotel. I've booked you a cab for four-thirty.'

'Right. You need to babysit Johnny McIntyre. He stayed at the hotel last night. All the *YourSong* judges did. Get over there now and keep him off the coke. I don't care how you do it. If he kicks off, call me. We can't have him speeding off his head like last time. No one's going to buy the "too much caffeine" story twice.'

'Sure.' She's taking her jacket off the back of the chair as Lily, the receptionist, walks in. 'The police are outside,' Lily says, her face pale. 'I've told them you're busy, but they're insistent.'

The police? My stomach clenches and sweat pricks at my armpits. I'm dizzy, lightheaded. Sue Fisher had promised to keep me in the loop, but I've heard nothing. Why would the police just turn up unannounced? My mind races through the possibilities. Maybe they've worked out Tyler is involved. Maybe they know who he was working for. Maybe they've found the bodies. Panic and fear rise up, blocking out every trace of grief. Christ. What if someone saw me at the scene?

Zero calories today. Control, Lola. Stay in control. Crisis management is what you do. Treat this like any other challenge.

I take another deep breath. 'Send them up,' I say calmly. 'Olivia, you'd better wait.'

'Do you think they've found Sam?' Her eyes are wide, and I see real fear in them.

'Let's see what they've got to say.'

As Lily buzzes them in, I wait in reception. Olivia looks stressed and is biting the skin around the edge of her nails, something she never does. Whatever they've got to say is best said here, not in front of all my other agents, though the news that the police are here has sent a ripple of whispers through the office and Anastazia keeps poking her head around the corner. I'm expecting Sue Fisher, but a younger woman with cropped short dark hair strides in, flanked by two plain-clothed officers. 'Ms Lovett? DCI Lauren Brown,' she says. 'Apologies for turning up unannounced. I'm working on Sam's case with DCI Sue Fisher. She has asked me to give you a lift to the station.'

'Is it Sam?' My voice is calm, with a hint of panic, but that's OK. Anyone would sound panicked if their friend was missing and the police turned up. 'Have they found him?'

'I don't have any firm details. DCI Fisher is on her way to Kingston Police Station now and has asked that you meet her there.'

Keep things normal, Lola. They must have found the bodies, and Sue wants to break the news in person. 'Of course. Anything I can do to help. I'll need a few minutes to cancel some arrangements. I have a launch tonight. *YourSong*. At the Mayfair Hotel. A cab is due to pick me up this afternoon. Olivia here was just on her way over there.'

DCI Brown turns to her. 'Olivia Carter?'

'Yes.'

'*Mary* Olivia Carter, I'm arresting you on suspicion of involvement in the abduction and murder of Sam Stevens. You do not have to say anything. But it may harm your defence if you do not mention when questioned something which you later rely on in court. Anything you do say may be given in evidence.'

Olivia? *Olivia* is involved in this?

'Sam's *dead*?' I splutter, but the shock on my face is genuine. *Olivia?*

'He's talked, hasn't he?' Olivia snaps. 'Tyler. I knew I should never have trusted him.'

She holds out her hands and one of the officers spins her around, clicking handcuffs in place. Lily, and several of the other agents are staring at her, but she turns her head to look at me. Only me. With a sneer on her face.

'You had it coming, *Mother*.'

'Mother?'

'*They* know who I am.' She gestures at the police. 'But *you*, the selfish, self-obsessed *bitch* who gave birth to me, doesn't even care enough to recognise your own *daughter*. Even when I'm right under your nose. I might as well tell you now, face to face. Embarrass you in front of all your staff. See you squirm.'

Her almond-shaped brown eyes. Her nose. Her quick mind. Her steely determination. The way she'd pestered me for the job.

'Olivia?'

'*Mary*, actually. Which you'd have known if you'd even tried to find me. But you didn't give a shit, did you, Lola? I was someone standing in the way of your success. And we all know what you do to anyone who does *that*, don't we?'

I can't tear my eyes off her. So this is what my child looks like. This is who she is, where she is. And she's being arrested for Sam's murder?

'Did you ever think about me?' she asks. 'Even once?'

'Of course I did,' I lied. I hadn't. Thinking about the baby was somewhere I couldn't go. If thoughts of it ever forced their way in, I shut them out. Fast.

'Well, why didn't you look for me? It's because you're the most selfish person I've ever met, Lola. You didn't care about me, and you don't care about anyone in this room. You *use* people.'

We all know what you do to anyone who does that. What did she mean? Did Sam tell her about Des Lethbridge? Maybe she'd tortured him enough in that stinking shelter to get the truth out of him. If she tells the police…

Suddenly my mind is razor-sharp, focused. Olivia is a problem that needs to be solved. And as far as they're concerned, I shouldn't know that Sam is dead.

'D-did you say she *murdered* Sam?' I ask, looking straight at DCI Brown. 'Is he really *dead*?'

'I'm sorry to tell you that two bodies have been found. We believe one is the body of Sam Stevens.'

'W-where is he?'

'We'll have more information for you as soon as we can.'

'You said *two* bodies?'

'We believe the other person is his boyfriend, Tyler Tipping.'

Olivia gasps.

For the first time in my life, I'm terrified. If Sam's told her everything, she can destroy me. Right here. Right now.

The world spins, and I reach out to steady myself, but everything goes black.

Chapter Twenty-Six

TWO YEARS EARLIER

M ary Carter sat on her pastel-pink bed in Chelsea, staring at a piece of paper. She'd found it, along with other documents and notes, going through her father's locked bureau at the house in Winchborough. He'd been dead for two weeks, and as far as Mary was concerned, that wasn't anywhere near long enough.

Lola Lovett. From Farnborough, Hampshire. She'd always known she was adopted, but seeing her birth mother's name unleashed an unexpected, slow-burning rage that gradually consumed her every waking moment. A social worker had registered the birth, and named her 'Mary'.

She had often thought about tracing her birth mother, assuming it would mean years of dead ends and blind alleys. But once Mary came across the paperwork by chance, it had taken ten seconds on Google.

Lola Lovett, PR guru. Pictures and videos of Lola were

everywhere on the internet. Endless snaps of her with the actor Sam Stevens, gushing over him like a new puppy. Find a red carpet video of Sam, and Lola was usually in the background, guarding him like a mother hen. Mary stared into Lola's brown eyes, at the distinctive shape of her nose, her lips, recognising herself, raging uncontrollably at this woman who had dumped her for a glamorous, childless life and had never looked back. This skinny woman, with her Chanel sunglasses and her celebrity pals, who had *no* idea what she'd put her unwanted daughter through.

Did Lola know *anything* about Jonathan and Penelope, she wondered? The adoption agency certainly hadn't. To the world, they were doting older parents, who gave her everything. To Mary, they were seriously fucked up.

Jonathan had wanted children, but Penelope hadn't, a fact she had loudly pointed out for as long as Mary could remember. Penelope had eventually agreed to adopt in her late forties, fearing – Mary suspected – that Jonathan and his money would leave her for a younger woman. She was cold and icy towards Mary, slapping her face if she cried. There was no love, no tenderness, and Mary was expected to be seen, not heard. Except when they had visitors. Then Penelope would dress her in a frilly frock and fuss over her like a doll, praising her latest pianoforte piece or schoolwork.

At seven, Mary – already tall for her age – was packed off to boarding school. It was a god-awful, draughty place, where, as Mary saw it, you had two options: bully or be bullied. She chose the former. Relationships to her were about getting what you wanted. Respect, love and friendship didn't come into it. They never had.

While other children's parents arrived at school with treats and hugs, Jonathan would turn up in the car at the end of term, place her trunk in the boot and remind her to be quiet when she got home as 'your mother has a headache'. He was old-school, ex-military, a distant figure who had little to do with her. Having a child, Mary realised, was about his standing in the community, having someone – even if it was a *girl* – to inherit his fortune, rather than 'that bastard of a brother of mine', or 'the dogs' home getting it'. Penelope, meanwhile, just deeply resented her.

Her birth father's name was there in the documents, too.

Believed to be Martyn Tipping, 18, but not confirmed by Lovett. Tipping has one other child, Tyler, in foster care. Lovett wants absolutely no contact and we should respect that.

A half-brother. The thrill of knowing there was *someone* out there, someone who was real family, surprised Mary. Finding him on Facebook had proved easy. And he was willing to meet. Someone she was actually *related* to, who shared a father with her. Someone who might want *in* on her plan.

Mary put the piece of paper carefully in her handbag, and stepped out into the Chelsea street, where Jonathan's black Jaguar was parked in a residents' bay. Since he died, she'd been driving it everywhere. Dressed in jeans and a blue cashmere sweater, Mary threw her snakeskin handbag on the front seat and drove towards the King's Road, joining the queue of traffic heading south.

Farnborough was an hour and a half's drive, an easy run around the M25 and M3 in the middle of the day. She was surprised to find herself nervous about meeting Tyler. He'd said very little in a text, suggesting they talk in The Golden Egg, a cheap café near the town's Meads shopping centre. Mary wanted to piece together her life, make some kind of sense of it. And make those responsible pay.

She'd moved out of the Winchborough farmhouse when she won a place at University College London to read maths, but the house had never felt like home anyway. Jonathan and Penelope – just like Lola – had been glad to see the back of her, Mary was sure of it. They were happy for her to use the Chelsea flat for free and give her an allowance, as they rarely went to London any more, and Penelope constantly worried about squatters. Since graduating a year ago, she'd taken a couple of temporary jobs, unsure of her future. But now she had Lola's name, Mary knew exactly what she wanted to do. And Tyler might be of use.

The Golden Egg was in an old, flat-roofed 1960s block, thick with the smell of grease, which also seemed to have a thin layer deposited on every surface. She was surprised how much she looked like Tyler. Even though they were only half-brother and sister, there were similarities.

'You must be Tyler,' she said, sitting down opposite him

at a Formica table, where an oily laminated menu was perched between a salt cellar and a giant plastic tomato full of ketchup. His pupils were dilated and she knew instantly that he was high. 'I'm Mary.'

He nodded. 'Thought so. Don't get many snakeskin handbags in here. Not real ones, anyway. You'll stink of fried eggs when you leave.'

For a moment, they looked at each other in silence.

'You're the first blood relative I've met,' Mary said.

'Weird, isn't it.'

'Yeah.'

'I met our dad a few times,' Tyler said. 'He visited me in the children's home. Sometimes at foster homes, too. But he stopped.'

'What was he like?'

'Nice. Kind. I can't remember much. He had dark hair. And he used to bring me sweets. Sorry, I wish I could tell you more.'

'So you weren't adopted?'

'No.' He picked up the greasy menu. 'Do you want something to eat? I'm starving.'

'Just a coffee. But have whatever you like. I'll pay.'

Tyler ordered a full English breakfast with extra fried bread and devoured it like he hadn't eaten for a week. He said he had been in care. Lavington Place. Mary had seen it all over the news a couple of years earlier. She didn't need to ask Tyler if it had happened to him. Mary could see it in his eyes, a darkness, a loss of innocence.

He'd left on his eighteenth birthday and ever since had

lived hand-to-mouth, renting cheap bedsits when he could find work, sleeping on the streets when he couldn't.

'Where are you living now?' Mary asked.

'Staying at a squat. It's OK. The people are nice. I sometimes pick up a bit of work in the local pub, washing up. And other stuff.' He looked down at the floor. 'Usually regular customers. All *straight* married men. Through an escort agency.'

Mary sipped her coffee. 'I looked up our dad. I'm not sure if you know, but…'

'He's dead. Yeah, I know. I found our grandad, Harry. He said Dad took his own life after his second baby was taken away. *You.*'

Mary hadn't expected that. All she knew was that Martyn Tipping's death had been registered shortly after she was born.

'Our dad wanted to take care of me,' he went on. 'You, too. That's what Harry said. But the social wouldn't let him. So I ended up at Lavington Place. You ended up wherever. And he ended up smeared along the train tracks.' He took a small vodka bottle from inside his coat and tipped some into his chipped mug of tea. 'I'm guessing you got luckier.' There was more than a trace of bitterness in his voice.

Mary nodded. 'I was adopted, by an old couple in the Cotswolds. Very rich. But they didn't want me either. Did you find your birth mother?'

'Yeah.' For the first time, Mary saw anger and hatred blazing in Tyler's eyes. 'Alison Brennan. She still lives near

274

our grandad. She's got four kids. And grandchildren. Dotes on them, the bitch.'

'Did you speak to her?'

'I wanted to. I wanted to scream at her that while she was pushing a pram round the estate and playing happy families, I was getting buggered. I wanted to shout, "Do you know what he did to me, Mother? The head of Lavenham? Afterwards he made me kneel with him on the wet carpet while we prayed the gay away."'

'That is so fucked up.'

'I know. But then I saw Brennan come out of the house with a baby in her arms. Probably one of her grandkids. Couldn't have been more than a few days old. I couldn't do it. I just walked off.'

'Have you seen her since?'

'Once. Later that day. I went home and got really high. She was at the bus stop. I...I punched her in the back of the head and ran off.'

'Did it make you feel better?'

'Yeah, it did. What about your birth mother?'

'I've only recently found her. She's big in celebrity PR. Sam Stevens' agent.'

'Sam Stevens? The actor? Are you gonna call her?'

'Better than that. I'm going to persuade her to hire me. Make her think I'm some media hot-shot. Find out all her dirty secrets and expose her for the heartless, selfish bitch she is.' Mary took a tiny sip of her cold, milky coffee, and looked at the track marks on his arms. 'I can help you, Tyler. If you'll let me.'

'Why would you do that?'

'Because I can. Because *you* can help *me*. And because you're the only family I've got.'

Tyler placed the shopping bags on the doorstep, hunting for his keys. He'd been living at the Chelsea flat for a month, since coming out of private rehab – paid for by Mary – and life felt good.

He didn't think for one second she'd persuade Lola Lovett to hire her. But Tyler was rapidly learning that Mary's posh voice, bullish attitude, icy emotions and refusal to ever take 'no' for an answer opened a lot of doors. Including Lola Lovett's. *Olivia* Carter was her new assistant.

It was his turn to cook, and he'd bought fresh pasta, tomatoes and basil down on the King's Road. Living with Mary had refined his tastes. Now he knew about buffalo mozzarella and flaxseeds, herbal teas and oat milk, Wagyu beef and oysters. In the children's home he'd been fed lumpy mash and fatty sausages, and in the squat he'd lived on one meal a day at most, maybe a cheeseburger or beans on toast, washed down with black Happy Shopper tea. Now he ran every day, looping around Chelsea and West Brompton, and sunbathed in the house's pretty courtyard.

His phoned beeped. It was Mary.

Gonna be late. Launch in Leicester Square is going on and

on. And on. Yawn. Put mine in the fridge. We can watch
the next ep of Succession when I get in x

Tyler smiled to himself. Mary was at a top showbiz party, but she'd rather be at home watching TV – like most of the people at these parties, as she often told him. They were there because they had to be, contracted by film studios, or, like Lola, watching over their clients. The only people who honestly enjoyed them were reality stars, who drank too many cocktails and slept with each other, basking in the inevitable headlines that followed.

He liked living here in Chelsea. Mary didn't have friends, only acquaintances, people who were of use to her. Tyler knew he was probably one of them. But he'd got clean, he was living in a gorgeous house, he had money, and he didn't have to wash greasy plates or be fucked bareback by frustrated married men. He'd enjoy it however long it lasted.

Her plan sounded simple. First, they'd find him a small flat to rent in Wandsworth, and a worthy job that would suit someone just out of rehab. A charity would be ideal. Then he'd go along to the weekly local AA meeting, which Sam Stevens always visited unless he was on location. He'd been an addict, so he'd know what to do and say. Mary wanted Tyler to befriend him. Worm his way into his circle. Win his trust with his 'pretty face'. Tyler was just his type, apparently. The fact Tyler was straight was irrelevant. He'd be playing a role. And finding out Lola's secrets, which Mary would then leak to the press.

He filled a pan with water and put it on to boil, chopping the tomatoes and basil on a large wooden board. Mary promised once she'd destroyed Lola's reputation, Tyler could move back here to Chelsea. Did he trust her? Not really. Did he think Sam Stevens would be interested? Not in a million years. But he was happy to go along for the ride.

Chapter Twenty-Seven

LOLA

I wake up to the sound of a machine beeping. My eyelids feel heavy, too heavy to open, and there's something around my arm.

'Status epilepticus,' a voice said. 'Basically, a seizure that doesn't stop. We've treated her with a large dose of benzodiazepines.'

'I didn't know she had epilepsy.' It's Sue voice, concerned and caring.

'There's nothing about seizures in her notes, though she may have seen a private GP. But she was extremely dehydrated. She had anorexia as a teenager. Judging by her weight, and the abnormal heart rhythms we're picking up, I'd say she still does. That could have triggered it.'

'What about stress?'

'On its own, in an average person, unlikely. But in *her* case, taking everything into account, her low bodyweight, then yes, it could.'

'When can we talk to her?'

'The meds should wear off enough for that in a few hours. But you'll have to be brief. I know you're on that missing persons case but I don't want my patient stressed out. Fortunately the ambulance crew got oxygen and meds into her rapidly, but we won't know if there's any lasting damage until she wakes up.'

'What sort of damage?'

'To the brain. Possibly the body too, if there's been a stroke. You realise this could have killed her.'

I hear their words, but I can't process them. I'm lost in a fog, a place where time has slowed down, a strange, drifting landscape of sounds and words, unconnected, alone. I try to think, but everything is hazy, my body unmoving, thick and leaden. Then she walks towards me, surrounded by light.

'Olivia?'

I whisper it, and I feel a hand on my arm.

'Rest, Lola.'

Sue's voice is soft, gentle. There are footsteps, she's gone, and I drift into the unknown.

Chapter Twenty-Eight

THURSDAY

Mary Olivia Carter sat in the interview room, composed and controlled, the duty solicitor at her side, her handcuffs removed, and a large, cool cup of tea in front of her. Across the table, Sue was sifting through her notes. Dev snapped on the tape.

'Interview with Mary Olivia Carter, Thursday 8 September. Present are DCI Sue Fisher, DI Dev Basu and duty solicitor Sarika Chopra.'

'Would you like me to call you Mary, Olivia or Ms Carter?' Sue asked. The woman in front of her seemed so calm, so demure, so emotionless.

'Mary.' She sipped her tea.

'Tell us about your relationship with Tyler Tipping.'

'He's my brother. Well, half-brother. But you already know that.'

'We've found Tyler dead at your parents' home in Winchcombe.'

There were no tears, but Sue could tell Mary was rattled. The first flicker of emotion.

'Yes. In the bunker where Sam Stevens was being held. And he's dead, too. You put Sam in there, Mary, didn't you?'

The solicitor laid his hand on Mary's arm, and whispered 'no comment' in her ear, but she brushed him away.

'Tyler and I both did. But it was my idea,' she added. Sue sensed a sickening sense of pride. 'I'm guessing he went back to try and rescue him.' She snorted. 'It was on his conscience. I knew I shouldn't trust a junkie.'

'What about Dafydd and Gwen Morgan, Sam's parents?'

'*I* killed them,' Mary replied triumphantly. 'The carving, that was Tyler. He got high, got carried away.'

'So you planned this meticulously?' Mary was clearly proud of this plan she'd executed, and Sue was sure she'd want to show off.

'Yes. I found Tyler online a couple of years ago. My *mother*,' she spat the word out, 'was always being photographed with Sam Stevens and I thought I'd get a job at her agency. See if I could befriend him, dig around, get some dirt on her for the press.'

'So how did Tyler come into this?'

'He didn't, at first. Not in any clear way. I thought there would be some kind of use for him. But he was a junkie. And he was my brother. My only family. I paid for rehab, got him straightened out, and he moved in to the Chelsea house with me.'

'So how did you get the job at Lola Lovett PR?' Dev asked.

'I turned up every day, on the doorstep, with my CV. Ambushed my *mother* and waved it in her face. After a week of it she agreed to an interview. They needed a new intern. It was unpaid, but I had plenty of money. My adoptive father, Jonathan, gave me a generous allowance. Anything to keep me out of the house.'

'Why Sam? Why target him?' Sue asked.

'Because my mother *doted* on him. I'd seen it on photos and videos before I started there, but working with her made it even worse. It was almost *incestuous*. She fussed over him endlessly, Sam this and Sam that, cancelling anything that got in the way of her plans for him. She *loved* him.' Mary's voice was becoming more animated now, revealing a deep, blinding rage that Sue had seen in other killers.

'So you engineered this relationship between Sam and Tyler? How?' Sue asked.

'Easy. He always went to an AA group near Wandsworth if he was in town. My mother seemed to like me – the *irony* – and promoted me to her assistant, so I had access to Sam's diary. Tyler was pretty, and straight, but he'd been a sex worker so had no problem doing what it took. It *was* a gamble. I don't like risk.' She paused. 'I studied maths at uni. I'm logical.'

'Why did you risk it?'

'Because I sensed Sam had dirt on Lola. Major dirt. I heard them arguing on the phone a few times, though I didn't know what it was about. There was trouble brewing, I could feel it, so trying to get Tyler into that mix seemed like a sensible shout.'

'Did you find out what it was?'

'Tyler said Sam shouted at her about a guy called Des Lethbridge. He wasn't happy with how Lola had treated him.'

'Who is he?'

'I don't know. Maybe another actor? Or a fan? I couldn't find anything about him.'

'So why kill Sam? Why not let Tyler stay living the high life until he found out more about this beef between Sam and Lola?'

'Because Tyler started using again. It made him unpredictable, dangerous. I couldn't be sure what he'd told Sam. He might have revealed everything about *me*. Sam was away a lot on shoots, and Tyler had the time, the money. He was bored. Sam even rented him a flat. He only did drugs there, never in any of Sam's houses. Or so he told me.'

'How did you know he was using?'

'He started becoming paranoid, almost psychotic. That was the crystal meth. He'd phone me up and rant about Sam's parents. He was *obsessed* with what they'd done to Sam. Especially the father. Rejected him, told him he was worthless. Sam didn't make any secret of that, but he also told Tyler his father was active in the men's public lavatories back in Wales, at Talbot Green. He'd been in there one night when his father came in. It was the hypocrisy that got to him. But Sam would never *out* him because he loved his mother.'

'So you killed them?'

'I had to do something. Tyler was determined to dish out justice. He was totally screwed up by what happened to him in care, and his hatred for Sam's father tapped into that. My plan was to kill Sam's parents and frame Sam for the murder. Case closed. No one would look for anyone. Sam could just disappear.'

'Why not just kill Sam, then?' Sue asked. 'Why tie him up and leave him to die slowly? You talk about risk...'

'There was no risk,' Mary said flatly. 'No one ever goes near the bunker, except for the occasional dog who strays off the footpath. I didn't want Sam Stevens to drift to his death in a happy, drug-filled haze. I wanted my *mother* to spend years wondering where he was. And then, when I sold the house and disappeared abroad, the truth would come out. She'd know how he'd suffered. How her beloved *baby*, as she called him, had spent his final days screaming and rotting in his own filth.'

'But wouldn't you have to spend the rest of your life looking over your shoulder? Even if you were overseas.'

'It would have been worth it. Anyway, I'd found someone on the dark web to get me a fake passport. I'd have had enough money to do whatever I liked. To disappear and start again.'

'You pushed Tyler into that bunker with him, didn't you?' Sue went on 'Forensics suspect he didn't fall in. Someone pushed him. He had marks on his wrists and ankles where he'd previously been bound. Like Sam. He'd become a liability.'

'I've already told you. I didn't.'

'So, Dafydd and Gwen Morgan. Talk me through what happened.'

'I had the day off, Friday, and drove to Tonyrefail. Penelope's carer, Sonia, keeps a stack of aprons and PPE at the house so I'd taken some in advance and changed into it when I arrived. I told them I was there to give them their next Covid jabs.'

'And they let you in?'

'Without any problems at all. Didn't even ask why it was going directly into a vein. They just kept thanking me and the NHS, bless. Tyler had scored the heroin and benzos earlier, and we'd mixed it together. Once they passed out, I gave them a second injection, just to make sure.'

'Why not leave them there?'

'That's what I would have done. But Tyler was obsessed with Camber Sands and I needed to keep him on side. They'd had a trip there from the children's home. Bad things happened. Very bad. He said it was a place that needed to be put on the map. Like Soham. Remembered for the hell that happened there. *Only* for that. He found the empty bungalow on a website he'd used when he was squatting that lists empty properties. I wrapped their bodies in plastic and put them into a couple of cheap wheeled suitcases. Drove back to Chelsea and waited for Tyler to finish work. Late that night we went down to Camber. Tyler had said the bungalow was "remote". When we got there, it damn well wasn't. I'd never have gone there, or taken the Jag, if I'd known. But Tyler was off his head, unpredictable, determined to go through with it. We put dark coveralls on with hoods, gloves too, and got the cases inside.'

'That's when he mutilated them?'

'Yes. I planned to leave them on the bed, but Tyler got carried away. He had a scalpel and I didn't feel safe stopping him. Besides, the carving just pointed the finger even more at Sam. My main worry was sobering him up before he met Sam on Saturday.'

'But you managed it?' Dev asked.

'I took him back to Soho, cleaned him up and put him to bed. Next morning, I stuffed him with black coffee and breakfast. All he had to do was get the train down to see Sam, act normal until Sunday. Which, somehow, he managed to do. We needed the bodies to be found, and we wanted *your lot* to think Sam was the suspect. Tyler needed an alibi for Sam's disappearance.'

'So who put Sam in the bunker?'

'I did. That was easy. I drove to Cobshott, gave him some "urgent" scripts to look at, and slipped a massive dose of sleeping tablets in his cocoa. Tyler didn't want to get involved at all. He'd started developing a *conscience*.'

'Is that why you killed Tyler?' Sue looked straight into Mary's cold eyes.

'I didn't. Why would I lie?'

'Because he's your brother?' Sue ventured. 'Because somehow killing your own brother crosses a line? Because he could have grassed you up?'

Mary shook her head and sipped her tea. 'All valid reasons. I can see why you'd think that. I had been wondering how to silence him. He started acting randomly, telling you guys Sam was on drugs again, which was clearly nonsense. So he was a risk. But no, I didn't do it.'

'And the tip-off call to Lola's agency? About the bodies in Camber?'

'Tyler put a call in from a burner phone. All we needed to do was have an incoming call logged on the office phone records as I knew you'd check.'

'So, if your plan had worked, and Sam was blamed for his parents' deaths, what was your plan after that?'

'Walk away happy, knowing I'd ruined Lola's life. Wait for Penelope to die and move back into Winchborough. Tyler could have come with me. And then, if and when I wanted to deliver the final agonising blow to Lola, sell the house, start a new life abroad with a new identity, and let his body be found.'

'If only you hadn't lost patience with Tyler.'

'I didn't.'

'Interview terminated.' Sue snapped off the recorder.

'What happened to *Mother*?'

'In hospital. She'll live.'

'Good. The scandal this court case is going to whip up will kill her.'

∼

Back in her office, Sue asked Dev to order a full psychiatric assessment.

'There's something, Dev. My guess is that she's a psychopath. Cold as ice. Won't affect the sentence – she knew right from wrong – but it will help explain what she did.'

'The defence might push for insanity.'

'They might. I don't care. So long as she's locked up. Charge her with the murder of Sam Stevens, Dafydd Morgan and Gwen Morgan. She's just denying Tyler's murder as one final attempt to keep control. I'm sure she killed him too, even if we can't yet prove it. I'm going to go back to the hospital, see Lola.'

'There's an email from DCI Lauren Brown, in case you haven't seen it. We're both copied in. Says she can't go into details, but they're still chasing leads from the Onslow Avenue paedophile ring and linking it to Lavington Place will really help. It will take time. Years, maybe. There's so much to investigate.'

'These things do. That's good to hear though. It's never too late to make abusers pay for what they've done.'

'Oh, and that paparazzo has turned up. Jim L. Full name is Ryan James Stewart-Longton. He'd gone sightseeing in Norfolk for a few days with his *Daily News* cash. Lots of photos of windmills.'

'Any luck on this Des Lethbridge character that Mary mentioned?'

'There's a record of a Desmond Lethbridge dying of an overdose in a Camden alleyway a few years ago. Aussie backpacker. Entered the UK from Greece. Bipolar, and off his meds, according to the medical records and post mortem. No suspicious circumstances.'

'Hmm. I'll run his name past Lola Lovett, see what she says. Though I doubt there's anything in it.'

Mike appeared in the doorway.

'Sue, we need to talk.' His voice was firm, controlled.

'I'll get on it, boss.' Dev nodded to Mike as he left the room.

'We've got her, Mike. The woman who killed Sam Stevens. And his parents.'

'Sue, listen to me. It's Tom.'

Sue sat in her office, pale and silent, her eyes red, as Mike gently placed a strong cup of tea in front of her.

'Drink this,' he said gently. 'Three sugars. It's good for shock.'

'H-how did you find him?'

'He called me. From the cliffs at Beachy Head.'

'It's all my fault, Mike. I've been a terrible parent. You kept trying to warn me that something was wrong. I *knew* something was wrong. And I didn't do anything. He must have been in so much pain. I'm sorry for everything, Mike.'

Mike picked up the tea and held it to her lips. 'Drink, Sue. Don't blame yourself.'

Sue took a sip of tea. 'W-where is he now? I need to see him.'

'I'll take you to him.'

~

The hospital room was dark, and cool. Tom was laid out on the bed, a sheet over him.

'It's all right,' Mike said softly, taking her hand.

Sue sat down beside the bed and rested her hand gently on Tom's.

'I love you so much, Tom. And I'm so sorry I wasn't there for you.'

Tom rolled over. His face was pale, his eyes dark. Sue took him in her arms and held him close to her, breathing in the smell of his hair, his skin, his life. 'I don't care about the drugs, Tom. I love you with all my heart. *All* of it. I couldn't bear to lose you. And we will get through this together.'

He began to cry, tears falling from his eyes on to her shoulder. 'I'm so sorry, Mum…'

'You have nothing to be sorry for. I wasn't there for you. I wasn't there for you with your dad. Not like I should have been. But I'm here now. We will sort this, love. And the people who made you feel like this will pay.'

'They said they'll kill you.'

'They won't.'

'I couldn't do it, Mum. I wanted to. I looked down and saw the beach below and I thought you'd be better off without me. But I couldn't do it without saying goodbye. And I knew you were busy. So I rang Mike.'

'We'll get through this, Tom. You've got so much to look

forward to. Uni will be a new start. And I'm never, ever too busy to talk to you. Ever. I've missed you so much.'

'What if they come after you?'

'With the intel you gave about them, Mike's team has already picked them up. Dealing that much cocaine will put them away for life. They're just cannon fodder for the distributors higher up. No one's going to come after a kid caught up at the bottom of their hideous chain, in county lines.' She smiled through the tears and kissed the top of his head. 'You've been watching too much *Breaking Bad*.'

'Can we go home, Mum?'

'As soon as the doctors give us the go-ahead. Dev can take care of the case for me. Hot chocolate, each other and a doze on the sofa are all we need. I'll even try playing you at chess later. Everything will be all right, I promise.'

In the hospital waiting room, Sue threw her arms around Mike and sobbed.

'You saved him, Mike. If it wasn't for you…'

'I just chatted to the lad,' he said thickly, through tears. 'Talked him down. And got Sussex police to pick him up.'

'I've been a shitty mum and an ever shittier partner, Mike. I've pushed you away. I've just been finding it hard, you know. With Tom leaving. And Rob gets in my head.'

'It's OK, Sue.' Mike had wished Rob dead so many times, but in the end even that wasn't enough to destroy him. The memories he left were always there, always would be, and he knew that being with Sue meant he'd have to accept that. Somehow.

'Can you forgive me?'

'There's nothing to forgive. I know I'm a boring old fart. Let's try some of those things you're always on about. What was it? Salsa classes? And date night. Every week, we'll go anywhere you like.'

'I do love you, Mike.'

'I love you, too, Sue.'

He couldn't tell her about Rob and Onslow Avenue.

Sue had never seen so many flowers. Lola had been moved into a private hospital, where she had her own, huge room, and it seemed each of her clients had tried to outdo the other in the size of bouquet.

After a couple of days at home with Tom, Sue felt confident enough to leave him for a hospital visit. They'd talked though what had happened in detail. Along with the dealers Tom knew, who were now on remand without bail, Mike's investigation had also picked up some from higher up the chain. Sue had stationed a couple of officers to watch the house, just in case.

Tom's closest friend from chess, Tania, had come round to see him. 'I'll be out for a couple of hours, but I'm on my mobile,' Sue had said. 'Mike's in the garden if you need him. Tania, love, help yourself to anything you'd like.'

'Thank you, Mrs Fisher.'

Lola was sitting up in her hospital bed, in full make-up, on her phone. She was wearing a pink silk kimono and Sue couldn't help but notice how beautiful she was.

'Sue!' She smiled. 'Thank you for coming to see me. Or is this a professional call?'

'Strictly personal,' Sue replied. 'I brought you these' – she proffered a small bunch of pink carnations from the petrol station – 'but I rather fear I've been outdone.'

'Don't be silly, they're *lovely*. I'll have the nurse put them in water. Everyone's been so kind. I had to get my boyfriend Peter to order extra vases off Amazon.'

Sue glanced at the label of a particularly large bunch of pink and white roses, and smiled to herself. 'With all love from Tim xxx.' Had to be Tim Thacker, editor of the *Daily News*.

'Lola, I'm so sorry about Sam.'

She sighed, and Sue saw a bleak sadness in her eyes. She knew that pain. Lola *had* loved Sam.

'And I'm sorry about Olivia,' she added. 'That you had to find out like *that*.'

Lola nodded. 'Me too. I remember the day she was born, on the bathroom floor. And I did wonder what had happened to her over the years, but most of the time I just shut it out. Couldn't go there, you know. Now I *definitely* bloody can't. Though when I look back, I can see why I hired her. She reminded me of me.'

'It's all over the press. Including the fact you're her birth mother. We didn't leak it.'

'You didn't need to. There were ten agents craning their

necks to hear what was being said in that foyer. They'll have told someone, who told someone, and...anyway, it's fine. I've already been on to the AdoptMe charity. I'll set up some photo shoots with me and children who need homes to get them some publicity. Win-win. Won't actually adopt any myself, of course. I'm far too selfish.' She paused. 'What will happen to Olivia?'

'Trial. Old Bailey, probably. Even if they plead insanity, she'll still be locked up for life. Just in a secure hospital rather than Holloway prison.'

'Good. She's no daughter of mine. If she ever writes to me it's going in the bin unopened. But she won't. And Tyler?'

'Olivia still denies she killed him. But we're not looking for anyone else. We suspect he'd visited Sam, felt guilty, tried to help him. Then she found out. The CPS says the circumstantial evidence is overwhelming and she doesn't have an alibi for Wednesday night, which is likely when he died.'

'I didn't trust Tyler from the start,' Lola replied. 'Always had a feeling he was up to something. I thought he was after Sam's money. What happened to Tyler's body?'

'His grandfather, Harry, will make the arrangements, but Forensics still have a lot of work to do. He'll be cremated, I understand. Probably only Harry as a mourner, so I'll go if I can. Poor man. Dev went down to tell him face to face. He was absolutely devastated. Thinking Tyler had made something of his life had given him hope.'

Sue thought of Harry, offering her the vodka, his thin frame hunched over, his eyes full of sorrow.

'One thing I need to ask you, though, Lola. Does the name Des Lethbridge mean anything to you?'

'Sadly it does. He was an Aussie backpacker, bit of a druggie, who took a liking to Sam before he was famous, and flew to London hoping to shack up with him. Sam didn't want to know him so I got Des a room at the Holiday Inn in Camden for a few nights, and a plane ticket back to Greece, where he'd come from. I'm assuming he went. Why do you ask?'

'Just something Olivia said. About you and Sam arguing over him.'

'Oh, he'd always bring up that old chestnut whenever we had a tiff. He was annoyed that I paid for the plane ticket out of his salary. Thought Des was a gold digger. But he seemed quite sweet to me. He was little more than a teenager, totally in love with Sam, bipolar, and I thought the best thing to do was send him back to Mykonos. Before Sam broke his heart even more.'

'He didn't make it. Des was found overdosed in an alleyway.'

'No! I'm sorry to hear that. When?'

'Oh, years ago. No suspicious circumstances. I just wanted to check.'

'Of course. I totally understand.' Lola sighed. 'That really is sad, Sue. He seemed like a sweet guy. Lost, but sweet.'

'When's Sam's funeral?' Sue added.

'Next Tuesday. Anastazia, one of my senior agents, has been helping with the arrangements. I wanted to hold it at the church in Hampstead. Sam always felt at home in that apartment. But we've got so many A-listers coming that Cobshott makes more sense, with the wake at his house.' She paused. 'Might as well use it before it's sold. I'm sure you know he'd left almost everything to his mum, so now the properties will be sold and shared between the Buddhist centres and his LGBT charities. Will you be at the funeral? Soozie Lightwater's on the guest list. And it's just down the road from you. Great publicity for the force. Front pages.'

Sue smiled. 'No. I've been in the spotlight enough. And I'm taking some time off. Six-month sabbatical. I'm going to settle my son into uni, just be around for him. He's had a bit of a tough time lately.'

'Tom, isn't it?'

'That's right. You've got a good memory.'

'I'd make a great detective.' Lola smiled. 'Well, if he ever goes into acting, send him my way. No fee.' She blew her nose gently on a pink tissue. 'I do miss Sam so much, Sue. And my own child killed him. I just don't know where to start with that.'

'Therapy?' Sue said gently. 'My son's been having some. We lost his dad a while ago. Lot of stuff we need to work through.'

'Good God, no. They've already been on to me here about that. I had an eating disorder when I was younger and for some reason they seem to think I still have one.

Nonsense. I told the doctor, it's the bloody *shock*. When did *you* last find out your assistant was your daughter?'

Sue smiled, looking at Lola's thin frame, remembering the uneaten pizza in the flat. 'I just wanted to ask you something. Why didn't you see Sam on the set of *Murder in the Lakes*?'

'We'd had a bit of a falling out. It had been bubbling for months. He was passionate about climate change and animal rights, wanted me to make the whole agency vegan. Chuck out the leather sofas, only serve vegan food at events. Ban anyone from coming in wearing leather or wool. Including *me*. Said I could set an example. I told him he was nuts. So we'd been keeping our distance a bit. But I still checked in on him regularly by phone. Besides, if there had been any trouble Simon Omeria would have been straight on the blower.'

'You should do it in his honour. Make the agency vegan.'

Lola smiled. 'That's not a bad idea. We'd get amazing publicity. If you get bored of detective work there's a job for you here in PR.'

'So what's next?'

'There's only one way through this,' Lola went on. 'And that's to get back to work. They're letting me out this afternoon. I've got the launch for this year's *Strictly* in three days. And sleazy footballer Michael King's wife is in it.'

'Sleazy?'

'You don't want to know. But it got her *Strictly*. And you might want your officers to check out those car parks around Wisley at night.'

Lola's phone buzzed. 'I'll let you take that.' Sue smiled. 'Just wanted to check in. Say hi. And wish you all the best.'

'Keep in touch, Sue.' Lola smiled. 'Seriously, do. You've got my number. Come and make a fuss of Cleopatra. Or *me*.' She paused. 'And thank you. The world deserved the truth about Sam. Now he'll be loved for ever.'

They parted as friends, and Lola watched Sue from the window as she walked off towards the Tube station. She'd covered her tracks. Six hundred calories today, well within her new target of 1,700. And she'd taken her meds. She couldn't risk losing control with seizures again.

Lola checked her phone. The video of her and Sue was still there, should she ever need it. *Keep your friends close and your enemies closer.* That's what her nan had always said. And no one was closer to her than Rick, the imaginary friend she'd had since childhood. She wouldn't be needing him anymore. Not at the moment, anyway.

Right, *Strictly*. She'd need a sparkly new dress. And a new assistant.

Acknowledgments

Huge thanks to my amazing publisher and editor, Charlotte Ledger. Charlotte's ability to turn something that fell out of my head into an actual *book* – not to mention her forensic eye for details and timelines – has made *The Publicist* a thriller I hope you'll love.

All the lovely people at One More Chapter and HarperCollins, and my awesome agent, Ed Wilson at Johnson & Alcock, whose support means more than I can say. I've learned that so much work goes into getting a book to market that my job – writing it – really is the easy part.

A big shout out to all the brilliant TV publicists I've worked with over the years for making my job as a journalist so much easier – and for *not* being like Lola. As far as I know, anyway!

Tarne Sinclair, for reading my drafts, and always being there.

My colleagues on the TV magazines, many of whom have become close friends. I'll never forget the laughs we had at round tables and set visits – or missing that Julia Roberts interview.

Gino, Jasper, Justin, Tiana, Coco and Birrle-Oove, who are the best family anyone could wish for.

And, as always, a big thank you to you, for reading.

ONE MORE CHAPTER

YOUR NUMBER ONE STOP
FOR PAGETURNING BOOKS

The author and One More Chapter would like to thank everyone
who contributed to the publication of this story...

Analytics
Emma Harvey
Maria Osa

Audio
Fionnuala Barrett
Ciara Briggs

Contracts
Georgina Hoffman
Florence Shepherd

Design
Lucy Bennett
Fiona Greenway
Holly Macdonald
Liane Payne
Dean Russell

Digital Sales
Laura Daley
Michael Davies
Georgina Ugen

Editorial
Arsalan Isa
Charlotte Ledger
Nicky Lovick
Jennie Rothwell
Tony Russell
Kimberley Young

International Sales
Bethan Moore

Marketing & Publicity
Chloe Cummings
Emma Petfield

Operations
Melissa Okusanya
Hannah Stamp

Production
Emily Chan
Denis Manson
Francesca Tuzzeo

Rights
Lana Beckwith
Rachel McCarron
Agnes Rigou
Hany Sheikh
Mohamed
Zoe Shine
Aisling Smyth

**The HarperCollins
Distribution Team**

**The HarperCollins
Finance & Royalties
Team**

**The HarperCollins
Legal Team**

**The HarperCollins
Technology Team**

Trade Marketing
Ben Hurd

UK Sales
Yazmeen Akhtar
Laura Carpenter
Isabel Coburn
Jay Cochrane
Alice Gomer
Gemma Rayner
Erin White
Harriet Williams
Leah Woods

**And every other
essential link in the
chain from delivery
drivers to booksellers
to librarians and
beyond!**

Read on for an extract from *The Nail Salon*

In a world where appearances are everything … you can't
trust anything.

Available in eBook and paperback now

The Nail Salon: Chapter 1

Melinda

She's been having the funeral fantasies again.

The ones where she swaps the Canderel for ricin or Novichok or some other deathly poison that she dreams of buying on the dark web.

She tells me, in hushed whispers, that a friend says there are *hit men* available. It's never going to happen, of course. She's far too anxious to go poking around the murkier side of the internet. This will end up like all the others – in a messy divorce with an obscenely huge payout. Enough to cover the housekeeper, the nanny, the Botox, the fillers, the Prada. She'll get the house anyway.

And that's when the rot really sets in. Soon it's daily trips to the hairdresser, to me – here in the nail salon – and slipping a vodka into the Evian to fill the gaping vacuum. I've seen it all a thousand times before.

But Soozie hasn't hit the divorce courts yet. She's still officially in the 'making a go of it' stage, even though she loathes her husband, Simon – forties, blondish hair, works out, pretty handsome as far as City bankers go – who has been having pretty wild sex with a brunette twenty-something for the last year and a half.

Soozie doesn't know that. But I do. I know all about their lives. Not just what they tell me.

Day after day, I listen to their stories as I file, paint, polish. I'm their confessor. I know *everything*. Just the occasional, sympathetic 'oh' is enough to unleash another torrent. And today, Soozie is on a real roll.

'It's just so *unfair*,' she wails. 'This dinner party has been arranged for *weeks*. Now he's saying the firm needs him in Manchester overnight. Overnight! On a Saturday. So I'll have to host it on my *own*.'

I make a sad face. If only she'd seen what I have. Simon in the back of his car, the brunette astride him, pumping up and down, pink flesh pressing against the damp glass. Not to mention their twice-weekly trysts they used to have at his secret second home – a secluded mock-Georgian mansion, Riverdell, on the nearby, private Crown Estate. The estate where Soozie longed to live, but Simon insisted they couldn't quite afford.

Soozie gazes down at her blue nails. 'He doesn't give a flying fuck about me.' We both know the Manchester trip is a lie.

But listening to her isn't enough. My clients keep

coming back because they genuinely believe I'm their friend. Their closest friend, I've been called.

I can't do without them. It's not just the money. I feed off their lives, their emotions. Their pain is my drug. Their joy, too. I soak it up, letting it run through my veins, feeling every betrayal, every divorce, every new baby, every school exam, every failed university application, every elderly parent whose mind is being eaten away by dementia. They rarely ask much about me. I like that. And I do have a soft spot for a few of them. Especially Soozie.

'Well, we'll have to make sure this is the most fabulous dinner party ever, honey,' I say brightly. 'What's on the menu?'

'Black cod.' She's not cooking it, of course. Some Nobu-trained chef is doing the catering. 'And there's a *vegan*.' She spits the word out. Soozie briefly embraced the whole clean-eating fad, before the lure of a steak and garlic butter became too much. 'I mean, *honestly*. I'm putting up with all this from the girls too. They won't touch dairy. As if life isn't complicated *enough*.'

It's the first time today that she's mentioned the twins. Both are complete teenage brats. Simon adores them and they know it. I've seen them climb into his Range Rover, all waist-length blonde hair, pink lipstick, tiny waists, fake tan and heels, and he drives off like he's won the lottery. And poor, irrelevant Soozie, with her creases and pot belly that no amount of sit-ups seem to shift, and the ever-present glass of wine, is yesterday's news.

She wasn't always like this. When she first came to the nail salon, five years ago, she was full of joy. Talking about how giving up her career in celebrity PR to be a full-time mum was the best move she'd ever made. How looking after the girls was the best job in the world (even if, as far as I could see, all she did was tell other people what to do). I didn't follow her then. Her story was too familiar, too commonplace. I didn't feel that connection. But when the twins started coming in, that's when I knew she'd be on my list. And Simon too.

It's always been my tactic – become their confidant, and then casually suggest other family members might like a session. Soozie came with the girls at first. But soon they were coming on their own, and that's when I began to breathe in their stories like a rush of terrible oxygen.

Her nails are dry, and Soozie's in no rush to go. But I've had my fill for the day. Even though I'm not on the guest list, I've got a dinner party to look forward to.

The Nail Salon: Chapter 2

The reflection in the bathroom mirror needed attention. Her face was fine. He was always careful about that. But as Detective Chief Inspector Sue Fisher let her silk robe fall gently below her shoulders, the livid bruising on the tops of her arms glared back, daring her to expose it to the world. She ran her fingertips over the marks where his fat, thick fingers had been, holding her, shaking her, and for a moment she was back in the living room, his voice distant and hollow as he ranted and seethed. Sue couldn't even remember what the latest tirade had been about. Spending too much time on jobs with her colleague Mike was usually behind it.

There was a little arnica cream left in the tube and she smoothed it over her shoulders, trying not to wince. Sunlight streamed in through the bathroom window, and her phone said it would be thirty degrees today. Even the water in the cold tap was warm. This summer had been the hottest on record so far, and to Sue's horror it showed no signs of abating. It was easy to cover up at work; people expected a shirt and jacket, but on her days off it was harder to explain a long-sleeved T-shirt when everyone else was sun-worshipping in strappy tops.

He was still asleep in bed. He'd be sorry, of course, there would be texts, tears, flowers and the broken-record promise to stop drinking. Keen not to wake him, she tiptoed around the bedroom, dressing as silently as possible, hoping that their son Tom hadn't heard the row. Being fourteen, he spent most of his time zoned out with headphones, oblivious to everything going on in the world.

On the way to work, Sue cranked up the car stereo, shouting out the words to 'Mr Brightside' as she screamed into a void.

The office was unusually quiet for a Tuesday morning. Mike, her deputy, was late as usual, but Sue didn't care. Tipping some of the murky brown liquid from the communal coffee machine into a cracked green mug, she was still logging on to her computer when the boss, Chief Constable Steve Biller, strode in.

'Missing person,' he said, throwing the file onto her desk. 'Reported early hours of this morning. Another underage runaway. Check it out, Sue. Rich kid. Probably putting on her parts when daddy wouldn't pay for a limo. Went AWOL once before and turned up like the proverbial bad penny having stayed the night in a Travelodge. Last seen 7am Monday. It's been twenty-four hours, so...'

'I'll get straight on it, sir.'

Sue picked up the thin file. A girl's face stared back at her, the full Instagram experience. Big hair, pout, green eyes, flawless – and obviously photoshopped – skin, looking far older than fifteen.

'I miss the days when kids looked like kids.' She sighed as Mike quietly slid into the seat opposite, his hungover eyes shaded by dark glasses. 'Good night? Twelve pints and a curry?'

Mike shook his head. 'Wine,' he said weakly. 'It's the Devil's work.'

'Oh, the *date*! I forgot. How was she? Anything like the photo?'

'No. And nothing like her description, either. I tell you, Sue, you're so lucky to have Rob. This online dating lark is a nightmare. I had to drink two bottles just to get through the evening.'

'How did you end it?'

'At Wimbledon tube. Thanked her for a lovely evening and said I'd be in touch. She wants me to go horse riding. In Richmond Park.'

Sue looked up from the file and grinned. 'Why not? Beats staying in watching *EastEnders*. You should give it a go.'

'And she's got kids. Three of them. All under ten. Two different fathers. Didn't mention that in her bio. Too much baggage. Anyway, who's this then?'

'Anna Littlejohn-Eaves. Fifteen. Lives in Kingston. The very posh bit. Tillingham Estate. Last seen yesterday morning. They've tried the local hospitals.'

'History?'

'Done it before, a year ago. Went out partying, stayed in a Travelodge with a mate, then rang Mummy at 7am to go and pick them up, completely unaware of the fracas she had caused.'

Sue took a slurp of coffee. 'Come on. We'd better go and see the parents.'

The Nail Salon: Chapter 3

Melinda

He's never been to the salon. Doesn't even know it exists. But the twins have put me on to Daniel. Soozie's twins. Sky and Star. The fifteen-year-old brats – with the ridiculous names and more spending money in their Prada bags than I'll ever have in a lifetime – waft in just as Soozie's leaving. She's popped in for me to touch up one of her nails. And a chat. They've been in the coffee shop opposite. Sky still has the remnants of a soya caffè latte on her top lip.

'Do you girls want me to wait?' ventures Soozie hopefully. 'I could give you a lift?'

'I told you, Mum, we're going shopping,' snaps Sky, rolling her eyes. 'We'll get an Uber.'

Soozie looks deflated. 'OK, well don't be out late. I'll see you at home.'

I watch as she closes the door behind her. She hesitates

for a moment, her fingers resting on the handle as if she's coming back in, then walks down the street towards the car park. Sky stifles a giggle. Poor Soozie. The girls are just cruel to her. And she knows it.

They don't glimpse the disappointment in my eyes. To them, I'm just 'staff', in the same invisible category as their housekeeper, the chef, their personal trainer – but they can't resist showing off when a captive audience of one is present.

'I met Daniel online,' brags Sky, as I begin removing the immaculate gold nail polish I applied three days ago. 'He's taking me out in London this afternoon. Told me to meet him in Leicester Square. Three o'clock. By the Tube.'

Soozie clearly doesn't know. It's a Monday in August, the school holidays, and she rarely had any idea what they were up to until she checked their pouting Instagram feeds.

'What's he like, this Daniel?' I ask.

'Probably a paedo,' Star says sulkily.

'He's not,' snaps Sky. 'You're just jealous. I've seen pictures of him. He's nineteen. A YouTuber.'

There is time. I have two clients booked for the afternoon whose stories have long gone cold. I can easily cancel. And to hell with any walk-ins. Daniel is worth a follow. Soozie won't be winning Mother of the Year any time soon, but at least I can keep an eye on Sky for her. Strip away the nails, the makeup, and she's just an insecure little girl. Fragile. I remember how that felt at fifteen.

The girls flounce out, Star with purple nails, Sky with

bright red. I flip the sign on the door to 'closed' and pull down the blind.

My salon is on a Surrey high street, Cobshott to be precise, where bankers' and footballers' wives, plus a handful of top 'creatives' – whatever the hell they are – dominate the handful of council tenants yet to be squeezed out. Vast, sterile mansion new-builds rise up from the ashes of old cottages. This is a land of triple garages and bifold doors, of interior designers and Range Rovers, of a quest for perfection and inner pain the like of which I never saw back home in Great Yarmouth.

There aren't many of us who make it out of the seaside town. The singer who did the jungle and the M&S ads, whatshername – Myleene Klass, I just googled it – maybe a few others. I never fitted in there. But here, in Cobshott, they love me.

My clapped-out mini is parked around the corner. I can't afford to live here, of course. Renting the tiny salon costs a small fortune, though I did a good cash deal with the owner. But image is everything. Reality is a bedsit twenty minutes' drive away, in Surbiton, the heart of suburbia. They'd never believe it, my clients. One room, with an overflowing wardrobe and a tiny TV. A sink in the corner. A dingy grey bathroom with damp, threadbare towels piled up, shared with five others. Mice in the kitchen and a solidified KFC bargain bucket, left on the table by two of the Kingston University students a couple of days ago. It's the closest place I can afford to Cobshott, near enough for me to have an easy, cheap commute, and right by the fast train to London. To my sanctuary. Where I can be me.

I find a space in the street nearby, lock the Mini carefully and walk up the weed-strewn front path. It's an old Victorian terrace, and I'm in the basement. The only blessing is there's no damp. Down the stairs, key in the lock, and I'm in. Now, what to wear?

My wigs live on a long shelf above the dressing table. I have everything – curly blonde, red bob, hipster, even clip-on man bun. Today I'm going for the shoulder-length brunette. First, some foundation. The cream darkens my skin tone and I set it with powder. Draw on my eyebrows and lighten my lids with MAC shadow in Nylon. Pale lips. Jeans, a baggy blue top, padding to make me more portly, and a thin baggy jacket. Trainers. Nothing too noticeable. I need to disappear into the Leicester Square crowd.

The train is half-empty. I take a window seat and gaze out as summer flashes by. Semi-detached houses quickly give way to terraces, then tower blocks. Run-down, brick council flats jostle with the steel and glass outline of new London. The Shard appears, reflecting sunlight against a crisp blue sky. Down the Tube, where tourists puzzle over the coloured train arteries connecting London, and parents are inflicting the horrors of a commute on half-terming kids. It's hot, too hot, and I spill out into Charing Cross road, with its familiar smell of urine-dried pavements and diesel fumes.

Outside the Hippodrome Casino seems a good place to wait. I lounge against the wall and scroll through my phone, furtively glancing round at potential Daniels. There's a nervous young lad in a baseball cap, clutching a cheap bouquet of wilting roses in plastic wrap. A handsome but slightly shifty-looking guy in his mid-forties, wearing a suit and a coat with the collar up, despite the stifling heat of the day. The lad meets his equally-terrified-looking date, and they disappear into Burger King. Classy. Two-thirty. Three o'clock. Then four. The shifty-looking guy has gone, replaced by irritating, fat American tourists loudly asking where they can find Lie-cester Square.

I'm starting to worry a little now. London is no place for a fifteen-year-old, especially one who thinks she's streetwise. I check Sky's Instagram, wishing I'd thought of it earlier. There's a shot of her and Star in their Cobshott pool, posted half an hour ago, all smiles, drinking cocktails on a giant inflatable unicorn and hashtagged 'summerdaze'. The shadows show it's late afternoon. And there, right there, are the freshly painted, bright-red nails with the two diamantés. She's home, and she's safe.

For a moment, I'm relieved, but then anger begins to boil in the pit of my stomach. She's lied to me. She's made me feel like a *fool*. I'm here, sweating, tense, wasting my time trying to look out for her when she hasn't even left the house. She's invented Daniel to wind up Star, and I've fallen for it.

I'm heading back to the Tube, furious and fed up, when I spot her in an alleyway. A newbie. Couldn't be more than sixteen. Long, carefully curled chestnut hair, ironed clothes, clutching a small rucksack but with a harrowed, fearful look in her eyes that spice, heroin or any other street drug has yet to numb. Sky might not need my help, but this young girl does. And she needs it now. Maybe this afternoon won't be a waste of time after all.

'You OK?' I say gently, crouching down beside her.

She shakes her head, but her green, desperate eyes meet mine. There's an asthma inhaler in her hand and she's wheezing.

'It's all right, honey,' I add. 'I'm Sally. I help out with London's homeless. Haven't seen you around before.'

'Just arrived,' she says, in a soft voice, politely taking my hand and shaking it. Well-mannered. I like that. 'First time. I'm… Karen.'

I gesture to a homeless man on the pavement, frozen, zombie-like, in the foetal position, his filthy, shoeless feet and stinking clothes resting on a urine-soaked newspaper. 'You've got to be careful on the streets, Karen. He's on spice. That's what it does to you. And there're a lot of dealers ready to push you into it. For free. At first.'

She agrees to a coffee in a nearby Soho cafe, one I know has no CCTV, where sweet, kindly Sally listens to her life story. From Margate in Kent. Absent father. An alcoholic mother who starts the day with a vodka. Severely asthmatic. Scars she hates from surgery to her belly when she was a baby. A second coffee, this time with a veggie 'bacon' sandwich. And cake. Soft Victoria sponge, with jam and cream, just the sort a loving parent would bake. She's fifteen, she's started talking and now she can't stop. Tears, pain, sexual abuse, it all tumbles out. I hug her, feeling her pain, more alive than I've been for months. I've been wanting another lost soul to help, to join my family. And Karen is perfect.

My long wig is itching, my makeup sweaty, the padding is making me overheat, and the anticipation makes me feel like I'm about to burst. But outwardly, I'm just sweet, calm Sally, the one person in London that Karen can trust. At last her words begin to dry up, her throat thick, and she gazes out at the warm drizzle now conveniently coating the shiny London streets.

'Weather's taking a turn,' I say softly. 'We really do need to sort you out a bed for tonight. It's too dangerous on the streets. Drugs, rape, even murder. And the hostels aren't any better. That's why people choose to sleep out here. They think it's safer.' My voice drops to a whisper. 'But it isn't.'

She clutches her rucksack to her chest like a teddy bear and puffs at her inhaler.

I sigh deeply. 'Look, I don't normally do this, but why don't you come and stay at my place? There's plenty of space and you can have your own room. We've chatted for so long, I trust you, and it's getting late. Tomorrow morning we can phone round to find you somewhere permanent. And a job, with training. A new start.'

Karen hesitates, but only briefly. On the pavement outside, a frozen spice addict suddenly stirs, and soils himself.

Her gaze flicks back to mine. 'Are you sure?' she says. 'I won't be any trouble.'

'Of course.' I smile. 'It's a bit of a walk, as it's on the

other side of town, but we can chat on the way to Waterloo. Then just a little train ride. Much nicer than the Tube.'

We leave the coffee shop, squeezing through the hordes of people spilling out of pubs onto Soho's warm streets, down to Trafalgar Square, and I point out where she'll be able to see the giant Christmas tree in a few months' time. Over the busy Hungerford footbridge, where the City skyline glitters in the failing light, towards home. The drizzle has stopped, and the summer sunset bathes London in gold, the colour Karen had always dreamed it would be.

Ready to find out what happens next...

The Nail Salon **is available to order in eBook and paperback now**